HOPE

REIGN ATKINS

For information, or to order additional copies, please contact:

Beacon Publishing Group
P.O. Box 41573 Charleston, S.C. 29423
800.817.8480| beaconpublishinggroup.com

Publisher's catalog available by request.

ISBN-13: 978-1-949472-76-9

ISBN-10: 1-949472-76-0

Published in 2019. New York, NY 10001.

First Edition. Printed in the USA.

Dedication

To John and Cherie for having to put up with my story ramblings and ideas. To my children, remember, nothing worth having comes easy, and to Kelly & Jorrell, always have hope! To my dad and my aunty Ronda, thank you for believing in me!

Prologue

In the ancient Olympian ruins of Greece, in
the middle of an excavation site, an American
archaeologist by the name of Mario Cruz dusted
away the thick sand that coated an old pottery jar,
complete with its tightly sealed lid.

It was sitting in what looked like an ancient
shelf built into the wall. He cautiously picked it up
and held it in his hands to get a better look.

"Yo, Cruz! What do you have there?" His
best friend Joey approached and rubbed his gloved
hands on his knees. The two of them had known
each other for most of their lives. Their nerdy
obsession for history had been their motivation to
get into an archaeology career in the first place and
this was their first trip to Europe.

Cruz was of Hispanic descent, with shoulder
length dark hair, brown eyes and a childish smirk
that would appear, generally following a witty
remark. His friend Joey, on the other hand, was a
taller, slender man with mousy hair and green eyes.

"It looks like a jar. A pithos, I think they'd
call it..." Cruz replied eyeing over the relic. He
shook it a little.

"Anything inside?"

Cruz shrugged his shoulders. "Beats me. Maybe we should just take it back to camp."

Joey took the pithos from Cruz's hands. "You can't be serious. Don't tell me that you aren't the least bit curious!" He studied the object with intent, brushing away the excess dust. "It certainly looks important. Besides, finders' keepers... Don't let David take that away from you." Joey handed the jar back to Cruz, who placed it into his backpack.

He was not willing to risk his career by opening and possibly breaking an ancient relic just to satisfy his own curiosity. Joey could certainly be a bad influence when he chose to be.

"Come on, Cruz... Lunchtime!" Joey led him out of the ruins and back to their large tent, where the sun was dry and hot.

"You boys look like you need water!" Hannah, the site doctor told them, once they had arrived.

"Only if you're offering, Han..." Joey smiled at Hannah, forcing Cruz to roll his eyes and sit down at their work table.

Hannah ignored Joey's flirtatiousness and handed them each a bottle of cold water, which Cruz took and drank thirstily before he set it down and pulled out his latest treasure. His temptation to open it was strong. It was almost as if it was beckoning to him. But, surely, that would be a crazy notion. It was just an old jar made of clay.

Hannah stared down at the pithos in Cruz's hands. "Ooh... what's that?" she asked, making him shrug. He didn't know what to tell her.

"Cruz found some sort of jar in the cave. He refuses to open it." Joey said. "Speaking of things that won't open... Han, when will you accept my open invitation for drinks?"

Hannah smiled. "When I know that it won't be a waste of my time, Joe."

"God, get a room you two..." Cruz said, not taking his eyes off the jar. He knew that he needed to put it away or to take it to his boss. But it was almost as if the jar was beckoning to him. "I seriously need to know what's in here... whether it's a million dollars or a jack in the box... I just need to know." He removed his gloves and brought his hand to the lid.

Hannah offered him a polite smile. "Maybe some things just aren't meant to be opened. But you'll have to hand it over to the boss, regardless..." Hannah left them in peace.

"She loves me... she just doesn't want to admit it," Joey said, while slumping down next to Cruz and drinking his water.

"Sure, man... whatever you say. Shit! I think I've loosened it." Sure enough, Cruz had managed to twist the old clay lid. He removed it from the container.

There was a sudden whoosh and what sounded like a thousand whispers all around him, as the dust fragments lifted into the air surrounding them. Joey breathed in some of the dust and started to cough. "Get Hannah, I think I'm having an asthma attack!"

Cruz threw the jar down onto the table and left the tent in search for Hannah on an impulse. He scoured the campsite until he found the doctor. "Hey, Hannah! Come quick! Joey's having an asthma attack!"

She followed him back to the tent to see Joey coughing and struggling to breathe. She raced over to the cupboard to find the Ventolin and a mask, but the dust that had settled into the air began to surround her, too, forcing her to struggle for breath.

Cruz was hit by panic. "What do you need me to do?"

The doctor looked over at the table where the jar was lying open on its side. "What was in that jar, Cruz? We need a quarantine team, now!"

Cruz looked over at the pithos on the table. What the hell was in that jar?

Chapter 1
One Year Later

On the seventeenth floor in a New York City apartment, one woman in her early twenties sat curled up on her couch with her laptop reading over some of the news headlines. There had certainly been a lot over the past year.

"Astrid Hope Sutherland! Get off that ass of yours and come shopping with me! Now!" Stacey demanded as she ran past her friend in their small apartment.

"Stacey... Must you really use my full name? You sound just like my mother!" Astrid barely looked up from the latest article to address her friend.

"Hey, at least it gets your attention... Please, I'm begging you... I really don't want to risk going shopping alone and bumping into Jules. Especially if she's out with my replacement!" Stacey pouted.

This time Astrid looked up. "Your replacement, Stacey? Seriously? You guys broke up because you weren't right for one another. In fact, you even told me that the only thing that you had in common was that you both love women."

"Is that your long way of saying 'no' to shopping?"

"Pretty much... yeah... I'm sorry... it's just these articles are really bothering me. It can't just be paranoia. The crime rate has seriously been on the increase all over the world! It seemed to have escalated from Europe... Here, look at this one... One man went on a shooting spree, he killed seven children and eleven adults... and why? All because he was angry! I just wish there was something I could do to help."

"Yeah, there is... stop reading and come shopping with me... seriously, Astrid! It's not that hard!"

Astrid put down her laptop and stood up. "Okay, fine... But this is the last time this week... Then I'm admitting you to shopaholics anonymous." Stacey smiled and flicked her long blonde hair. "Thank you... now that wasn't so hard, was it?"

Astrid and Stacey had always been very close, but they were also very different in just about every way. While her friend was a tall blonde, blue-eyed girl, Astrid was much shorter with medium-length light brown hair, green eyes and a personality that Stacey depended on to keep her in check.

The girls arrived at the mall and Stacey immediately began piling items of clothing, that she just had to have, into Astrid's arms.

"Oh, this one is beautiful! But, I can't decide if I want the blue or the black... oh, I'll just get both." Stacey continued to ramble on as she shopped.

"Stacey... I think you have enough," Astrid said as she eyed the price tag on one of the dresses. "I don't think that your dad would be pleased that you've spent... wow, that much money... on his card."

"He'll be fine. Don't stress so much." Stacey took the pile of clothes and placed them on the counter. She eyed a set of earrings from the nearby rack as the sales assistant scanned all the items. "These, too. Thank you!"

Astrid watched as her friend swiped her father's card. "Declined?" Stacey snapped. "There has to be some mistake!" She swiped it again, once more she got the same result. She attempted to call her father.

Astrid looked around them. A long queue of customers had gathered behind them and they were growing impatient. "Stacey, let's just go!"

"No! I'm not leaving without my stuff!" Stacey waited for her father to answer the phone.

"Er... miss...?" the sales assistant stammered.

"What!" Stacey snapped, startling the young woman.

"Could I please serve the next customer while you make your phone call?"

"No! They can just wait their turn! I have just recently had my heart ripped out, and I'm sorry, but right now all I need is to..."

"...Stacey!" Astrid interrupted, as she attempted to lead her friend away from the counter. "I'm sorry, miss, I'll just take my friend to..."

"I'm not going anywhere! We're not leaving until I have what I came for!"

"The card was declined. This is the fourth time you've been shopping in three days. I don't think your dad will be willing to pay this time..." Astrid made an attempt to lead her friend out of the store, only for Stacey to pick up the black coat and the earrings and run off out of the store with them in hand, ahead of Astrid.

"I'm so sorry, miss... I'll catch up with her... I'll get them back!" she pleaded.

"I'm sorry, but I still have to call security..." the sales assistant replied.

"No, don't... I promise, I'll get them back." Astrid ran out of the store after her friend. Stacey had disappeared.

Later that night, back in their apartment, Astrid had managed to handle the situation with the authorities. She snapped at her housemate for her foolishness. "Really, Stacey? I get that you are going through a rough time right now, but stealing a two-thousand-dollar coat and high-tailing it today? You've seriously hit an all-time low! You're just lucky that I was able to convince the police that you're just suffering from a mental breakdown... God, you could have gone to prison!"

Stacey stared at her friend. She wasn't willing to back down, either, which was not like her usual happy self. "Look, I don't need your crap right now! I'm going out!"

She went to leave, but Astrid grabbed her and spoke calmly, "Stacey, you need to calm down and..."

"What I need is for you to get off my case! I'm going out!" Stacey left, stealing Astrid's purse and slamming the door on the way out.

Astrid grumbled and slumped down angrily on the couch, flicking on the television and picking up her laptop. It was just after seven, so the Diane show was on television.

"Drama, drama, drama!" Astrid mumbled under her breath as she scanned over more news articles. Rapes, murders, riots and shoplifting all in her usually safe neighbourhood.

"...So, Cruz… what you're saying is that the global increase in crime is all because you found some relic... some ancient pot in Europe..." the female host, Diane, spoke to her guest speaker, on her television show. The man had long dark hair tied in a ponytail at the back of his head. He was sitting nervously facing Diane. The host's words

5

had grasped Astrid's attention enough to turn up the volume with the remote control.

"Yes, Diane... that's exactly what I'm saying," the dark-haired man said. "...I get that this all sounds rather... coincidental, but I believe that we may have found the resting place of Pandora's Box."

"I don't think that 'coincidental' is quite the word that I would use... Cruz, is it?"

"That's right..."

"Well, I don't believe that coincidental sounds all that accurate... I'd say that it all sounds a little far-fetched... Let me get this straight... You are trying to tell me that you have uncovered the object of a myth... a somewhat holy grail and that the world's crimes are all because you released an ancient curse all over the world... To anyone else that would sound..."

"...It sounds like absolute nonsense! Yeah, I get it! But I saw my own colleagues go from sane one minute to entirely unstable the next... Greed, anger, pride, lust and the rest, just amongst my own team... it was..."

The blonde host leaned in close to Cruz. She was clearly mocking him. "So, your team was affected?"

"Yes, they were... My friend Joey was..."

But once again, Diane interrupted him. "If they were affected then why weren't you? You did open it, so surely you would have suffered from the effects firsthand."

"I'm not entirely sure. Maybe it's because I opened it? But..."

"...and where is this 'Pandora's Box' now? Do you have it on you?"

"No, I don't. You see... it was removed by my supervisors and then the military got involved and..."

"...Thank you... Cruz, the archaeologist..." Diane said, cutting him off. "We have to cut to break now, but it was nice speaking with you! When we return, we'll be looking at the effort that I go through each day, to look simply amazing!"

Astrid turned off the television and looked back down at her laptop in amazement. There were just too many coincidences to everything that had been going on as of late. Her friend's sudden change in behaviour for one thing and the increase in crime were just to name a few.

She clicked on the search bar and typed in 'Europe Excavation site, Pandora's Box' in which she found multiple forums all relating to conspiracy theories and hoaxes. But then, when she added Cruz's name to the search, she was able to pull up his social media profile.

The man had written multiple blogs over the past year, which had all been trolled horribly. He

clearly felt that he had found the resting place of
Pandora's Box and he seemed to be on a mission to
find a cure for the world.

She laughed at the thought that she might
have been giving in to the notion. She was a logical
person and an atheist. This man sounded like a
lunatic. Regardless, she decided to send him a
message just the same.

'Hi, I just saw your segment on the Diane
show. She really seemed to come off as a bitch. My
friend has just recently experienced a sudden
change in behavior. I'm a psychologist, so I have
been putting it down to stress. But, I think you
might be right. There's just something odd going
on.'

She clicked 'send' and wasn't sure if she was
waiting for a response or not. Suddenly, she heard
something smash out in the hallway. It was
followed by loud yelling and a high-pitched scream.

Astrid jumped to her feet and ran over to the
door to look through the peephole. There was a
group of men in the hallway running in and out of
apartments and taking things. Fear swept over her
forcing her to lock the door.

Of the five years that she had lived in this
apartment she had never once experienced a break
in. But now there was a group of men going through
her neighbors' homes taking everything.
Furthermore, by the looks of things they were
clearly assaulting the people who lived there.

Astrid's breath caught in her throat in terror as the men hurried towards her door. She needed a place to hide. She grabbed a sharp knife from the kitchen as well as her phone and made haste to find a spot to hide in. She could hear the banging and the voices of the men trying to get into her apartment.

She ran into her room, locked her bedroom door and hid under her bed, as she dialed for the police.

"Hello, you've reached 911, what is the nature of your call?"

"I need the police, there are some men out in the hall. They've robbed and assaulted my neighbors and now..." She had to fight against her fear for the will to speak.

The men continued to bang loudly on her door. They knew that someone was in there and they were telling her to let them in and make it easier for them.

"...I'm sorry, ma'am... what did you say?" the operator on the phone spoke.

Astrid choked on her fear trying to speak clearly. "There are men trying to get into my apartment... please... they have weapons..."

The operator sighed. "I'm sorry, miss... but you'll need to wait two hours. We will send a patrol car out then."

"I don't understand! But, the precinct is only ten minutes away!" Astrid could hear the banging of her door being beaten in. With one large bang, she knew that they had succeeded in opening it. They were now standing in her living room.

"Come out, come out, wherever you are..." one man said.

"Hey, it looks like women live here... I could have some fun!" another man said.

"That's the latest laptop out... it's mine!"

"Help yourself... I'm looking for the women."

Astrid knew that it was only a matter of time until they found her, and by the sound of the woman on the phone, the authorities would not make it in time. She would need to protect herself.

She eyed her window and knew that it would be a long drop if she fell. But, there was still a ledge that she could walk along, provided she kept close to the wall. She could make haste for the window that led to the stairwell and climb the stairs to the lower floors.

Astrid climbed out from under the bed, clutching her phone and her knife close to her. She struggled to open the window. But after a few heaves, it opened.

She stepped her left foot out the window and rested it carefully on the ledge below. The ledge wobbled a little, but she knew that it would hold her weight. It had to. Her life depended on it!

She took a deep breath and heard as the men began to rattle her bedroom door from the other side. They were trying to get into her room, and by the door being locked, they knew that she was in there.

"Come out, girlie... we just want to have a little fun..." one of the men said with a menacing laugh. Astrid placed her right foot onto the ledge, alongside her left foot, and followed it to the right, facing the weathered brick.

"Alright, Astrid... don't look down." She told herself as she began to sidestep the ledge, heading for the fifth window across, which would lead to the stairwell.

She heard the bang the moment her bedroom door had been slammed open. The men were searching for her and they had made it to her bedroom.

A loud involuntary whimper emerged from her throat as she picked up her pace. While a fear of falling seventeen floors was certainly present, the fear of what might happen if they caught her dictated her actions. She passed the second window and heard the voice of one of the men. "Oh, look here... I found her!"

She didn't bother to look at him. Instead, she continued to sidestep to the next window.

"Come back! I won't bite... not unless you want me to." The man added a biting sound for emphasis, as he stepped out on the ledge to follow her.

Astrid felt the pinch in her gut and her tears willing themselves to come. She told herself to keep going as she reached the third and then the fourth windows. The next window was the one that she needed. Her hands were still tightly clutching her phone and the knife. Her nose was pressed up against the cold brick wall before her.

Alas, she had reached the window, but the glass was closed shut. She wobbled it. Fortunately, it wasn't locked. She had to muster her strength to pull the window open.
The man was catching up fast, he was only a few steps behind her. With one large heave, she pulled up the window. It opened, so she climbed in and dropped to the floor in a panic.

"You can't run anymore, honey." He said as he had reached the window. Astrid clambered to her feet and pulled the glass down fast, locking it in place with him on the outside.

She ran as fast as she could down the stairs and out of sight. She was on the seventeenth floor and it wasn't long until she heard the glass from the window smash. She continued to run as fast as she could, down the stairs, almost out of breath.

But she knew that he would eventually find her. She needed a diversion. He was still two floors above her, yet he couldn't see her, and she couldn't see him. She slipped out the door on the tenth floor and hid in the storage cupboard close by.

The storage cupboard was empty, but from her spot, she could hear the echo of his footsteps when he eventually reached the floor. He didn't exit the stairwell, though. He kept on running down the stairs to find her.

Astrid was surprised to see that her floor wasn't the only floor that had been terrorized that night. The tenth floor was no different, which explained the empty storage cupboard. She waited in the cupboard until she was sure that there was no one after her.

#

Cruz sat alone in his apartment at his desk, riddled with the frustration that sat well with the guilt that he had been dealing with for a year now.

His television interview on the Diane show had been a complete failure. He had ended up looking like nothing more than a nutcase. A crazy man on the street hassling passerbys and telling them that the end was near.

But to him, that's how it was.

Outside his apartment, he could hear the chaos going on. However, they wouldn't be able to make it through his door or his windows. He had upgraded them himself, as soon as he had returned to the United States.

The dim glow of his laptop lit up his dark apartment; he kept his apartment dark at night as it discouraged looters.

Cruz rested back in his desk chair and brought his hands to the back of his head in frustration. He thought back to that day that he had released chaos onto the world by opening that damn jar.

He remembered the last time that he had seen Joey. The man had been overtaken with an anger that had caused him to lose control of who he really was.

Hannah had been overcome with lust, which took over her entire body. She had become nothing more than a wild animal attempting to seduce anyone who passed her by.

Their boss David had become so greedy, that when the military had come to collect the pot, he had caused a major scene getting himself locked up. Even the military and the officers in quarantine suits had become affected.

Cruz had been the only person who had managed to prove immune to the object's curse. He wondered if it had something to do with the whispers that he had heard. But, the thought of whispers making him immune to the Pandora's Box curse was a crazy notion.

Hell, this whole thing was insane! But, as he arrived back home without his friends, and began to watch the news unfold, he realized that this was his new reality.

People became unstable, giving into their weakest desires. The seven deadly sins; rage, greed, lust, jealousy, vanity, sloth and fear.

Cruz had poured himself into survival and research, in his bid to relocate the artifact and put an end to this apocalyptic hellhole.

Fortunately, unlike all the movies he had ever seen in relation to the end of the world, technology and communication was always the first thing to go. But he had figured, that in a world where the prideful people still existed, he could be thankful that he wasn't left to go without.

Cruz was ripped from his thoughts as a notification box came up on his screen. One new message from an Astrid Sutherland. "Another troll, I'm presuming..." he muttered under his breath.

Regardless, he clicked the notification and saw the display picture of the girl. "Hmm. A cute troll," he muttered to himself.

He clicked into the message and read.

'Hi, I just saw your segment on the Diane show. She really seemed to come off as a bitch. My friend has just recently experienced a sudden change in behavior. I'm a psychologist, so I have been putting it down to stress. But, I think you might be right... there's just something odd going on.'

Cruz reread over the message. "Huh! Someone actually believes me? And they're a psychologist?" He typed in his response. 'Is this a joke?'

She must have only just messaged him, so he was surprised when she didn't respond right away. He tapped his fingers on his desk impatiently.

"Come on, Cruz... you're getting anxious waiting for a girl to message you back... And now you're talking to yourself again." He sighed and got up from his desk, making his way through his dim city apartment.

He walked over to the kitchen and pulled out a beer from the fridge. He sipped it as he analyzed his cold food supply. He would need to go and get more food and beer in the morning. He was beginning to run low.

He directed his attention to the hallway, the noise had died down again. Even before he had returned, he had been used to hearing the crime from outside his door. People screaming, gunshots and arguing, he had heard it all.

He lived in that part of New York. But things were getting bad everywhere and not just in his own neighborhood. He sat on the couch and switched on his television, drinking his beer.

The Diane show was just finishing. He wasn't sure what he had been thinking, by choosing to guest on there. Maybe, it was to create an awareness or to get help. But deep down he was giving up hope.

He envisioned Joey throwing his water bottle at his head, just skinning him. The bottle had bounced off the post, splashing water all over him.

"I miss you, man!" Cruz mumbled as he wondered where his friend was, hoping that he was still alive.

He must have dozed off for a little while, as he opened his eyes to the sound of his laptop. It made a quick beeping sound as it received a message. He got to his feet and slumped back to his desk to see that he had a new message from Astrid Sutherland. He clicked on it.

'No, this is not a joke. I need help. Please. I'm stuck in a storage cupboard with only a knife and my phone. The police won't be here for a while and there are men after me. If you know of anyone who lives in my area, can you please send them to help me? Please! I wouldn't normally give out my address, but this is urgent.'

Cruz brushed his hair out of his face and reread the message. Was this a prank? He read the location, it was on the other side of the city.

He would need to find a car if he were to help her. He would be risking his own survival if he did so. But what if she wasn't there? It could all be for nothing.

His conscience got the better of him. If she was telling the truth, and there really were men after her, she might not have much time left. It would not be a pleasant way to die.

"Man, I'm such a sucker for a pretty face!" He got to his feet, collected his survival backpack and pulled out his handheld pistol from his desk. He had never used it before, but he knew how and he kept it for emergencies.

He placed the pistol into his jacket pocket, slung the bag over his shoulder, walked over to the door and listened for sounds in the hallway. Still, there were none. He held the mirror under the door, maneuvering it to check for anyone.

The coast was clear. He unlocked the door, opened it and stepped out into the hallway, locking the door behind him. Remembering every 'Mission Impossible' movie that he had ever seen, he made his way out of the apartment and onto the street.

He tried a few cars, all were a no-go. But then he saw a motorbike sitting casually on the street. Someone had left the keys in the ignition clearly looking for a better ride.
Cruz picked up the keys and sat on the bike. "Okay, let's do this!" He took off and headed for the other side of the city.

Chapter 2

Astrid sat in the storage cupboard, staring at her phone. She had sent the message to Cruz twenty minutes ago when she had heard people in the hallway. The group were currently looting apartments and banging on doors at the other end.

There were multiple groups of looters throughout the building, and not just the ones that had forced her out of her own apartment. Astrid and her knife were certainly no match for any of them. Fortunately, nobody seemed interested in the small closet that she was hiding in.

She thought back to what Cruz had said on the Diane show, about discovering Pandora's Box. That would certainly explain the chaos. People had clearly given in to the Seven Deadly Sins.

But she had always thought of that as nothing more than a myth, and certainly not something that would happen in today's modern society. Astrid glanced back at the message that she had sent the man, asking for help.

She knew that it had been a long shot, but she had sent the same message to multiple people on her social media contact list and he had been the only one who had seen it but had not yet responded.

She had given him her address and her exact hiding spot; the storage cupboard by the stairwell on the tenth floor.

But what if he was just as insane as the rest of them were? He didn't seem to be insane on the television. Quite level headed, actually.

She hoped that he knew someone who lived in her area and had contacted them to help her, and that that was why he hadn't replied. It was an act of desperation.

Astrid waited another twenty more minutes, watching the clock on her phone tick away. She sent another message to Stacey, telling her that it was too dangerous to return home and to find somewhere safe to hide. Suddenly, she heard someone approaching. She locked the screen to her phone, leaving herself in total darkness.

She held her breath, but the footsteps seemed to disappear again. She wanted to leave her hiding spot, but fear only made her stay.

Suddenly, her phone beeped loudly, making her jump. Her battery was going flat. Unfortunately, she wasn't the only one who had heard the beeping.

"Did you hear that?" One man asked from down in the hallway.

"Yeah, I thought I was imagining things... it sounded like a phone."

"It sounded like it came from over there..."

Astrid's heart began to thud as if it were beating out of her chest. Her breathing stopped entirely. Her entire mouth had gone dry. If she kept going the way she was going, she was bound to go into shock from fear alone.

The men began to approach the storage cupboard. She could hear them. She could sense them only a few feet away. She heard the screech of the stairwell door and knew that someone else had arrived.

"Hey guys... so... er, what ya' doing?" The newcomer sounded as if he was standing right in front of the storage cupboard.

"Who does this guy think he is? Back off, Alice Cooper! This place is ours," one of the guys said.

"Seriously? You're going with Alice Cooper? My hair isn't nearly half as long as his... But I can play guitar... and sing, so..."

"Are you a moron?"

"Huh... I suppose I've been called worse... I mean... I was on the Diane Show earlier... seriously... no kidding! She kind of insinuated that I was insane... So I think that's a little worse than moron, because she said it in front of the whole world! Anyway, so what's with the storage cupboard? You guys are looters, right? I bet the goods are all upstairs... isn't that the way the rich people live? I'm not here to steal anything... I promise! I just want to check out the place. Just think guys... all that expensive jewelry and money, just waiting for you upstairs... so, why don't we let each other pass peacefully."

"He's right, boss... insane... but right!" the man who had remained quiet said.

"Shut up, Mark!" his accomplice said.

"Fine, we'll let you leave," he said. The stairwell door screeched again and then banged shut, forcing Astrid to flinch. Was she alone?

"Psst! Astrid, was it? The coast is clear!" The voice of the man who had convinced the other two to leave whispered. "You are still in there, aren't you? Don't tell me that you're not and I did all that for nothing..."

Astrid hesitated before she got to her feet and opened the door. But when she did, she recognized the man from the TV.

"Wow! Oh my god! You actually came!" She blurted out, still in a state of shock. She had dropped both the knife and her phone in the storage cupboard.

"Yeah, of course I came... you needed a hero, right?"

In one swift moment, the stairwell door opened up again, and the man known as 'boss' was standing there with a gun aimed at Cruz.

"Look out!" Astrid gasped as she knocked Cruz backwards and onto the ground, and landed on top of him.

She immediately rolled off of him and he reacted by pulling out his pistol and shooting the other man in the stomach. He dropped the gun in a panic, surprised that he had just used it to shoot someone.

"You asshole!" the man yelled at him in pain, crippling over, trying to shoot at Cruz again.

"Come on! We have to get out of here!" Astrid demanded of Cruz. "Take the gun."

"Sorry, what?" was his response. Astrid picked up the pistol and grabbed him by the hand, leading him down the hallway to the stairwell on the other end of the floor.

Once they had reached the second stairwell, they continued running down the stairs and eventually made their way into the street.

On the street, they found a car, which Cruz hotwired to drive them back to his apartment.

\#

Cruz invited Astrid into his apartment and relocked the door behind them as she immediately went in search for the lights. "Where's the lights for this place?"

"No, no, no!" He gasped, grabbing her hand from the switch beside the door.

He switched on the television instead. "We stick to dim lighting only... it draws much less attention."

Astrid bit her lip and then apologized. She eyed the door's reinforced materials and lock system. "You're prepared," she said.

"You heard my segment. I've been ready for this. It's just going to get worse... Seriously... I just shot a man... I don't know how to get passed that, I don't even know if he's still alive... crap, I might have just committed a murder."

Astrid placed the gun onto the coffee table.

"Keep that thing away from me!" he gasped.

"Relax... the safety's on. It was in self-defense, the man was going to kill you and then... god, I don't want to know what would have happened to me. But, thank you for coming."

Astrid sat down on the couch.

"You know guns?" Cruz asked.

"Of course, I do. I used to go to the gun range with my dad... But, enough about that... what the hell is going on?"

Cruz gave her a full explanation of things from his perspective, starting with him discovering the artifact, the military taking over, all about his research and how it all led to the changes in people's behaviors.

He then went on to say, "You don't seem like you were affected. To be honest, you seem quite calm!"

"I could say the same for you. I mean... if not, a little insane... sorry, that was a joke. But I'm not sure why I wasn't affected. I've been reading into the news reports... a whole lot of drama... and then my best friend Stacey has been a little unstable since she and her ex broke up... but this... the way she's been acting... it's just so out of character for her. She's never stolen a thing in her life... and then she takes a two-thousand-dollar coat in broad daylight... and then my purse..." Astrid gave a deep yawn and then apologized.

"No need to apologize. You yawned... if you're tired I have a spare room."

"Thanks... but I'm still just trying to wrap my head around all of this... Why did it take a year for our city to be hit?"

"It spreads like a virus... it seems somewhat airborne... but it even went through the quarantine suits... so, it's just... it's strange... you know? I remember hearing whispers when I opened the jar. I'm guessing that that's what kept me safe. It's like some sort of curse. My friends began coughing pretty badly, when they were affected... I thought that I had killed them... But you... you're something else. It actually has me wondering if there are more like us out there. I've been trying to work out where Pandora's Box is now located. The military were infected, too... so they could have gotten sloppy. I'm thinking if we can find it, we can study it... and if we can study it, then we can work out how to stop it."

"How to stop it? I'm not a scientist, but I'm guessing that that will be no small feat... this thing... it's like a zombie movie... or the apocalypse, or something... But, very different..." Astrid yawned again.

"The spare room's in there. Go get some rest." Cruz pointed towards the room.

"I'm sorry... but, I've just met you... it's probably not a good idea to...

"...Astrid, if I was infected by lust or something, I would have made out with you the moment you fell on top of me back there... but I quite literally risked my ass to save you. Trust me, you're safe."

Astrid stood up, said "goodnight," and made her way towards the spare room, as Cruz spent the next hours researching on his laptop. This had clearly become his life.

"There has to be some sort of pattern here..." he mumbled to himself. They were located in New York, but her question plagued him. Why had it taken a year to get to the city and why did it last so long once it was coursing through an individual's bloodstream?

He knew that he needed to find a doctor. He considered their immunities. There had to be a doctor, who was just as immune to the virus as they were and was just as intrigued in finding out the answers.

After a few hours he had run a search of medical forums in relation to the Seven Deadly Sins. No one really seemed concerned except for one man, who came off as if he had a superiority complex going on. Dr. Gregory Reynolds.

He had lost his career and family due to his beliefs. He had claimed to have synthesized a treatment for the current behavioral plague that had taken over mankind.

His current whereabouts were unknown. "Another brick wall, meant to be broken down... wherever you are, Reynolds, I'll find you." Cruz mumbled, very tiredly.

He began searching for an email address, as Astrid's voice made him jump. "At least I'm not the only person who talks to myself... Sorry for startling you... I just keep tossing and turning and it doesn't matter how tired I am. I just can't sleep."

"There's coffee over there if you want some... I think I might have found someone who can help us put the world back to normal. I just found an email address."

"I'm sorry... I get that you're on a mission, but I still need to go back and check on my friend. I still have a job to get back to and a li..."

"Seriously! What you just saw back there has become the world that we are currently living in. I lost my friends because of this, and if your friend has been affected by greed, like I believe she has... she will be nothing more than a monster. If you want to help her, your best option is to help me... otherwise you're more than welcome to go back to your home..."

"Okay, I'll help." Astrid rolled her eyes. "Just let me put on some coffee... I can't half tell you've been alone for a while."

Cruz shook his head slowly. Of all the women that he had to be saddled up with, she was turning out to be a real pain in the ass.

Cruz sent an email to Dr. Reynolds, informing him that he held some sort of immunity for the virus, but he was willing to join forces and work together to put a stop to the chaos.

With her coffee cup in hand, Astrid sat beside him and looked over the articles that sat on the desk. "Wow, you've done a hell of a lot of research in a year." She exclaimed. "So, what can I help with?"

"I normally do all of this alone, so I'm sorry, but I don't have any jobs for you." He spoke as his eyes were glued to his screen.

"You sure know how to make a woman feel needed." She replied. She made her way over to the couch and flicked through the TV channels with the remote.

The news displayed nothing but chaos. The reporters were all characterized by vanity and laziness which made the delivery of the news reports very interesting to watch.

"Wow, I'm surprised that Nick Bellows even turned up to work, look... he's eating at the desk..." Astrid laughed at the news reporter on the late news.

"Hmm? Yeah..." Cruz muttered from over at his computer, entirely immersed into his research.

Astrid rolled her eyes and got back to quietly watching the news and feeling like a burden, as Cruz was delighted to see a message from Dr. Reynolds.

'Hi, Cruz... I watched your segment on the Diane show. We should meet. Signed, Dr. Gregory Reynolds. M.D.'

The email continued to give his location. "This guy lives on the other side of the country!"

"Who does?" Astrid looked up at him from her spot.

"This Dr. Gregory Reynolds. He believes that he might have a treatment for the curse... he wants to meet, but he needs us to go to him."

Astrid finished the last of her coffee. "Okay... the sooner we get this over with, the sooner we can go our separate ways..."

"You're sure?" he asked her. "You don't want to go back to your apartment to collect anything?"

"Like what? Those guys robbed me... My friend is nowhere to be found and this world is going to shit. We may as well join forces and get this over with."

"Alright, then we leave now!"

#

Fortunately, the car that Cruz had picked up to bring both he and Astrid back to his apartment, was still in the parking lot. They loaded it up with enough supplies for the trip and climbed in.

As Cruz pulled out of the parking lot and onto the road, Astrid questioned him. "So, if this guy lives on the other side of the country, why don't we just catch a plane?"

"Because right now, flying would be very dangerous. We can't trust the pilots. They'd be too unstable."

"I guess that makes sense... but a road trip to San Francisco, it seems kind of dangerous and very long. Not to mention we're going to have to find motels to stay at... and I'm going to need to cancel my credit cards, and get my cash from the bank... So, we will need to deal with unstable people and..."

"...Do you realize that you talk a lot? And considering I've been living in solitude for a year now... it's a big difference to what I'm used to." he replied, focusing on the road. "But seriously, yeah, I get it. Let's just try not to make any unnecessary stops, shall we?"

"Sorry, I talk when I'm nervous... Plus, I'm just trying to be logical... Look, if you and I have to do this, let's just try and get along."

"Do I make you nervous?"

"Yeah, a little bit. Especially when you act like a patronizing dick. Besides, I think that I have a right to be nervous... look at everything I've had to deal with tonight... At least you've had a year to prepare yourself. I've barely had a day and I was forced from my apartment by a group of men."

"Alright, sorry... let's just listen to the radio." He switched it on. The radio host had chosen not to play any tracks, but to sing his own tone-deaf covers of famous songs.

"Yikes!" Astrid exclaimed as she turned off the radio again. She raided the compartments for music and was relieved to find some good old classic rock. "Okay... this will do..." she said as she inserted the cd into the stereo.

Cruz continued to ignore her humming, as he managed to get to the outskirts of the city. "Whoa! Turn that down!" he told her, as he did so himself.

"Why?" she asked as she looked up to see a major road blockage of police cars up ahead. "Oh crap." She added.

She retrieved the pistol from the back seat and placed it into the pocket of her coat. She applied the central locking to all the doors from the middle control panel.

"Let's just hope that they don't ask for papers," Cruz said as he reached the intersection, pulled off to the side of the road and opened his window.

Aside from the three police cars, there was no one else about. An officer approached the window and peered his head into the car, giving the vehicle an overall look.

Astrid examined him, trying to determine what sin the officer was suffering from – if any at all. It wasn't obvious at first, but after a close examination of his perfectly neatened hair, his button-up collar and his perfect composure, she worked it out immediately.

"Hi guys... where are the two of you headed this early, at five in the morning?" he asked them. Astrid eyed the rest of the officers.

Two were arguing and one was sitting eating in his car, with another officer. 'Three police cars, five officers... there's one officer missing,' Astrid thought to herself.

"Sorry, officer, my girlfriend and I were headed out on a road trip... You know what they say about the early bird, right?" Cruz said casually.

He took hold of Astrid's hand for her to play along. Astrid took his hand and interlaced his fingers into hers.

There was something about their hands interlaced together that way that felt so right to them. It was clear that they could both sense the chemistry between them.

"I'm sorry, sir, but I've been at my job for a long time so I know how to spot a liar. You're going to have to step out of the car, please." The officer said. He had clearly been hit by pride.

Cruz glanced at Astrid, to reassure her, let go of her hand and turned off the central locking. He had no choice but to comply. He unbuckled his seatbelt and attempted to open the door.

"Hey, officer." Astrid said, stopping Cruz mid action. "My boyfriend and I really wanted to beat the rush... and I can tell that you are absolutely amazing at your job. I also know that you guys get a pretty bad rep around these parts...

So, how about you just let us go? I'll even put in a compliment to your supervisor at the precinct... what do you say?" She gave an award-winning smile in the officer's direction.

The officer shuffled on his feet, a little bashfully. "You'd really do that for me, miss?"

"Of course, I would... You're busting your asses off out here... and for what? Probably not enough to pay the bills."

Cruz sent Astrid a smile and then glanced back at the officer. "Yeah... you just have to love that about her." He added. "She's always the first person to stand up for the middle man. You bet your ass she will. I'm guessing the minute that you let us pass, she'll be on the phone calling your superiors and begging that they give you a raise."

The officer pulled out his notebook and leaned on the roof of the car as he scribbled something down. "You're good." Cruz mouthed to Astrid with a smile. She continued to watch the officer, hoping that her plan had worked.

He approached Cruz's window again and handed Astrid the slip of paper. "That's my superior's number, and that's the accurate spelling of my name. Thank you, miss."

Suddenly, there was a gun shot. One of the officers who had been fighting had shot his partner.

"Alright, you two... get out of here... Now!" the officer told them.

"You don't have to tell me twice!" Cruz said. He put his seatbelt on and sped off down the road, as the officer called for backup and went to apprehend the shooter.

"Wow!" Cruz let out a large sigh of relief, as he drove them down the road, as fast as he could, without getting a speeding ticket.

Astrid glanced behind them and saw the stand-off between the two officers. It didn't seem like anyone was coming for backup.

"I take it you've had practice with sweet talking officers?" Cruz asked her.

"Not officers... I've dated a few egotistical jerks, though. It's all about reading people, Cruz."

"...and what do you read when it comes to me?"

"That you're a loner and that's how you'd like it to stay... Maybe I should call the precinct, I just hope that officer was alright."

Chapter 3

In his mind, Cruz could remember the moment that he had been frozen in his tracks. Joey and Hannah were both coughing severely, while he had just come off the phone to the quarantine team. But then, just as instant as their coughing had begun, it came to a complete stop.

They both seemed fine. That was until Joey had begun rambling angrily at Cruz, and Hannah had quite literally offered to sleep with Joey right there in the tent.

"Whoa, guys... what's going on?" Cruz asked them, entirely confused.

"You should know! You asshole! You caused this!" Joey yelled as he threw the bottle of water at him. Cruz managed to duck, but the open bottle splashed water into his hair.

"Naww... Cruz, why don't you and I go somewhere private to dry you off," Hannah said approaching him with a towel, and patting his hair lovingly. The way that she had looked at him scared the hell out of him.

"What the hell is wrong with you!" Joey demanded. "Cruz, you're supposed to be my best friend! Not sleeping with my girl!"

Cruz backed out of Hannah's vicinity, just as their boss, David, had entered the tent. "What's going on in here?" he demanded.

Cruz ran over to the jar and tried to put the lid back on, hoping that it would stop the curse, but it would not seal. It was as if there were some negative force repelling it from closing again.

"We found this, David... I think it has some kind of power." Cruz handed the pithos over to David to examine, holding the lid over the opening.

David begun coughing and dropped the pithos. Amazingly enough, the artifact did not smash. By this time, Joey and Hannah had begun making out in a fierce aggressive frenzy and the quarantine team arrived on to the scene.

One of the men demanded to know what was going on as David picked up the jar and refused to hand it over. Cruz wasn't sure how to answer, and the quarantine staff began coughing through their masks.

He had no choice but to leave the tent. He was astonished to find that people had been affected outside of the tent, too, and they weren't even close to the artifact.

He tried to enter the tent again, but no one would let him back in. Then the military arrived. Cruz managed to slip out before things got much worse.

#

"Cruz! Pull over, now!" Astrid's voice broke in over his thoughts. He had been falling asleep while driving. He pulled to the side of the road and parked. "I'm sorry... I just..."

"You're tired, you've been driving for hours. We're lucky that I woke up when I did, we could have had an accident. I'll take over, you just get some rest."

He knew that he couldn't be bothered to argue, so he did as she demanded, and fell asleep the minute that he had climbed into the passenger seat.

Astrid smiled over at him and continued driving amongst the traffic in the middle of the day.

She was hungry, so she decided to stop in the next city to get a bite to eat and cancel her credit cards, hoping that Stacey hadn't made too many purchases on her behalf.

Cruz awoke the moment that the car had come to a stop in the parking lot of the bank. He joined Astrid as she entered the building. He waited at the seats as she approached the clerk at the counter.

The clerk had been filing her nails and barely looked in Astrid's direction. "I need to cancel all my credit cards, as my purse was stolen. I also need to get some money out from my account, please." The woman stared at her, sighed and got back to filing her nails.

Astrid took a deep breath. "Can you please just take the time from your nails and do this for me? It's your job and you're getting a line up. I really don't want to piss anybody off."

The woman sighed very loudly and put down her nail file and began typing slowly. "What is your name, your date of birth and your address?" the woman asked with a very bored tone.

Astrid gave her details and then gestured for Cruz to join her at the counter. When he arrived, the woman was still typing very slowly.

"Did you ever see that kid's movie, 'Zootopia?' Cruz asked Astrid, making her stifle a laugh. The clerk stared up at them, as if slightly offended, but did not bother to say anything further.

"Yes, there has been a large amount of purchases on your card... Would you like to report this as a crime? We can have them arrested immediately..."

"Please just cancel the cards..."

"You will be held liable for the purchases unless you report this to the police, miss."

Astrid hesitated for a moment, but gave in. She knew that she couldn't let Stacey get away with her actions.

"Sure, make a report... and please cancel the cards... I also need to get some mon..." before Astrid could finish her sentence, the woman handed her a large stack of forms to fill in.

"Please sign these!"

Astrid glanced at the forms and looked at Cruz, but took a pen from the desk, regardless. They made their way towards the chairs in the waiting area to fill the forms out.

They looked back to see that the woman had gone back to filing her nails, and had entirely ignored her other customers.

As Astrid filled in the forms, Cruz analyzed the people standing in the queue. Most of them seemed to be suffering from fear, clearly they sought comfort in the bank's high security. Fortunately, none of them seemed like an issue.

But, there was one man who was clearly dealing with rage. He had been arguing with someone on his phone. He threw the phone across the bank, just missing one of the clerks. "I'm sick of this!" he stormed up towards the woman at the counter, who was still filing her nails.

"Serve me, now! You lazy bitch!" he demanded of her.

Please, sir, you'll have to get back in line and wait your turn..." she said casually.

"But you're not serving anyone!" the man pulled out a pistol and aimed it at her. "Serve me now! I'm not here to hold up the place or steal anything! Just serve me!"

The clerk barely battered an eye lash, but the customers in the line started screaming and running for shelter.

Cruz swore in Spanish and then mumbled, "They were afraid enough as it was, and now they're all in shock."

He got to his feet.

"What are you doing?" Astrid asked. She stood up beside him and placed the papers down on her chair. "I'm going to help... you stay here." He instructed.

"No, I'm coming with you."

Cruz shook his head annoyed that she could be risking her life, but then made his way towards the man.

"Hey, we don't need to cause any trouble here, man. Why don't you just put the gun down and then this lovely woman will help you." He looked over at the clerk who stared at Cruz, as if to say: 'are you kidding me?'

"Who the hell do you think you are?" the gun wielder demanded of Cruz as he waved the weapon in his face.

Cruz took a few steps back, inching closer to the wall behind him. "Whoa, hey, it's okay... I'm just the guy trying to keep the peace."

"You have to the count of three to put the gun down!" A male clerk said. "Get out of my bank! You'll spill blood on the carpets."

41

"Oh no... don't play the hero." Cruz whispered under his breath. The angry man instantly turned and released a bullet into the clerk's chest with perfect precision and a loud deafening bang.

"Hey, hey, hey! Please don't hurt anyone else!" Cruz pleaded, but the weapon was now being aimed at him again.

Astrid who had been trying to help the scared customers to safety, couldn't bear to see her friend in such a predicament.

The sight of him in danger forced her to take action to protect him. She subtly stepped up from behind the man who was holding the gun, and instantly disarmed him.

She was standing in between him and Cruz, holding the gun that she had taken, aiming it at the angry man.

"Now, you can continue being angry, sir... but you're going to have to leave. You're scaring everybody." she said sternly.

"Why... you fucking bitch! Give me back my gun!" he shouted. He went to charge for her, but she shot at the ground by his feet, just missing him. He stopped, but he was still angry.

"Now leave... or I promise... the next one won't miss!"

They could hear sirens blaring outside. The man knew that he wouldn't make it far.

Nonetheless, he grumbled loudly and made haste out the door furiously.

Astrid spotted another clerk at the counter. He had seen everything that she had done and was trying to hide away in fear. "Cruz, can you get my forms for me, please? I want to get this over with and be out of here."

She walked towards the young scared man. "Look... I'm not going to hurt you. I just need you to process a few things quickly and retrieve my money out of my account. Can I trust for you to do it quickly?" she asked in a comforting tone.

Cruz handed her forms over to her, and the clerk nodded quietly. "I don't even know why I come to work anymore." The clerk said as tears streamed down his face.

He was shivering in fear, which brought Astrid to feel nothing but empathy. However, he obliged and did as she had requested very quickly.

When they were done, Astrid handed him the gun that she had taken from the man. "Give this to the police, tell them what happened. I'm trusting you to look after it until then." Then, she and Cruz left quickly out the bank doors to find their car.

#

Astrid and Cruz picked up some hot dogs from a street vendor and immediately carried on with their trip.

"Why the hell did you do that, back there? You could have gotten yourself killed!" Cruz demanded of her, as he had taken over the driving. This was the first thing that he had said to her since the incident at the bank.

"Calm down. I knew what I was doing..."

"You knew? So it wasn't just some freaky adrenaline thing? Because... that back there..."

"...I saved your ass, Cruz. So, you're welcome. Now, just drop it! Okay?"

He took a deep breath and sighed deeply. "I don't mean to sound ungrateful, because I'm very grateful that you did that for me... no one has ever risked their life for me like that before... I just don't understand why or even how... how did you know how to do that? I thought you were just some pretty uptown girl... but that?"

"Naww... you called me pretty." Astrid joked.

"I'm serious... that was very unexpected. Where did you learn that?"

"My dad was a general in the military..."

"...so what? Like father like daughter?"

"Not exactly... there's more to it. But, I really don't want to bore you."

"Well, now you have to tell me..."

Astrid sighed. "Well, my first boyfriend wasn't exactly the nicest guy. Very handsome... but a bit of a jerk with an ego to boot... let's just say that something happened, my father was pissed and pushed for him to be charged as an adult and then he made sure that I learned how to defend myself. He had been away when it had happened... and while he was out protecting the country... he felt that he had failed in protecting his only daughter."

"I'm sorry to hear that. Where's he now?"

"He died a few years back."

"Ouch! What about your mom?"

"She's currently upstate. Dementia settled in quite early with her. Now, enough about me... I just told you my story... You can tell me yours."

"Ha... the old 'I show you mine, you show me yours' routine, huh? Okay... I've had a typical life. I was born in Puerto Rico, though I was too young to remember much. My family moved around a lot and then I moved to the city. I went to college with my friend Joey, we studied archaeology together... man, we did everything together. And then we went on the excavation trip to Europe... and that's pretty much it."

"So, what happened to Joey?"

Cruz sighed, but didn't take his eyes off the road, nor could he find the right way to answer her question.

"He's the reason you want to fix all of this, isn't he?" she asked sadly.

Cruz nodded. "I mean... he could still be alive... but if I hadn't convinced him to do this with me... if I hadn't of opened that damn thing... he wouldn't have changed... but hey... at least he got Hannah. Man, that guy was the closest thing I had to a brother."

"Don't worry. We'll help them all. I promise."

Astrid sent him a comforting smile.

Cruz smiled back at her.

There was a moment between them, where neither one of them needed to say a word. It was almost as if they could read each other's minds. It was clear that the two had a lot of chemistry between them, but there was also much more to it than that.

"You should... er... probably keep your eyes on the road." Astrid said, blushing a little. She turned to stare out her window. While he stared back at the road and smiled to himself, amazed that such a beautiful woman thought of him highly enough, to risk her own life for him.

Cruz continued to drive as far as he could, barely stopping unless necessary, until the night time hit, along with a sudden downpour of rain.

"We should find a motel or something." Astrid said,

"It's getting too dangerous."

"We should be fine."

Just as Cruz had spoken, a large bolt of lightning struck a tree up ahead, along with a loud rumble of thunder.

"Alright... point taken," Cruz said. "We'll stop at the next motel that we come across."

#

It took about twenty minutes until they came across a shady looking motel on the side of the road. Fortunately, the motel owner was clearly suffering with sloth.

He had fallen asleep at the counter and proved to be a real struggle to wake up. When they finally managed to wake him, he handed them the key and went back to sleep, no questions asked.

"Wait, isn't he even going to take our money?" Astrid asked. But Cruz took the money instead and led her to the motel room.

"We might need the cash later."

#

The room was small and only had one king bed, a couch, a small table and a television which clearly hadn't been upgraded since the nineties. The lighting was already very dim.

"I don't mind sleeping on the couch... you can take the bed," Cruz offered as he closed and locked the door behind them.

Astrid set Cruz's survival bag down on the table.

"But the couch is so small... I'm shorter than you, it would just make more sense if..." She stopped talking, to see Cruz staring at her, asking that she not argue with him on the sleeping arrangements.

"Okay, you can have the couch then, wow... it's just a couch!" She made her way towards the bed and sat down to take off her shoes.

"Wow, you always have to get the final word in, don't you?" he laughed at her.

"Not always!"

He smirked and shook his head. There was no point arguing with her. "Would you mind passing over one of those pillows?"

She leaned over and picked up the pillow that she wouldn't be using and threw it at his head.

"Er... Thanks," he said calmly as it bounced onto the floor. He picked it up and placed it on the couch. Cruz turned on the television. The volume was already very low, so he turned off the light and then laid down on the couch.

Astrid crawled into the blankets on the bed and attempted to get comfortable. She really needed a shower and a change of clothes and she couldn't get comfortable knowing that she was still in the clothes that she had worn the day before. She continued to move around in the bed restlessly.

"Are you okay over there?" Cruz asked.

"I can't get comfortable. I need a shower and a fresh change of clothes."

"Hmm... we can always pick you up something tomorrow before we head out."

"Thanks, I appreciate it..."

Cruz thought that that was the end of their conversation for the night when Astrid brought up another question that had been plaguing her. "Cruz, has any of your research given you a theory on how to reverse the effects?"

He sat up and gave her his full undivided attention from his location on the couch, so she, too, sat up. "I'm not sure, but if Greek mythology has told us anything, it's that the seven deadly sins have been with mankind since day one... back when Pandora first opened it. But, when I found the pithos, it was sealed as if someone had glued it shut and hidden it. But then, as the story went, there was one last thing that was left inside the jar... and that was hope. So, my first theory is that we relocate this indestructible inspirational artifact for pottery barn... shake it up a little and see if we can bring it out... but, honestly, I'm not sure if that will even work... because the lid wouldn't go back on... But I guess that I'm hoping that we can do it."

"That we can bring out hope? Even if it's invisible?"

"Mm hmm." he nodded.

"...I hope it works, too," Astrid said sadly, knowing that he was clutching at straws. "Well, for what's it's worth... it's certainly been fun riding with you. You're not as antisocial as I thought you were."

"Thanks, and you're not as much of a pain in the ass as I thought you were..."

"You thought I was a pain in the ass?" She asked with a smirk.

"Yeah... a little bit... I mean, you still are... just not as bad as I once thought."

Astrid could feel herself blushing again. "I think we should get some sleep. I'll see you in the morning." She laid back down and this time managed to get comfortable.

Cruz smiled back at her and got comfortable on the couch. He said "goodnight" and smiled to himself when she said it back. He fell asleep instantly.

Chapter 4

The next morning, Astrid took the car out early to go shopping, while Cruz slept. This was the first time that she had hotwired a car, since he had shown her how.

She was looking for clothes, accessories and a new purse and managed to locate a store that wasn't very busy.
The woman that served her at the boutique had a very prideful persona which wasn't too much of a strain to deal with.

However, as she was placing her bags into the car, she saw a sharply dressed suited man throwing himself onto a woman out of lust. Before Astrid could offer any assistance, the woman pulled out a gun and shot him angrily, releasing multiple bullets into his chest.

Astrid gasped and climbed into the car before the woman could turn the gun on her. She had left Cruz's pistol in the motel room amongst their luggage, and she knew that disarming the woman from such a distance would prove to be reckless.

She arrived back at the apartment, where Cruz was still asleep, and hopped into the shower.

The water running must have woken him, because by the time she had showered, dressed, done her hair and stepped out of the bathroom, he was sitting at the coffee table with his laptop and breakfast.

She wasn't sure if it was the way his hair was sitting, his stubble that had begun to cover his face or even his intense look that he got whenever he was busy, but there was something about him that had captivated her attention.

He could clearly feel her gaze on him, because without removing his eyes from the screen, he sipped his coffee as he spoke. "I went down to the café for breakfast, the guy was actually afraid of me... like hiding behind the counter, afraid... but I managed to get some coffee and breakfast croissants. Hope you're hungry." He gestured to the breakfast that was sitting on the table beside his laptop.

She sat down beside him and took a sip of her coffee. "Thanks... What are you reading?" she asked, removing her eyes from him and looking over at the laptop screen.

"It seems my interview on the Diane show the other night has been sparking a little controversy. Though, these people clearly aren't immune to the curse like we are. This is an entirely biased post from a very angry man, calling me a 'whacko'... he goes on to say that 'humanity is just as fucked up as it has always been' and that it's no different to the way it was before. And that I'm just trying to get my 'five minutes of fame'. Everyone is such a critic... but you see the difference, right? I'm not going crazy, am I?"

He looked at her for the first time since she had entered the room. He marvelled at just how pretty she looked when she was dolled up.

Astrid sighed, as she read over the man's comments about Cruz. "No, you're not going crazy. I've seen a lot of crazy things and a lot of unstable people... Try to think of it this way, it's the ones who think they're going crazy that are the..." before she could finish her sentence, he leaned over and kissed her.

He pulled away for a moment, surprised that he had given into his own temptation.

He cleared his throat. "Sorry... I probably shouldn't have done that without asking you first. I promise... I'm not that kind of guy..."

Astrid blushed. "No, don't be sorry... you just caught me by surprise." She leaned forward and kissed him back. They wrapped their arms around each other and began to give in to their urges.

It was the type of kiss that you would see in the movies, filled with passion and an urgency of two people who just needed to be together. This sudden elevation in their relationship had both surprised them, but at the same time it felt absolutely right. It was almost as if they were meant to be together.

But, before it could go any further, they were interrupted by a loud thump at the door, which startled them and forced them to look up. The thump was followed by the loud voices of two angry men yelling at one another from outside.

"It doesn't seem like they're trying to get in," Cruz said with a flirtatious smile, "...plus the door's locked, anyway." It was clear that he wanted to keep kissing her.

But Astrid stood up trying to regain her composure. "...we should... ahem... we should probably get back on the road, or we'll never make it to San Francisco... Have you been in contact with that doctor recently? Does he know that we're on our way?"

Cruz was surprised by her sudden change of behaviour. Nonetheless, he didn't persist. "Yeah, apparently things are getting pretty dire there. I can't see how it could be any different to what we've already seen... and this treatment that he's been talking about, it's like some fancy mood-stabilizer or something. So, I guess we'll just have to see for ourselves."

He stood up and they began to pack their things again. They heard the sound of glass smashing from outside but thought nothing of it.

Once they had packed everything that they needed, they stepped outside of their motel room and locked the door behind them.

"Hey, Cruz... I think I know what that smashing sound was earlier," Astrid said, with fear in her tone.

"What?" Cruz asked, but as he turned to see what she was referring to, he saw that a man's head had been smashed into the window of their car and it all made sense.

#

Cruz borrowed the phone in the main office, beside the still sleeping owner, to call the police. As he did so, Astrid sat on a chair in the waiting area, in complete shock at what they had just seen.

Her entire world was spinning. She took a sip of her water bottle. She knew that hydration was important when it came to dealing with shock, but she could barely think straight.

She had been to many open casket funerals in her lifetime, so a dead body was nothing new to her. But the way the man had died was traumatizing to see.

She thought back to the post that the man had written about Cruz, saying that the world had always been this way. No, it hadn't. Everywhere they went people were giving into their own inner demons. Even the upstanding citizens and police officers had become criminals.

Astrid knew that the police would not attend to the matter, they had become too vain and too lazy to do so. She wasn't sure if Cruz's plan to put the world back to normal would work, but the fact that they weren't going to just stand back and do nothing, was a start.

"That was useless," Cruz said as he approached her, interrupting her from her own thoughts. "The police aren't going to do anything, and now we don't have a car, either. How are you coping?"

She sighed. "I'm coping."

He sat down beside her and put his arm around her shoulder. "Astrid, you don't need to play it tough. You can talk to me."

"Yeah, I know that I can... But right now, I don't want to. So, let's just find a car, fill it up and get the hell out of here!"

Astrid pulled out some money from her purse and left it with a note addressed to the motel owner, saying 'thank you' for the room and the rental of his car, promising that they would return it. She felt that this was a good gesture, which was currently very rare to see in this world.

They took the man's car keys and left in search for his vehicle in the parking lot.

"Who would have thought? That sleepy motel owner has a pretty sweet ride," Cruz said smiling as they loaded their bags up into the backseat of the black impala.

"I'm thinking midlife crisis... But, doesn't it remind you of that TV show?"

It was clear that he was trying to make her laugh, but it wasn't working. They climbed into the car and he pulled out of the parking lot.

He continued to glance over at her as she rested her head on the glass of the window. He spoke after a while, though not expecting for her to respond. "I know that this has been a real eye opener, but we will get through all of this. You being immune to the curse has given me hope that not everyone has been affected. We will find Pandora's Box, and we will put the world right again. I just know it."

Astrid smiled up at him. This man, although they had only just met, gave her hope. There was a childlike optimism in him that he seemed to be clinging to. It seemed to be the only thing that he had left to stop him from giving up.

#

They had been driving for hours, listening to nothing but silence, when Astrid finally spoke up. She had been shuffling around the compartments looking for music.

"This man has no music..." she sighed.

Cruz was surprised to hear her speak up again. He needed to say something to take her mind off of the traumatizing scene that they had both witnessed. He forced himself to say something witty.

"Who needs music? I'm pretty sure that you and I might have shared a pretty steamy kiss back there... and I don't know about you, but, ah... I like to kind of know everything about a girl before we start locking lips."

Astrid was surprised, she hadn't expected him to bring that up so soon, but she realized what he was trying to do. "It was pretty steamy... wasn't it? Well, what do you want to know about me?"

"Okay, first... what's your favorite color? Do you have a middle name?"

"It's blue... and my middle name's Hope."

"Hope?" Cruz smirked and raised his eyebrows. "That has a sweet irony to it... I mean, the myth with Pandora and all... We need hope to defeat this curse."

"It is pretty ironic, isn't it? But now it's my turn for a question... so... what got you into archaeology?" His plan to take her mind off the scene from earlier was actually working.

"Honestly?"

"Mm hmm," she said with a smile.

"Okay... but you can't laugh, alright?"

"I won't. I promise."

"Well, er... when I was a little kid, I wasn't the coolest... or the most popular... I never really got the girl. But, I was really obsessed with the Indiana Jones movies, I guess that wouldn't have helped my case. But I remember saying that I wanted to be just like him and find something amazing. Some historical treasure... but now, I guess that I'm eating my own words, huh?"

Astrid couldn't help but laugh.

"Hey, you promised that you wouldn't laugh... you lied." Cruz laughed back.

"I'm sorry... I just couldn't help myself... that's just so cute. I mean that doesn't actually sound anything like you... even in the slightest. It's so hard to picture it... But how obsessed are we talking here, like, seen every movie over a hundred times obsessed... or?"

"We're talking about me knowing every word to all the movies off by heart obsessed."

"Okay. That's pretty obsessed."

"Yeah, so now it's my turn again..."

"Wait... hold that thought," Astrid said noticing the current town that they were in. "Take a look around us!"

Cruz took in what she was referring to. While there were multiple vehicles lining the streets, there didn't seem to be one person in sight.

He pulled over to the side of the road. The instant that they hopped out of the car, they were met by a strong distinct smell. They had to hold their noses as they walked up the street to thoroughly examine the ghost town that they were in.

"I don't like that smell," Astrid groaned.

"I know what you mean... the smell of the dead. It's quite potent."

It was clear that this town had allowed for the seven deadly sins to take over. Rubbish and rotting carcasses lined the streets. There was not a thing in sight that had not been smashed up in some way. It was a scary site to behold.

"Well, I think we know how mankind is going to die out," Cruz said as he caught the image of a body lying on the ground beside a dumpster in his peripheral vision.

"Cruz... let's just go, please?" Astrid said as she turned back in the direction towards their car.

"That won't be happening, missy!" They both looked up to see just who had spoken. There was a group of men standing beside their car with weapons, eyeing the two of them like fresh meat.

Astrid took Cruz's hand in her own out of fear.
There was no way of getting into their car without bypassing the men.

They stared at the four men before them, trying to decipher not only what sins they had been affected with, but also what their motives were.

They seemed relatively calm, but at the same time, it was as if they were planning something. They were dressed casually in jeans and shirts. But their shotguns clearly meant business.

Cruz and Astrid felt that maybe these people might have been immune to the curse. "I'm sorry... but we were just leaving," Astrid said, afraid to step out of line.

"You clearly didn't hear me earlier, missy... you will not be going anywhere," The man said.

"Why not?" she asked, but Cruz squeezed her hand tightly, trying to tell her not to piss the men off.

"Because we will not allow it," the man replied.

"I need to ask," Cruz said, trying to shift the limelight from Astrid and on to himself, as he stepped in front of her subtly. "You guys are clearly aware of what's been going on around here... but why do you all seem so calm?"

The man nodded at his men, and they approached and pointed their weapons at Cruz and Astrid.

"Get down on the floor, before we shoot you and have some fun with your girlfriend here," The leader demanded. Cruz nodded at Astrid, they had no choice but to comply. They slowly kneeled on the ground obediently.

Astrid and Cruz were led into the back of the van and were taken to the town's old police department, which the men had turned into their own base of operations. They were locked in a holding cell as the men left to determine just what to do with them.

"Cruz, we need to find a way to get out of here," Astrid said, as she sat down on the metal bed, looking around at their new environment.

"I don't think that those guys were affected. They didn't seem to be acting as if they were," Cruz replied as he examined the office on the other side of the bars, trying to make sense of their captors.

"It's not the point. Even if they haven't been affected, I don't trust them."

Cruz turned to face her. "Astrid, I won't let anything happen to you. As soon as we get the moment, we'll find a way to escape. But until then, they must know something and I'm going to find out."

Just as he had finished speaking, the door opened and three of the men returned into the office. Cruz sat down beside Astrid and held her hands in his.

"We're sorry to keep the two of you waiting, but you see, we can't be too careful with intruders in our town," the leader said, addressing them from the other side of the bars. "There's been a lot of... unstable characters as of late. It's almost like a zombie virus... right? But then, my friend here...well, he recognized you from the television... said you might be of some use to us."

"What sort of use?" Cruz asked. "I mean you seem pretty immune to the curse... why?"

The men laughed at him. "It's funny that you call it a curse... but regardless, I could say the same of you... I'll be blunt, we want the medicine!" he demanded.

"What medicine?" Astrid asked.

The sound of her voice seemed to anger him. "Don't play stupid! The mood stabilizers!"

Suddenly, the door opened again. It was the fourth member of the group. He shook his head at the leader and then gestured to speak in private.

They left, leaving the other two guarding Astrid and Cruz staring at them like wild animals in a cage and making them feel very unsettled.

When the leader returned, there was pure anger in his face. He charged for the bars and rattled them. "Lucas tells me that you don't have them in your car... which means, you would have to have them on you... give them to me!" He intimidated them both.

"We don't have any!" Cruz demanded.

But the man didn't believe him. He nodded at his men and one of them opened the cell door, while the other two aimed their shotguns at them. Cruz and Astrid immediately got to their feet.

"Now... where are my manners?" the leader said. "My name is Vince and this is Lucas, Tony and Gabe... I figured that I should be polite before we take the medication from you."

"What the hell are you talking about?" Cruz demanded. "We don't have any medication! You need to understand that!"

Lucas and Tony restrained Cruz, just as Gabe grabbed a hold of Astrid. He was a large muscular man, who she had no chance of fighting against.

"You get away from her!" Cruz demanded.

Vince held his shot gun at Cruz's head. "Give us the medication... or we'll take them from you both... starting with your girlfriend... and while you might hate our method, I'm guessing that she'll love it."

Cruz glared at him angrily. "Stay away from her! Don't you touch her!"

Vince shook his head. "Still uncooperative... do you know why I don't believe you? Because I have gone from town to town, only to find that no one is immune to this... what did you call it? A curse? Yeah... no one! And you'll never guess what happens when the medication wears off... Anyone who has ever taken it needs to be put out of their own misery. It isn't pretty... So, that's why I'm going to tell you one more time... hand over the medication!"

Cruz glanced at Astrid and then back at Vince. "We lost it," he finally said. "There were

some men down the road, and they took it from us...
we were actually on our way to San Francisco to get
some more."

Vince stared at Cruz long and hard. "While I
might believe you... it's been a while since I've been
in the company of a beautiful woman... you
wouldn't mind if I borrowed her, would you?"

It was clear that he wasn't asking as for
permission, but giving them an insight in to what he
had planned.

Cruz spat at Vince and demanded in a low
growl, "Stay the hell away from her," but Vince
punched him in the face, giving him an instant
bloody nose.

Then, Astrid had an idea. "Vince, is it?" she
asked casually. "How long's it been?"

Cruz raised his eyebrows at her. What the
hell was she thinking?

Vince turned to Astrid and gave a confused
smile. "Let's just say... it's been a while."

"Well, we can't have that now, can we?" she
asked coolly. Her tone reminded Cruz of the way
that Hannah had acted after having been affected by
the curse.

He knew what she was doing and he
couldn't let it stand. "Astrid, what the hell are you
doing?"

But she kept her eyes locked on Vince as
she spoke. "It seems that my medication is wearing

65

off, and you see, my boyfriend over there... while he is immune to this curse... I'm not... I was hit by... what he calls 'lust'...

I'm just too much for him, but he wants to mellow me out a little and take me to see some doctor for a refill. So, what do you say you and I go and find somewhere a little more private? And I promise... if you fulfill my desires, I'll bring you some medication on our way back... I promise."

Vince smirked at Astrid. "I like your way of thinking," he said.

He demanded that his men keep an eye on Cruz as he led Astrid out of the office.

As they disappeared before his eyes, Cruz yelled out angrily for them to come back and for Vince not to lay a hand on her.

Astrid was led down a long corridor and to what had clearly been an old policeman's office. Vince locked the door behind them and placed his shotgun on the desk.

Feeling ready to vomit with a mixture of fear, disgust and anger, Astrid forced herself to kiss the man. He seemed to be buying it. "I have an idea," she said with a smile. "I like to be in charge." She kept kissing him as she spoke.

"In charge?"

"Mm hmm."

"So, be in charge," he told her. She found a set of handcuffs sitting on the desk and held them up seductively.

"Do you think I'm stupid?!" he demanded.

But she continued to kiss him. "But... please..." She was really trying to play the part of someone who had been affected by lust. She undid her top button.

"Fine." He gave in.

Astrid smiled as he offered her his wrists submissively. But she didn't cuff him yet. She made him sit on the seat.

When he did, she cuffed him to the chair and ensured that he couldn't break free.

She took the key and pocketed it as she stood up to find something to use as a gag.

"This is pretty kinky," he told her. She found an old tie. It clearly belonged to the officer who had once worked there. She tied it around his mouth so he couldn't speak.

She smirked at how easy it had been, and turned to leave, making him realize exactly what she had just done. He began to muffle angrily and even tried to scream out as she picked up the shot gun and made haste for the door, locking it behind her and running down the corridor.

She headed back towards the holding cell where they had left Cruz to try and help him. But when she got there, the men had all disappeared with Cruz in tow. Now she needed to find them.

Astrid raced through the precinct looking through the offices, searching for any sign of Cruz and Vince's men. She stumbled across the surveillance room and locked herself inside.

She rested the weapon on the desk and played with the security footage until she had figured out how to scan from one location to another. "Come on, come on... where are you?" she mumbled to herself.

She looked around at the screens until she saw the men standing in the parking lot. Two of them were holding onto Cruz and the third was punching him in the stomach. Cruz looked very weak.

Astrid picked the weapon back up and noticed the set of keys on the desk. She wasn't sure what they would open but she took them and placed them in her pocket.

She ran down the corridor making her way for the exits.

From the entrance door, she could see them all. Cruz was badly wounded and still being beaten.

She crept outside and hid behind the post, observing the weapon that she held in her hands. She had only ever used a pistol before, although this was very different. She aimed at Lucas, who was punching at Cruz, and managed to shoot him in the leg.

The kickback of the weapon threw her a little, though it brought him down and alerted the others of her presence. Gabe dropped Cruz, leaving him with Tony and ran towards her. Fortunately, he didn't have his weapon.

Astrid aimed the shotgun at him, trying to fight back her own fear and adrenaline, while Cruz managed to fight off Tony.

Cruz's face was covered in blood and every inch of his body hurt. At least with Lucas wounded on the floor, he had a chance to fight against the other man.

He had been fortunate that the men's rage had been subdued thanks to the medication, though he knew that it wouldn't last long.

They needed to get out of there fast. He sent one last punch at Tony, bringing him down instantly and ran towards Astrid and Gabe.

Astrid saw Cruz approaching, but he brought his finger to his lips so that she would not blow his cover. Cruz found a large thick piece of wood and knocked it over Gabe's head, knocking him out cold.

"Alright, Astrid! Let's go!" Cruz yelled, taking her by the hand and leading her, as they ran through the parking lot.

They found a police patrol car, though the doors were locked. "We need the keys!" Cruz cried.

Astrid smiled at him and pulled out the set that she had found in the surveillance room. "Nice!" he replied. She threw the keys to him and he unlocked the doors.

Suddenly, there was a loud bang and Astrid screamed out in pain as she had been shot in the arm by a piercing bullet.

Vince had managed to escape from the cuffs and was currently standing with his men holding a gun aimed at her. He had taken the shot.

Astrid managed to open the passenger side door with her left arm, and climbed into the car, still clutching her shotgun. Cruz took off out of the parking lot as fast as he could go.

"How bad is it?" he asked, as he drove back to the main street, where they had left their other car. "It hurts. It needs a doctor. But I can cope."

He parked up alongside their other car, which had been smashed up.

"What are you doing?" she asked him.

"We have to get my laptop back. All my research and my survival gear is in there. Plus, our water bottles, your money and our clothes. I'll be quick, I promise."

As he went to collect their things, Astrid could see a second patrol car approaching in the distance. "Cruz... I think they're coming!" she cried out.

"Oh, crap!" he exclaimed. He threw what he had managed to retrieve, which included the pistol that they had tucked into one of the bags, into the back of the car and got back in, taking off before he had a moment to put his seat belt back on.

They kept their eyes on the rear-view mirror and managed to lose the patrol car, finding their way back out of the town and onto the highway. Astrid's arm was bleeding heavily. She had already bled through the bandages in Cruz's survival bag and had managed to find one of Cruz's shirts to use as a tourniquet, but it still hurt.

#

A few hours down the road, Cruz needed to stop for gas. "Astrid, I want you to lock the doors. If I'm not back in ten minutes, go without me..."

"Are you kidding me? I can barely move my arm... I'm not abandoning you. Take the pistol. And can you get me some strong pain killers? And see if they have any alcohol and more bandages, please!"

Cruz nodded. He clearly knew what she had planned as he raised his eyebrows at her. He took the pistol and hopped out of the car as she locked the doors behind him.

She pulled the black shirt away from her right forearm and checked the wound. The bullet was certainly lodged and she would need to get it removed.

The wound made her weak to her stomach just to look at. She felt around for the bullet. Just touching it hurt.

She remembered a story that her father had once told her about having to remove a bullet from one of his men on the battle field.

She bit into Cruz's shirt and felt dizzy as she tried to dig around for the bullet with her fingertips. "Oh god, oh god, oh god..." she mumbled as she found the bullet. She pinched it between her finger and thumb, but it only sunk deeper, making her muffle a scream.

She needed to try again. She felt like she was ready to pass out. It was now or never. This time when her finger and thumb found the bullet, she pulled it out instantly. An involuntary scream followed as she dropped the bullet onto the floor of the car. She held the shirt back up against her arm as dizziness set in.

A knock at the window on Cruz's side of the car made her jump. Fortunately, it was only him, so she unlocked the doors. "There was no one in there... Are you okay?" he asked as he climbed into his seat. "You look pale."

She nodded, so he handed her a cold water bottle, which she drank and then held up against her arm, cooling it down. "I removed the bullet," she stammered.

"Let me look," he said. She shifted her body to show him her right arm as he pulled the supplies out from the bag. He looked squeamish at the sight, but poured a little rubbing alcohol onto a fresh bandage, all the same.

"This is going to hurt," he said, as he tucked a lock of his hair out of his face, and behind his ear, so he could see better.

She bit into the shirt that she had been using to muffle her scream as he cleaned her wound. It hurt like hell. But after a while it stopped hurting as much, and he was able to bandage it up for her.

"There... all better," he said giving her a comforting smile.

"I didn't know you were so good with bandages."

"Blame Hannah... She was persistent that we knew what to do in case of emergencies."

"Hannah? Is that a girlfriend or something?"

"Hell no! Not mine, anyway... the love of Joey's life. But a good friend of mine. Before all this happened, he was forever chasing her. She was our site doctor, too."

"Well, that's good."

"What about you? You never told me if you had a boyfriend, before all this started happening."

"Nope. But according to everyone who has met you and I... apparently we're a couple," she said with a grin.

Cruz stroked her hair from her face. "I'm actually pretty okay with that... but, while we're sitting at a deserted gas station... we're practically sitting ducks. So maybe we should just get going... or I'll most likely wind up kissing you again."

"Well, we wouldn't want that now, would we?" Astrid said, as she blushed a bright shade of red. "...Hey can you hand over those pain killers? My arm really hurts."

He smiled at her as he handed her the medication, and they continued with their trip.

Chapter 5

Cruz continued to drive well into the night as Astrid slept. He made another stop for gas and coffee and then continued on again. The further he travelled, the more he saw the aftermath of the seven deadly sins curse. This was well and truly an apocalypse.

He pulled over to the side of the road behind a tree to check his emails. He had received one from Dr. Reynolds. The man had gone into hiding as there were people after him. Cruz sent a reply, telling him about the men that they had encountered and about Astrid's current condition.

He received an instant reply, listing a series of numbers that were clearly coordinates for the doctor's location. He ran a search in relation to the coordinates and then continued on his way. He knew where he was going, and fortunately they would be there in a matter of hours.

Cruz glanced over at Astrid who was in a deep sleep. He ran his hand through her hair and rested it on her cheek. She was burning up, and she barely reacted to his touch. It wasn't a good sign. He knew that things were getting dire.

She had lost a lot of blood earlier, and he was concerned for her welfare. Astrid was a tough woman, but it seemed as if she were going into shock.

It amazed him as to how she had removed the bullet herself. But still, he vowed not to make any more unnecessary stops. He was not going to let her die this way.

His feelings for her had certainly changed since they had first met, and he knew that he couldn't fight them any longer. He was falling for her very fast and he couldn't remember the last time that he had felt this way about anyone.

He could see the sun rising in his rear-view mirror, he was tired and his whole body hurt from his earlier beating, but he knew that it would be another four hours until he reached the doctor's new hideout.

He heard Astrid murmur in pain. He glanced over at her for a moment as he mumbled, "We'll be there soon. I promise, just hang on for me."

When he glanced back up, he noticed a man standing on the side of the road with his thumb out. A hitchhiker. "I'm sorry, man... not today. I've seen too many movies where that ends badly," he mumbled to himself.

He bypassed the man in the car and looked in his rear-view mirror as the man pulled something out of his pocket.

Suddenly, there was a loud bang. One of the tires had been shot.

Cruz mumbled a few curse words in Spanish as he pulled the car to the side of the road and parked. He punched at the steering wheel in a fit of anger, put the pistol in his jacket pocket and climbed out of the car.

"What the fuck, man!" Cruz yelled.

The hitchhiker who had shot the tire was charging for him. "I want your car! Now, give it to me!"

Cruz looked at the police car that had Astrid and all their supplies in it. "Sorry, hombre. It ain't happening. Not today... and look... you've shot the tire... What use will it be to you now?"

"I'm sure you have a spare... it's a cop car, and you don't look like any cop to me... so I'm taking it!" The man aimed his gun at him.

Cruz raised his gun at the same time. He considered the alternative if this man did take the car. What would happen to Astrid? "Where are you headed? Maybe we can come to some sort of deal," Cruz suggested.

Suddenly, he heard Astrid's door open and she began to vomit. The man attempted to walk over to her, but Cruz released a warning shot in his direction. "Stay away from her," he demanded.

"What's wrong with her?" the hitch hiker asked.

"Never mind... just be on your way and leave us alone!"

"Cruz... my arm... I think it's infected. We need to go," Astrid groaned from her spot on the floor beside the road. She started vomiting again.

"She's wounded... The next doctor isn't for miles... so, the two of you should start walking, because I'm taking your ride," the hitch hiker said.

Cruz glared at him. "Astrid... I need you to hop back into the car and lock the doors... please," he called out to her.

She didn't respond. "Astrid... please?" Cruz pleaded, not taking his eyes or his pistol off the man. The hitchhiker still had his weapon aimed at Cruz.

But then he turned it on Astrid, and before Cruz could pull the trigger of his own pistol on the stranger, there was a large deafening bang. The sound of another gun.

The hitchhiker dropped to the floor, and Cruz studied his own pistol. He hadn't shot it, but who had shot the man?

"Mr. Cruz, right? Mario Cruz? I'm Dr. Gregory Reynolds!" A tall slim man with dark hair, approximately in his mid-forties approached him. He held up one hand for Cruz to shake and a pistol in the other. He had been the one who had shot the hitchhiker.

"Please, just call me Cruz... Mario was my father," Cruz said, shaking the man's hand, absolutely baffled by what had just happened. "You shot him?"

"Well, with the lives of the only two people on earth who are immune to the Seven Deadly Sins at stake... I couldn't exactly risk the only hope mankind has now, could I? Now, get the girl... pack your things and follow me!"

Dr Reynolds walked over to Astrid. She had passed out on the ground in a pool of her own vomit. "This is why I came looking for you," he grumbled. "Pick her up and bring her to my vehicle."

Cruz lifted Astrid up off the ground and cradled her in his arms. He followed the doctor to the waiting ambulance. "Wow, first a patrol car, now an ambulance," Cruz mumbled as he helped load Astrid onto the bed in the back.

"You told me that she was badly wounded... it seemed fitting... now load in the rest of your things and take over the driving. I need to work on her immediately. Her gunshot wound is highly infected and she's still bleeding out... It's not looking good."

Cruz did as he was ordered, and after having been given the directions of the doctor's hideout, he drove the rest of the way there, praying that Astrid was in safe hands.

Dr. Gregory Reynolds directed Cruz to drive them to a small clinic in another small ghost town, despite Cruz's hesitation. They hid the ambulance around the back and locked the doors behind them.

#

Dr. Reynolds spent the next two days working on Astrid. It had grown apparent that when she had attempted to remove the bullet herself, it had sunk deeper, causing more damage as well as an infection. Her body had also experienced a high loss of electrolytes.

As the doctor worked, Cruz continued to pace around in frustration, until the doctor had done all that he could do for her. "You're both very lucky that I found you when I did. She wouldn't have survived, otherwise," Gregory said.

"Gracias! I don't know how to repay you."

"Well, you can start by telling me why you're both immune! If I can harness that, I might be able to make a cure and distribute it around the world."

Cruz told the doctor everything he knew, which included the whispers that he felt may have protected him from the curse.

"I'm a man of science... I don't believe in the supernatural! And that doesn't explain why that woman in there is also immune... it has got to be something to do with your blood types. Are you sure that the two of you aren't related... even remotely?"

"Absolutely sure. You can analyze my blood if you like. So, tell me about this mood stabilizer. The men we met down the road said that when it wears off it has some serious side effects."

Dr. Reynolds prepared the needle and took Cruz's blood from his arm as he spoke. "...That's why, Cruz... when you start taking the medication... you don't stop... You ensure that you take it at the exact same moment, each and every day and not a minute later... otherwise, whichever emotion you have been poisoned with will take over your entire body... I've seen men kill themselves over wanting something as simple as a blue colored sock."

Cruz raised his eyebrows in response to the doctor's statement, as Gregory handed him a tissue to wipe the blood from his arm and packed away the needle and blood-filled canisters. "Which emotion were you infected by?" Cruz asked him.

Dr. Reynolds adjusted his glasses on his nose and stared at the floor sadly, but he said nothing. Whatever secret he was hiding had affected him deeply and he didn't want to talk about it. "You should go and check on the girl in there. She should wake up soon."

Cruz nodded and stood up from his seat. His arm was no longer bleeding from Dr. Reynold's blood test, so he threw the tissue into the bin.

He made his way to the next room, where Astrid was still sleeping and closed the door behind him. Her vitals were normal.

He listened to the beeping coming from the monitors and watched the subtle rise and fall of her chest as she slept. For the first time in a while, he felt that the two of them were safe for the moment.

He sat down beside her and stroked her hair from her face. The instant that his hand made contact with her skin, she twitched and her eyes opened.

"Hey, girl... remember me?" he asked with a comforting smile.

Astrid sat up and stared at him. "I'm sorry... have we met before?" she asked.

Cruz opened his eyes wide, he hadn't been expecting that.

"Um, Astrid... It's me Cruz... You know, we met the other day when I saved your ass from those men at your apartment? We've literally taken this road trip from one side of the country to the other..."

Astrid's confused look turned into a humored smile, which was followed by a laugh. "Sorry, Cruz... I know it's you... I just wanted to make you sweat a little. So, where are we? And what the hell happened?"

Cruz laughed out of relief. "Ay dios mio, girl! Don't ever do that again! Do you remember that bullet that you took out? Well, your whole body went into shock. Dr. Gregory Reynolds found us and now we're safe in his hideout. You've been out for two days! That's a lot of silence."

"Two days, really? Wow. Okay, so what do we do now?"

"The both of you will rest until we can determine our next course of action," Dr. Reynolds instructed as he entered the room. "I'm Dr. Gregory Reynolds... the man who saved your life, miss. And if you value your lives, I would appreciate if you both stay here so we can work out just why you're immune."

"Do you need to take my blood or something?" Astrid asked as Cruz sat down beside her on the bed.

"I already have... I've been studying it, which is why I would like you to fill out these forms for me so I can gather a background check. Also... have any of your family members been affected?" Gregory asked as he handed them each a stack of forms and sat down in the seat where Cruz had originally been sitting.

"My whole family was," Cruz said sadly.

Astrid frowned. "I'm not sure. My father died a few years back and my mother's in a nursing home."

Gregory looked over at the clock on the wall and shook his head. "I'm going out for a little while, mind the damn place!" He stormed out of the room and slammed the door behind him.

"What was that all about?" Astrid asked.

"I think it has to do with the medication. He said something about having to take it at the exact same time, every day. But, enough about him... I need to talk to you, and it's serious..." Cruz took the forms from her and put them down on the chair.

She stared at him in confusion. "Is everything okay?"

He stood face to face with her. "Everything's fine... but this is about... us... Now, I know that we haven't known each other for all that long but seeing you in that position... so close to death... well, it scared me... a whole lot more than I'd like to admit."

"Wow, is this really the right time? I mean, I've been out for two days..."

"Horrible timing, I know... But, while I'm not the kind of guy to kiss a woman that I've only just met... I am the type of guy to not let something amazing pass me by. So please, I need you to hear me out… I get that I really shouldn't feel this way... it's just so early... but, I can't risk losing you. I don't want to lose you... even after everything goes back to normal. I need you to know that." Cruz knew that he was rambling. But he couldn't help himself.

Astrid thought for a moment. She knew exactly how she felt about him. "Okay... I guess it's a relief that I'm not the only one who has been feeling this way... I don't want to lose you either..."

"Really? Wow. That is a relief... So, when we were talking in the car about us being a couple..." His voice faltered and he stopped speaking.

She was making him nervous. A dorky smile spread across his face, reaching to his soft brown eyes.

Astrid's logical side was telling her that it was normal for two people, who were attracted to each other and were spending so much time together, to develop feelings like this. But she was skeptical as to if it was real or just an infatuation.

Nonetheless, after everything that the two had been through in the past couple of days, they decided to give in to their own impulses. They kissed.

They allowed for their kiss to travel further, as they gave in to their passion for one another, in the safety of their surroundings.

#

An hour had passed as Gregory Reynolds strolled along the small town. He had lost track of time, thinking back to when things had been simpler. He had a family; a beautiful wife and two teenaged children.

But his rage had caused them to fear him. His theories in relation to this new onset of emotions and humanity's mental instability made them believe that he was crazy.

His son had given in to gluttony, his wife had given in to pride and his daughter had been taken over by jealousy. Deeming himself a threat to his own family, Gregory left to create a treatment for them. But when he had succeeded and returned home, they were no longer there. He was all alone.

However, the medication was no permanent fix and he knew that. But it was currently all that he had. When the news had spread that he had created a super strength mood-stabilizer to treat these new emotions, he had become the target for thefts and even assaults. Everyone wanted a piece of the action, and he was running out of supplies even for himself.

He had witnessed men overdosing on generic substitutes that were nowhere near as strong. He had also witnessed what would happen if a man was to stop taking the medications so suddenly. Neither one of those scenarios had been pretty.

Gregory had only just taken his medication before he had gone for his walk. He had a two-week supply remaining of the tablets. He would need to return to his lab in San Francisco and create an injectable treatment to continue.

Dr. Reynolds continued his way down the quiet road until he saw vehicles entering the town. Normally, he would just hide behind a tree and wait for them to pass. But it was the type of vehicles that they were that caused him to run back to the clinic and find the others.

#

"Why didn't either of you tell me that the military was following you?" he demanded, the moment that he found them still in the patient room.

By the way that they were adjusting their clothes, it didn't take a scientist to work out what they had been up to, but he ignored it.

"The military? What do you mean?" Cruz asked, as he adjusted his hair nervously.

"Don't lie to me! Their trucks are entering the town now! They must have found the patrol car down the road! We need to hide! Follow me!" Dr. Reynolds demanded.

Astrid and Cruz followed him out of the clinic, keeping to the walls until they found an underground bunker in the backyard of an abandoned house, which they sought shelter in.

"Wouldn't the military be the best way to find Pandora's Box?" Astrid asked.

"While that might be true..." Cruz said, "we can't trust them. They must be looking for me because of my immunity! Why the hell did I offer to do that stupid segment on the Diane show?"

"...Or they could be looking to obtain more of my medication," Dr. Reynolds said. "I made a great deal of money selling them supplies six months ago. They could be after more."

"Alright, either way... we hide out here," Astrid said. They heard the roar of a loud military truck up above them. Gregory lifted a mat in the far corner, which revealed a trap door, going even further underground.

"Hey, how did you know about that?" Cruz asked him.

Gregory put his finger to his mouth, telling him to be quiet and gestured for them to hide inside.

They obeyed, and he followed them into the hole in the floor that led beneath the bunker. He pulled over the mat to conceal their hideout.

They could hear a nearby truck come to a complete stop. The soldiers climbed out and began to raid the town looking for someone. Dr. Reynolds stood at the top of the ladder entrance to their hideout, listening in.

The soldiers shook the bunker door and managed to open it. They stepped inside. "Any sign of them?" one soldier asked.

"They don't seem to be in here. They must have disappeared," the soldier who was standing inside the bunker said.

"We have an hour and then we'll leave this town..."

"You go up ahead... I'll finish here." The soldier had currently spotted the disheveled rug on the floor. He waited until he was alone and stepped towards it.

He pulled out a black marker and scribbled something on the wall, then left the bunker closing the door behind him.

#

Astrid, Cruz and Dr. Reynolds waited in the bunker for at least two hours until they had heard the trucks disappear. When Dr. Reynolds ran a check above ground to ensure that they were safe, he allowed for the other two to come up.

They stared at the black writing that the soldier had left on the wall. It was a name, 'Roger Charlie.' Cruz and Gregory were confused as to why the soldier would have left a name behind, but it triggered something inside of Astrid. There was something familiar to it that she couldn't quite put her finger on.

Nonetheless, they made their way back to the clinic and ensured that their property had not been taken or tampered with. It just didn't feel right that their things had been entirely left alone.

#

The military did not return, and the three of them stayed at the clinic for a week, making themselves at home.

It was a Sunday, as Astrid assisted Cruz and Dr. Reynolds with their research, with the television on in the background.

A proud news reporter that continued to boost his own ego, by delivering full coverage of the world's current state of ruin, kept them updated.

Along with the Seven Deadly Sins, the health of the world was diminishing. Disease was spreading fast and wiping out millions.

"Ok, I get that you don't believe in the Pandora's Box curse, Reynolds... but this... this just can't be argued with!" Cruz said loudly. "It's just like the myths. We need to find the pithos and do something now! Before we have nothing left of the world to save."

"Cruz is right," Astrid agreed. "That must have been the reason that the military were after us. They must need our help. We can't just let the world destroy itself."

Dr. Reynolds stared at them both. The truth was that he had one week's supply left of his medication. They needed to leave as soon as they could.

He had also found some interesting results with their blood samples, which he needed to discuss with them. Just maybe, Cruz was right about this being something on the realms of the supernatural.

"I need to speak with you both about your blood tests," he said staring at them.

Astrid joined him and Cruz at the table. "Is everything okay?" she asked.

"Well... normally, the virus shows itself in the form of an extra protein present in the blood stream, and while there are no traces of it in either one of you, that is good, because it means that none of you have it... Unfortunately, Cruz, there is no explanation as to why you are immune... but I decided to consider your 'Pandora's Box curse' theory and it led me to discover that Astrid's blood type is a very old blood type, one of the first original blood groups that once coursed through the veins of mankind. Astrid, you also wrote down on your background check that your ancestors originated from Europe..."

"If you're saying that she is immune due to her European background, that just doesn't make sense, because so many of the locals were still affected," Cruz said.

"In part... but still, not what I'm getting at... so don't interrupt! There was only one woman who proved immune to the seven deadly sins. That was the woman who opened it. But, while this time it was Cruz who opened the box... Astrid, there is no other theory to go on. What if you are actually a descendent from Pandora herself?"

Astrid laughed. "That's ridiculous. While I can see how Cruz could be protected with that theory, with the whispers and everything... my ancestry came from various parts of Europe. I'm certain that I would know, were that the case. I think we're just clutching at straws here."

"Astrid... it could make sense..." Cruz said, considering the possibilities. "Pandora was a human created by the gods... who went on to have children.

91

If I managed to find the box... who's to say that you're not one of her distant granddaughters?"

"So, what? You're telling me that I'm the descendent of a pawn, who was made and used by the gods to seek out their revenge on mankind? Nope, I'm not buying it! Why don't we just stop talking about this and consider our next course of action." Astrid stormed away, leaving both Cruz and Dr Reynolds alone in the office.

"When she puts it that way, it's a little hard to believe... even for me..." Cruz began.

"... I get where you're both coming from... but come here... take a look at her bloodwork... also consider that her middle name is Hope... which even in the myths was the answer to saving mankind. I don't believe in coincidences. It's why I got into science a long time ago."

"So, if she is... what do we do?"

"We keep her safe... and we hunt down Pandora's Box... But first, I need to go back to my lab in San Francisco and stock up on my treatments, or I'll be of no use to either one of you."

"We keep her safe? Have you met that girl? She quite literally risked her life for me... She's not afraid to throw herself into a fight if she needs to... So, what's your plan? Tie her down or something?"

"I'll leave that up to you. Just remember, when it comes down to it... if my theory is correct, we will need her to end this once and for all."

"Well, it's not going to be easy... she's not exactly what you'd expect from the descendent of Pandora..."

Dr. Reynolds stared at Cruz. "Get Astrid and gather your things. I'll go find us a car."

#

Astrid had gone into another office and pulled up a search in relation to the children of Pandora. The woman certainly did go on to have children. Surely, it could have been possible that a branch of Astrid's bloodline could be linked to the woman, somehow.

But it seemed a little too far-fetched for her liking. Most of the images depicted an old-style portrait of what the artist believed that Pandora would have looked like.

Seemingly beautiful.

The door opened, startling her. Cruz was standing there. He approached to see what she was reading and placed his hands on her shoulders. "I know how crazy it sounds..." he said.

"About as crazy as you finding the resting place of Pandora's Box itself. But, while I don't think you're crazy... this link... that I'm of some relation to her... that just..."

"...Sounds impossible? I know, I get it." He wrapped his arms around her, and looked at the screen in front of her. "But people believe that she was beautiful... so that must run in the family."

Astrid glanced up at him, so he continued on, "It would also make sense... I mean, the curse is what brought us together. I was losing hope, and I found you... the perfect embodiment of hope... you gave me a reason to not give up, and even your middle name is Hope... I also fell for you in such a short time, that doesn't generally happen to me. I like my space... but, it's almost like we're..."

"...if you're about to say meant to be... I swear that I will slap you." She smiled at him.

"Okay, I'll go with 'a match made in heaven'?" he said with a laugh.

Astrid went to slap him, but he took a hold of her hand and brought it to his lips, leaving a kiss on her knuckles.

"You're so corny," she laughed.

"Mm hmm... but, I was also sent in here for a reason. Reynolds wants us to pack our things. We're leaving today."

He hugged her from behind again and kissed her on the top of her head, making her smile.

"Alright, let's go, lover boy..." she giggled as he helped her to her feet and they left the office to pack their things.

Chapter 6

Astrid took the shift of driving the SUV that they had acquired for their ride, while Dr. Reynolds sat in the front passenger seat beside her.

"So, Dr. Reynolds. We've known each other for a week now and we barely know anything about each other. If we are going to be working together we need to trust each other... Can you tell us something about yourself?"

"I think that me saving your life is a sign of my loyalty, Astrid. Keep your mind focused on the road and not on my private affairs. Thank you."

"Hmm. Tough crowd," Cruz joked from the back seat.

"Excuse me?" the doctor said, slightly offended.

"Nothing." Cruz smirked as he looked back out the window from his seat behind the driver's side.

"The way that the two of you see this as some kind of romantic road trip is the reason that you almost died last time! Now, when you start thinking of this as strictly nothing more than a mission, we might have a chance to survive!" Dr. Reynolds barked at them both.

Astrid glanced at him and then back at the road. "Have you taken your medication, Dr. Reynolds?" she asked.

"Actually, yes I have. But this whole 'Romeo and Juliet' thing that the two of you have going on, it will not help any of us. It will just prove to be a burden later on."

"What's that supposed to mean?" Astrid snapped at him, pulling the car over to the side of the road.

"Well... Look at this from a logical perspective. The world is crumbling all around us. Everybody that we love has become so unstable that we can't be around them... or they are dead. The two of you have already had a few brushes with death... and right now, you're the only hope that this world has... But, if I've learnt one thing, it's that love only complicates matters. It's the question that plagues every hero's nightmare. Could you really risk the one that you love to save the world, if it came down to it?"

Neither Astrid nor Cruz could answer him. Instead, Astrid pulled back onto the road and continued driving.

After a while, things began to make sense. "You lost your wife, didn't you?" she asked, making Gregory look at her. "You still wear your wedding band... Either she passed away just recently, or she left and you haven't been able to come to terms with it just yet."

Dr. Reynolds stared down at his ring just as they were nearing the outskirts of San Francisco. It was still bustling with chaos.

"Why don't you let me take over the driving," Dr. Reynolds decided. "…at least we should make it to my lab in one piece."

Astrid did as he asked, and Dr. Reynolds drove them through the bustle of San Francisco's streets.

The city was filled with car accidents, wreckages and crime. There was a smashed-up police car on the side of the road filled with graffiti. There were traffic jams lining the road, where the drivers had decided to just stop and sit.

When it was clear that they wouldn't be able to push past the traffic any further, Dr. Reynolds hid the car in a deserted parking lot and they got out on foot, carrying emergency kits and weapons.

Dr. Reynolds handed them all a medical mask and requested that they put them on. "What's the mask for?" Cruz asked, fixing his to his face.

"The news report earlier said that disease is spreading throughout the world, and if that is true, we don't want to risk any of us getting sick. Just because you're immune to the seven deadly sins doesn't necessarily mean that you would be immune to disease now, would it?" he said as he handed them a set of blue latex gloves to put on as well.

"I suppose that makes sense," Astrid added, as she applied hers also. Dr. Reynolds led them through the streets, surrounded by chaos. They continued to keep their heads down to not draw too much attention on themselves.

Acts of aggression, lust and greed were carried out all around them, but fortunately the individuals committing the acts were so focused on what they were doing, that they barely noticed the three strangers making their way towards the laboratories.

#

When they had finally arrived at The San Francisco Laboratory, Dr. Reynolds led them to his own research department where he immediately got to work. The lab had been smashed up, but fortunately, he was able to salvage all the things that he needed.

Astrid and Cruz found a space by the window to watch the streets below. "How long do you think we'll need to stay here for?" Astrid asked.

"I'm not sure... but he seems pretty preoccupied. So, maybe hours?" Cruz suggested.

"I thought as much." She removed her gloves and mask, and so did he.

"Are you okay?" he asked her.

"I'm fine... Do you trust him?"

"Who? Reynolds?"

"Yeah... He seems... I don't know... odd?"

"He seems committed... I'll give him that... but I trust that he wants to end this thing just as much as we do." Cruz said. Astrid nodded and glanced over at the doctor who was busy at work.

Cruz held her in his arms and smiled down at her as he added, "We will end this thing... I know we will!" He kissed her on the head and the two of them stared out of the window, watching the chaos down below.

After a few hours, Dr. Reynolds managed to synthesize another strain of his treatment, incorporating a new secret ingredient, some cells taken from Astrid's blood.

"I've done it! I've altered the strain a little and we're going to need to test it out. I would test it out on myself but..." Dr. Reynolds said.

"...But, it could have some very bad side effects?" Astrid questioned him, annoyed. "So you're willing to risk an innocent person with no disregard for his or her life."

"Astrid... if it helps our cause... it's just an altered strain, we know the other one works and I'm sure that he knows what he's doing..." Cruz defended the doctor's case.

"Okay... we'll go out and find some people... guinea pigs as you would probably prefer to label them as..." Astrid said as she made her way out of the laboratory.

"Good, the two of you can go. I'll stay here and create some more," Dr Reynolds said, waving them out.

Cruz shook his head and followed after her.

#

Astrid and Cruz made their way outside and studied the streets around them. They were surprised that, despite the chaos, some of the stores were still in business. "Wow, San Francisco," Astrid said in awe.

"You say that like you've never been here before."

"That's because I haven't."

Cruz was surprised by this news. "Well, maybe we should make the most of it..." He glanced over at a café, hinting about going for a meal together.

He changed his mind, as they noticed a man sitting outside the café, feeding his face hungrily. He looked as if he had been sitting there for days, doing nothing but eating. His clothes, his face and his hair were all a mess. They both groaned at the sight.

"Man, he's hungry..." Cruz commented.

"He looks like he's going to be sick," Astrid replied.

"He could be our first guinea pig?"

"No... let's move on to the next."

"What about those two lovely ladies right there?" Cruz asked, referring to the two women, a blonde and a redhead, who had clearly given into lust, and were making out on the side walk. Cruz gave a humored smile.

"You're such a pervert," Astrid joked. "But I suppose that they would be safer coming inside with us as opposed to giving everybody a live performance from the street."

Astrid led him over to the couple, who seemed absolutely exhausted from making out, but couldn't resist on continuing.

"Er... hi?" Astrid stammered. "We don't mean to interrupt, but would you two like to accompany us across the street?" The women didn't even bother to look at them.

Astrid gave Cruz a look for him to try something. He moved his mask from his face, stuck his fingers in his mouth and whistled loudly, startling Astrid, the two women and a few people passing by. "Hey, ladies!" he said.

They both looked up at him and stood up, marveling at his attractive features. "Hey, yourself," the blonde woman said flirtatiously.

"Would the two of you like to accompany my girlfriend and I to the labs across the street? We might be able to help you," Cruz said.

The women ignored Astrid entirely and approached Cruz. "We'd love to," the redhead woman said as they began to run their hands up his back, his shoulders and his arms, lusting all over him.

"Er... Astrid?" Cruz stammered, realizing that their sense of lust wasn't gender specific. Astrid giggled at him.

"You're the perfect bait. Let's just get them over to Dr. Reynolds."

As Astrid ran up ahead, Cruz hurried behind her, with the two lust-filled women closely on his trail. He managed to catch up to Astrid as they entered the building.

"We might have to tie them down to give them the medicine," Cruz said under his breath. "They're like the brides of Dracula."

"Mmmm... I like that idea," the blonde woman said.

"Mmm... me too," her friend said.

"No...no, that's not what I meant... Astrid? A little help?" Cruz said.

Astrid pressed the elevator button to open the doors and they all stepped inside. The women pushed Cruz up against the wall and attempted to move his mask from his face again and kiss his neck as Astrid pressed the button to take them to their floor.

Cruz tried to hold the two women off, as Astrid attempted to break up the display. "Okay!" she said loudly. "That's enough."

She stood between Cruz and the two women daring them to make a move while she was standing there. "Now, we want to help you... But to do that, we need you to cooperate with us."

"You're just so beautiful," the redhead woman told her. She approached Astrid and ran her hands through Astrid's hair. The blonde woman approached her also and ran her hand up Astrid's arm. "Oh, shit," she groaned.

Suddenly, the elevator doors opened to Dr. Reynolds' floor. "Oh, thank god!" Cruz said taking a hold of Astrid's hand and leading her out of the elevator, with the two women on their heels.

"Hey, Reynolds... We have two guinea pigs for you," Cruz said.

"And please hurry," Astrid added.

The women looked around the floor, examining everything around them. Dr. Reynolds readied his first injection and struck the blonde woman in the arm first.

"Hey! Hey! What the hell!" she screamed at the doctor, sending her redhead friend into a frenzied state.

Dr. Reynolds prepared his second injection and went to administer it to the next woman. She tried to fight him off, but Cruz restrained her. "Shh... it's for the best," he whispered to calm her down.

Astrid approached the blonde woman and knelt down beside her. "Are you okay?" Astrid asked.

The woman was confused. "What am I doing here?" she asked, looking over at the other woman. Then it all made sense to her. "Oh my god!" she gasped, bringing her hand to her mouth in embarrassment. The serum had clearly worked. She was in control of her own mind and body.

By now, Gregory had administered the second serum and the other woman was also coming to her own senses.

"It worked! It actually worked!" Cruz exclaimed excitedly.

"Of course, it worked," Dr. Reynolds said. "I know what I'm doing."

#

Dr. Reynolds, Astrid and Cruz continued to monitor the women after having given them their treatments. The blonde woman who went by the name of Ashley, and the redhead, who went by the name of Tara, had never met prior to being affected and were currently dealing with the embarrassment of their actions.

"You shouldn't feel so embarrassed," Astrid told them. "The world is currently going through some sort of apocalypse and nobody is acting like themselves. We're just trying to do what we can to help people."

"This stuff that you injected us with... is it some sort of cure?" Ashley asked.

"No. It's just a treatment," Dr. Reynolds said. "We're working on a cure."

"I have to ask... how long do you need to monitor us for?" Tara asked. "I remember him calling us guinea pigs earlier, which will mean that you're just trialing the medication on us. So, are we talking an hour, maybe two?"

Cruz and Astrid both looked over at Dr. Reynolds as he said, "Two days... maybe a week?"

"A week?" both the women gasped.

"Do you expect us to stay here for the week? In this laboratory, like animals?" Ashley demanded.

"No, we can pay for you to stay at a motel," Dr. Reynolds said. "The same motel that we will be staying at. I imagine it will be a much safer option with the rest of the city dealing with their own instability."

"Treatment and a place to stay?" Tara asked. "You drive a hard bargain. I'm actually a tourist to the city, so that sounds pretty perfect to me."

"I thought it might," Dr. Reynolds said. He returned back to his desk ending the conversation abruptly.

Tara looked over at Astrid and Cruz, who were now standing with their arms around each other. "Is he always so..." Tara began.

"So blunt? Rude?" Astrid finished.

"Yeah..."

"That's just his way," Cruz explained. "Well, we should probably go and search for somewhere to stay."

"Are you all leaving?" Dr. Reynolds asked, as the four of them began to make their way towards the elevator.

"Yeah... it beats staying here," Astrid said.

Dr. Reynolds began piling ready-to-go injections into a smooth metal briefcase and handed it over to Cruz. "This is in in case of an emergency. You know what to do." He then handed Astrid a phone. "So is this. Call me if you need me. My number is listed in there."

Astrid took the phone. "When did you manage to get a phone?"

"It was my work phone, I left it here in case I returned. Now it's yours."

She pocketed the phone and the four of them left the floor via elevator.

As they made their way towards the exits, they noticed that many of the facility's employees were mentally stable. "I think I know where most of Reynolds' supplies went," Cruz suggested. Astrid nodded. She had been thinking the same thing.

#

It didn't take them long until they found a motel in close proximity to the labs, although the front desk wasn't tended to.

"Hello!" Astrid called out, dinging the bell. But no one turned up.

"I think that means free accommodation!" Ashley grinned as she hopped over the counter and helped herself to the keys.

"Hey, stop! What are you doing?" Astrid asked.

"What does it look like? I'm guessing the honeymoon suite would be perfect for you two, and no offense, Tara... but I'm not sharing a room with you." Ashley said as she handed out the keys.

"None taken," Tara said, taking her key happily.

Astrid refused to take the key from Ashley, so Cruz took it instead. As Tara and Ashley ran off to find their rooms, Cruz dangled the key in front of Astrid's face with a flirtatious smile. "Let's go check out this honeymoon suite."

"You go on ahead. I'll be there in a minute," she replied. Astrid pulled out some money from her purse to pay for the rooms and left it on the counter by the computer.

She signed the guest book, leaving a comment saying that they paid for the rooms, but no one was tending the counter.

As she put the pen back down, she noticed the name just above her own. The same name that had been scribbled on the wall, back at the bunker. 'Roger Charlie.'

Astrid looked at the room number that the man had stayed in. Room 24. She looked up to see that the room key was on the wall. On an impulse, she took the key. She needed to know just why that name was so familiar to her.

#

With the key in hand, Astrid went back to her own motel room, where Cruz had already started putting away their things. She showed him the key. "What's that for?" he asked.

"Do you remember back at the bunker when we were hiding from the soldiers? That man wrote a name on the wall. Roger Charlie. That same name was written in the guest book, and he had stayed in the room that this belongs to. But that just doesn't make any sense... why would a soldier need to stay at a motel?"

Cruz shrugged his shoulders and took the key. He wasn't sure, either.

"I know that this sounds crazy, but I know the name. It's just so familiar. I think my dad might have known this man. Maybe he wants to help us," Astrid added.

"Or maybe he doesn't. Do you really want to take the chance?"

She snatched the key from him. "If it can give us some answers, then yes, I do." She ran out of the motel room with him following her outside.

108

"Astrid, I didn't mean that to sound like a jerk. I just don't want to see you get hurt."

She ran up ahead of him searching for the matching room number. "So come with me," she said, turning back and smiling at him.

Cruz caught up with her, just as she had managed to locate the room and put the key into the lock. She turned the key and the door opened instantly.

The room was empty. Regardless, she began searching the draws and in the cupboards. "What are we looking for?" Cruz asked.

"Anything that might be a clue... maybe even just his name. Come on, you're an archaeologist... isn't searching for things kind of what you do? You found Pandora's Box of all things."

"Ha! Ha! That's not the same thing, and you know it..." Cruz said sarcastically. "Fine. I'll help... but I've seen how these movies go, so don't say I didn't warn you." He joined in the search.

Astrid pulled up the bed sheets and ruffled the pillows, unsure as to what she was looking for, but she was determined to find something, anything all the same. Why else would the man have left his name in the guest book? If only she could remember the context so that she could remember it.

As she entered the bathroom to look around, Cruz called her back. He had moved aside the large brown picture frame of a ship at sea, and an envelope had fallen out.

"Yo! Astrid... you were right. Come and check this out. It's addressed to you."

She approached and he handed her the envelope. "See, Cruz? A clue!" she joked.

She went to open it, but he stopped her. "Whoa. Don't open it, yet! I've had bad luck when it comes to opening things... It could be laced with something that could kill us."

"It's just a letter."

"Yeah, and I thought Pandora's Box was just a jar..."

"So what do you suppose we do?"

Cruz took the letter from her and held it up towards the light that was coming in from the open door. He shook it cautiously, checking the weight.

"We're wasting time," Astrid said, taking it from him. Before he could stop her, she opened it. There was a note inside.

'But the rest countless plagues, wander amongst men; for earth is full of evils and the sea is full. Of themselves diseases come upon men continually by day and by night, bringing mischief to mortals silently; for wise Zeus took away speech from them. So is there no way to escape the will of Zeus.'

"That's Hesiod!" Cruz announced. "Whoever the guy is, he's toying with us... Hesiod was an ancient poet and this is what happened to the earth when Pandora first opened the box. It's what's happening now."

Astrid looked at her name on the envelope. Whoever it was had used her full name and written her middle name in capital letters. "This guy's been following us since the beginning," she stammered. "He knew that we were in the bunker, yet he let us go free. I think they're trying to help us."

"Astrid. Promise me that whoever this is, that you will be careful."

"Only if you're willing to help me find out who this guy actually is."

Cruz stared at her for a moment in silence. "Fine... I'll help. Argh! Why do I have to be such a sucker for a pretty face?"

"What do you think he was talking about in regards to the mischief?" she asked looking back down at the note.

Cruz took another look at the note. "Hmm... it could be anything... death maybe? But we've already seen that... back in those ghost towns."

"Unless... it is quite literally the end to come and that there's nothing that we can do about it?" Astrid suggested. They stared in fear, as they contemplated the possibilities of what the message could possibly mean.

#

That night, as Astrid slept, a series of dreams flashed through her mind, causing her to toss and turn restlessly. She watched as the gods created a beautiful woman, the perfect tool for revenge on the earth and sent her as a gift to the man known as Epimethus.

But then the direction of the dream changed. She was no longer seeing it as an onlooker. She was Pandora, and Epimethus had turned into Cruz.

But then when she looked down at her hands, she was holding the pithos. She knew that she shouldn't do so, but she opened it. The room began to swirl around her and her vision faded to black. Her dream had ended.

Her next dream took her to her childhood. It was less a dream, and more a memory. She was playing 'pretend' with her father on the grass outside. They were playing with toy guns and pretending to shoot each other.
She had held hers up and made a 'pew' sound at her father, pretending to shoot him. He had fallen onto his back dramatically, clutching at his chest and gasped "Oh no! Roger Charlie is down!" It was a name that he had made up when they had played together.

Then just as her realization sank in, she woke up instantly, startling Cruz who had been sleeping beside her. She jumped out of the bed and opened his computer that was sitting on the table.

"Hey, are you okay?" he asked her.

"Yeah... I know who Roger Charlie is! Just as I know the real reason that we are feeling the way we are about each other this soon in our relationship."

The screen was requesting a password, which she didn't know, so Cruz climbed out of the bed and typed it in for her. "I'm all ears," he said.

"I should have been the one that opened Pandora's Box. But you did, so whatever those whispers were... I think you were right... it was some kind of protection spell. In my dream, you were that man... Epimethus. You and I were married and I opened the box instead. It's like it was calling out to me and... like it still is, but through my dreams. It's all part of some silly spell for me to find Pandora's Box."

Astrid was rambling, and Cruz was trying to make sense of her rambling. "So, what you're telling me is that I only have these feelings for you because I was the one who opened the box?"

"That's exactly what I'm saying," Astrid said, not taking her eyes off the screen as she tried to run a search for the name Roger Charlie.

"So, none of this is real? None of what we feel for each other is real? It's just some kind of love spell. No! That doesn't make sense at all. There was never a love spell on the pithos."

"No, there wasn't... but Pandora was given her beauty by the gods. It sounds pretty poetic that the man who ended up opening the pithos would wind up..."

"...Falling for the descendant of Pandora?" Cruz said glumly. "Well, it's good to know that it's all because of some stupid spell... look, I need to take a walk, I'll be back soon." His tone was filled with frustration as he threw on some clothes and headed to the door.

"Cruz, no... I didn't mean that to offend you," Astrid said, realizing that she had said the wrong thing.

"It's fine... You should just keep researching that Roger Charlie, guy." He opened the door and left her alone in the motel room, as she felt disappointed in herself, but continued her search, regardless.

Astrid researched into the early hours of the morning for anything related to the man Roger Charlie but turned up nothing. She was tired and knew that she had exhausted all her possible leads.

She looked up at the time, it was close to six a.m. and Cruz had not yet returned. Maybe he would be back for breakfast. She got dressed and left in search for the café down the road.

#

She arrived at the café, where the greedy man from the day before had died at his table outside and the prideful owner was struggling to move him from the spot.

"Miss! I assure you that our food isn't poisoned. It was just so good that this man couldn't stop eating." The café owner was pleading that she come inside and eat at his café. His face was filled with exhaustion from literally killing the man by feeding him too much.

Astrid shook her head and pulled out one of the vaccine treatments that she had taken from the suitcase. She needed to put this man out of his misery. She struck him in the arm and he collapsed to the floor.

As he remembered everything that had happened, he broke down into tears. "I killed this man," he cried.

"No, no you didn't," Astrid told him.

"I did! I just kept feeding him and feeding him. He was a food critic! I needed him to love my café, and it killed him."

Astrid's heart softened. "Look, I just gave you a treatment that should help you with your emotions. My friend Dr. Reynolds has been trying to work on a cure. Unfortunately, that treatment won't cure you, but he is willing to help you by giving you more, if you like." She handed him one of the doctor's cards.

He read the card and looked around them, where people were still slaves to their own mental instability. "Thank you. But I should go home and sleep. I've been working night and day without rest, since... I can't remember when."

"You worked here last night, didn't you?" Astrid asked.

"Yes... that was when this man here... when he died."

"Did you happen to see a guy with wavy dark hair, brown eyes and a dark blue jacket? Very good-looking? He would have been acting normal, as normal as you and I are now."

The man thought for a moment. "He actually came in two hours ago, needing a coffee. Mumbling something about 'fixing his mistakes, alone'."

"Do you know where he went?"

"No, I can't say I do... but he took a car and left down the street. Now, can I go home and sleep or is there something else you need to know?"

"No, you can go. Thank you."

The man turned and left in an exhausted hurry, making his way for home as Astrid headed to Dr. Reynolds' laboratory.

#

Dr. Reynolds had been up all night, working on his treatments. "Cruz is gone!" she exclaimed. "He took off a few hours ago."

Dr. Reynolds stared at her. "What do you mean, Cruz is gone?"

"I mean that the café owner heard him say something about fixing his own mistakes and he took off in a car down the road."

"And what would have forced him to do that?"

"I might have said something about us only being together because of the curse."

"...And that, Astrid, is exactly what I warned you about. But neither of you wanted to listen to me... regardless, we can do this without him... can you hand me that beaker right there?"

Astrid handed him the beaker angrily. "What do you mean we can do this without him? He's probably gone to find Pandora's Box by himself. He's going to get himself killed."

"And that will be his own fault. Now, while I'm finding the whole supernatural theories a little hard to believe, I believe that Pandora was real. But what we need to do is find the location of Pandora's Box. Before he left, did he happen to give you any hint as to where they might be keeping it?"

"The military should have it! There's some other news that I need to discuss with you. Yesterday, I received a letter reciting Hesiod." She handed him the note and he read over it. "I think it was by a man by the name of Roger Charlie. It was a name that my father used to use when I was a little girl," she added.

"The same name from back at my bunker," he mumbled under his breath, handing the note back to her.

"Your bunker? That was your old family home, wasn't it?"

Dr. Reynolds nodded. "...yeah, and that clinic was where I used to work. I lost my entire family because of this virus... this curse, so losing Cruz is nothing new to me."

"Right, I get where you're coming from, but none of us would be here if it weren't for him. We should be out looking for him. But, I promise you that we will find your family." She felt that he had not heard her.

Suddenly, Dr. Reynolds' face changed dramatically. He got to his feet, stormed away from his desk and towards a shelf of glass beakers.

He pushed the shelf over in a fury, shattering everything onto the ground. He went to his counter and began throwing beakers onto the floor.

Astrid gasped. "Dr. Reynolds! What are you doing? Dr. Reynolds!" But he seemed to be in a fit of his own aggression. He picked up a glass beaker and threw it in Astrid's direction, just missing her head.

She stormed towards him. "Gregory Reynolds! Stop!" But he kept going.

Astrid hurried over to the desk and picked up one of the treatment vaccines and struck him in the arm with it. He stopped instantly.

He stared at the mess around him, and then looked back at Astrid. "I'm... I'm sorry! I don't know what came over me..." He saw the needle in her hand. "Wait... which serum did you just use?"

"The one from the counter... why?"

"Oh no! No! No! No!" He began rummaging around his lab aimlessly and then he turned back to her. "Why would you use that one?"

"Because it's the one that you gave us? The one that worked on Ashley and Tara... and the café owner."

Dr. Reynolds stared at her in horror. "Astrid... the virus has been getting stronger... that new treatment... I used the cells from your blood to synthesize this new strain. Have you spoken to Tara or Ashley? Have you even checked in on them? I did, and they're both very sick!"

"What do you mean? They were just fine yesterday," she snapped back at him with concern. Dr. Reynolds led Astrid back to the motel and instructed her to put on her mask and gloves. They peered their heads into Tara's and Ashley's rooms. The women were laying in their beds in their own vomit and their entire bodies were covered in very large sores. They looked as if they were dying.

"Oh my god..." Astrid gasped as they closed Ashley's door.

"...and you injected it into me," the frightened doctor said.

Chapter 7

Astrid returned to her room and turned on the television. She was having a hard time dealing with everything that was going on. Because of her, Cruz had left, and Dr. Reynolds was in the process of trying to synthesize a solution to ensure that he would not get sick, just as Tara and Ashley had.

She thought about the café owner that she had injected with the serum. Was he yet suffering as Ashley and Tara were? How long would it take for Dr. Reynolds to succumb to the sickness?

She was angry that he had used her blood without her consent. She assumed that her blood would have been the ingredient that had turned the treatment into a toxic poison.

Astrid looked up at the television. It seemed that reality shows and the news had become the only programs that plagued the television.

She decided against watching the sixty-minute reality shows that represented nothing but greed, pride, lust and gluttony, just as they had always done before and opted for the news instead.

She was just becoming immersed in the weather report, where the woman was flirting with the camera and forgetting what she was saying, when the television suddenly turned itself off. The power had gone out.

She tried to switch the television back on, but there was no power running to it at all. The electricity had been cut.

As if on cue, the phone that Dr. Reynolds had given her started to ring. It was an unknown number. She answered it. "Hello?"

"Astrid... we have Cruz... There's a car waiting for you outside. Tell no one." The phone call ended abruptly.

She put the phone into her pocket, ran out of the room and into the parking lot. There was an expensive-looking black car waiting for her with the back door open.

She was hesitant for a moment, but she remembered that they were claiming to have Cruz. She wasn't going to risk his life for her own doubts. She climbed into the car, closed the door and put on her seat belt. There was no one in the back with her.

"Where are we going?" she asked the driver as he drove out of the parking lot, ignoring her. "Where's Cruz? What have you done with him?"

Still, the driver did not say a word.

#

He continued on until they reached the fisherman's wharf. The tram was no longer in service, and the area seemed entirely abandoned of people, all except for a grey military boat, waiting on the water.

The driver came to a complete stop and opened her door, instructing that she hop out of the car. She climbed out and made her way towards a black suited man that was standing on one of the piers, facing the boat.

"Astrid Sutherland," the man said, turning to face her. "I've been expecting you."

He was clearly only a few years older than her, with blue eyes, very short dark-blonde hair, clean shaven and very handsome.

Astrid looked around at the abandoned wharf and then back at the man. "Are you Roger Charlie?" she asked.

He laughed. "Follow me if you want to see your friend again."

He led her onto the boat. There were a few men who all seemed mentally stable, tending to the boat.

"How have none of you been affected?" she asked the man.

"Do you really think that Reynolds is the only doctor who has worked out a treatment?" he asked as he led her into the cabin and directed her to sit down, which she did.

"Where are you keeping Cruz? You better not have hurt him in any way!" she snapped, but the man just laughed at her again.

The boat took off, making its way towards Alcatraz Island. "You will know all in due time, Miss Sutherland," the man said.

#

When the boat arrived at the island's pier, the soldiers had to undergo a high clearance check. Astrid was in awe of her surroundings. It seemed what had once been a prison, and then a tourist attraction, had been taken over entirely by the military.

Soldiers stood on guard ensuring that no trouble was caused, as the man that had brought her there was saluted by them. She realized at that point that he must have been someone of high ranking. A sergeant or something.

He led her out of the boat, up the ramp and to the very first building. Once again, they met with soldiers with their guns at the ready, performing further clearances.

"Who am I meeting with?" Astrid asked her escort. "When will you take me to Cruz?" Still, he did not answer her.

Finally, they were standing outside an office with the door closed. He knocked on the door and said, "We have the girl."

Astrid wondered what was going to happen to her. She felt like running away, but she knew that she didn't stand a chance.

The man from inside spoke briefly. "You may enter." His voice was strangely familiar.

Her escort opened the door and led her inside. As Astrid stepped into the room, she stood in shock as she saw just who had been waiting for her arrival.

Cruz was not being held against his will in any way. He was standing with his arms crossed, until he saw her.

"Astrid!" he gasped. He ran towards her and held her tightly.

But it was the man sitting at the desk that made her speechless. It was as if she had just seen a ghost, for he was a man that she knew very well and had once believed to be dead. It was her father, and he seemed to be the lead authority of this base and very much alive.

"Dad?" she stammered.

Astrid examined the green eyes and the light grey hair of her father. He had surely aged in the past few years.

She was in shock, and at the same time, very angry to see him just sitting there. Knowing that he had been alive all this time and hadn't contacted her, affected her more than words could express. Yet, there was still a small part of her that was relieved to see him alive. She was speechless, as was Cruz, who did not know that he had been speaking with her father all that time.

But that didn't matter, for General Sutherland addressed them both as he got to his feet. "Now, you have been brought here, ultimately for your own safety. Astrid, Cruz, you are both being hunted because the military would like nothing more than to use you to end the curse..."

"Whoa, whoa, whoa! Dad! You have got to be kidding me! You are the military!" Astrid interrupted him. The soldiers that had followed her into the office readied their weapons.

The General raised his hand at his soldiers. "Leave us!" he ordered of his men. They heeded his words and left obediently, leaving only Astrid and Cruz in General Sutherland's presence.

"Help me understand this, dad! You work for the military! In fact, while we thought you were dead, you have been working with them all this time! How could you lie to us this way? Mom went insane believing that you were dead. And now you capture me and Cruz in a military boat saying that the military are after us? What the hell!"

General Sutherland stared at her. "I no longer work for the same branch that I once did. I work for myself. When you thought that I had died, I needed you to believe it. But now, with everything that has been happening I need to know that you are safe. I am risking a lot just by being here."

"So that was you back in that town? You knew that we were in that bunker?"

"No... that was Sergeant Davids. He infiltrated a group that were after you. They would have taken you, had he not thrown them off your trail."

"Do you mind if I sit down for a moment?" Cruz asked nervously. "This was not how I anticipated meeting my girlfriend's father..." General Sutherland nodded, so Cruz sat down in the chair by the window.

"Nor had I anticipated that Pandora's Box would be opened by someone not of my wife's bloodline," General Sutherland replied.

"Yeah... about that... I'm sorry... Wait, Astrid actually is the descendant of Pandora? Great... so we *are* only together because of the curse," Cruz added sarcastically.

"So, it's true?" Astrid asked her father. The General picked up the folder that was sitting on his desk and handed it to her.

"This folder contains everything that you need to know... no need to snoop the internet, this information has never been released to the public."

Astrid opened the folder and glanced at the first few pages, but barely read them. Cruz stood up beside her and looked at the pages, interested in what they had to say.

Then, as if they were of no importance, Astrid handed Cruz the entire folder and glared at her father. "So now what? You expect me to believe you? To stay here with you? No, Dad! I'm finding that box and ending all of this!"

"...and I want to help you... but we can't do it by sitting here in the ruins of Alcatraz prison. But, at the same time... I can't have you doing anything reckless..."

The General's comment about Astrid acting reckless made Cruz stifle back a laugh. "What's so funny, Cruz?" she demanded.

"Nothing... just... you are a bit reckless..."

"No, I'm not!"

"You quite literally disarmed a guy who was about to shoot me... that's a little reckless."

The General cleared his throat abruptly, demanding their attention. They both looked up at him. "Have something to eat, get some rest and report back at fifteen hundred hours. We will be leaving then."

"Dad... I'm your daughter... not a soldier. So don't treat me like one... Besides, I can't leave Dr. Reynolds at the labs," Astrid argued.

"Dr. Reynolds is not my priority. You are! You will not be leaving and that's an order that I am giving you as your father... And you will obey it!"

Astrid glared at him and stormed out of his office angrily.

Cruz attempted to follow her, but General Sutherland told him to stop. "Cruz, that's my little girl... I haven't got to where I am for being nice... do you understand what I'm saying?"

Cruz felt himself tremble in fear. "Yes, sir."

"What was that?" the General asked.

"Yes, sir!" Cruz said loudly, even scaring himself. As nervous as Astrid made him feel, this man made him feel like he could need a change of pants at any moment.

He clutched the folder tightly to his chest and followed Astrid as they were led away from the General's building.

#

The soldiers who had led Astrid to her father's office prior, were the same ones that led them to the cafeteria, where they were provided with breakfast.

"I can't believe he's been alive all this damn time!" Astrid snapped as they found a table for themselves.

Cruz took a hold of her hand. "Yeah... that must be..."

"Unbelievable? Yeah, it is!" she interrupted him, sighing as she spoke.

"He's actually a little scary," Cruz said under his breath.

"You know, you're not the first person to tell me that... but I am glad that you're talking to me again. I was worried about you when you didn't return."

129

"Yeah, I'm sorry... I needed time to think... there's just a lot to think about... I mean, what if the world ends before we could fix things? Or what if..."

"Cruz! Stop worrying. Right now, all that matters is the present. Plus, I need to speak with you about something important."

"What's that? Aside from the fact that all these soldiers make me feel quite inferior in every way."

"Dr. Reynold's treatment... it had some very bad side effects."

"What do you mean? Are Tara and Ashley okay?"

"Well, they are sick... They're dying."

"Wow... I bet Reynold's isn't too happy."

"No, he's not... But, prior to that, he kind of freaked out and I didn't know the side effects and... I gave him the injection... I injected him with the serum... I might have just sentenced him to death!"

"Wow... Astrid... I... I don't know what to say. I mean, Reynolds could come up with a treatment... He could be fine. It's too bad that your father won't let us go and check on him..."

It was evident by his surprised, and then disheartened tone, that Cruz was upset by the news. But unfortunately, there was nothing that he could do to change things.

They finished their meals in silence and then Cruz opened the file, studying everything that it held on Pandora's Box and Astrid's bloodline.

"Wow, you should check this out. It's pretty amazing stuff," he said after a while. "It actually dates back to the ancient times! They've translated it and everything!"
He was getting very excited.

Astrid laughed at him. "You were saying before that the soldiers were making you feel inferior... but this right here... is why I'd pick you over them in a heartbeat."

Cruz blushed and kept his face down.

"The General recommends that you train with the rest of us," the Sergeant that had escorted them down for the meal said. "In case you have a use for it later."

"...and if we refuse?" Astrid asked, casually.

"Well then, Sutherland... you'll die an easy death out in this ever changing world... This is not summer camp! We're training for an apocalypse! You and your boyfriend will both receive adequate training tomorrow morning on the ship with the rest of us!"

"What's your name, soldier?" Astrid asked him.

"Davids. Why is that of any importance to you?"

"Well, my father seems to have appointed you as my watcher... I just like to know the people that I'm surrounded by. That's all," she told him with a smug smile.

Sergeant Davids stared at her, as if trying to determine her second agenda, but then left all the same. He couldn't have been any more than five years older than her, yet he was clearly her father's second in command.

"He was a real dick," Astrid said under her breath.

"See? You always have to have the last say, don't you?" Cruz joked.

"Hey, watch it, you! But now, it looks like you'll be made to train like the rest of the soldiers. So, you'll have no reason to feel inferior."

"Meh! I'd prefer to stick to my research and excavations... Much more exciting!"

"I suppose it can't hurt knowing how to defend ourselves..." Astrid sighed, knowing that they had no choice in the matter. But then she looked over at Cruz and grinned. "Now, you're not only going to be smart and sexy... you'll be strong, too... a triple threat!"

"Well, querida... This should be just a walk in the park for you, then."

"What did you just say?"

"Nothing... I said nothing." Cruz smiled to himself as he got back to his reading.

#

By the afternoon, Astrid and Cruz had boarded the General's ship as per his request. While Astrid had been granted her own cabin, Cruz had been ordered to sleep in the bunks with the rest of the soldiers.

As the day turned into night they stood at the bow of the ship, as it left San Francisco. The General had refused to give them any information about where they were headed.

"I can't believe that he refused to go back and get Dr. Reynolds!" Astrid vented to Cruz.

"Me neither. Though, I hate to sound heartless, but he's kind of right. We're dealing with the end of the world here... and you know that Dr. Reynolds would agree... especially if..." Cruz's voice trailed off, as he thought about the possibility that the man could be dead.

"I get that. But I'm allowed to be pissed off!"

"Yeah, you are... but why don't we channel that into our training tomorrow and use this moment to watch the sunset... How many more are we going to get?" Cruz put his arm around her and held her tight as she nestled in to him.

They stood in silence for a moment and then he asked her a question that had been plaguing him. "Do you think your dad will make me cut my hair like the rest of these soldiers? Because that's where I draw the line."

Astrid laughed, but before she could speak, her father answered for her. "You can keep your hair, Cruz... just as you can keep your hands far from my daughter in my presence."

Cruz did as he was told, and they turned around to face General Sutherland.

"Leave us," the General ordered of him. Once again, Cruz obeyed him, out of fear, and smiled at Astrid as he left.

"He's a good guy, dad, and he's afraid of you."

"Yet, he's a fool like Epimethus."

"I'd appreciate it if you got off his case."

"Okay, I will for now, because I wanted to talk to you about the artifact. Do you even know what it will take to end the curse? Does your boyfriend know? Because if you did..." the General stopped speaking in the middle of his sentence.

"Don't stop there, finish your sentence, dad. What will it take?"

"The blood of the true descendant... and while I'd hoped it might have been your mother to spare you of this burden... she is unsuitable for the mission. You are our only chance of survival which is why we need you to be ready."

"Ready for what? You need to spell it out for me! My blood? How much of my blood?"

"I'm not certain... that's why we need to keep you safe. The men who are currently in possession of the pithos are looking to end both your lives. I would like to learn if there are any loop holes before we take such drastic actions."

Astrid was overcome with shock at his words. "So I need to die to save the world? Would you really end your own daughter's life to do that?"

"Astrid, I promise that we are looking to find another way!"

"Dad! The world is quite literally ending. People are going insane thanks to the Seven Deadly Sins! Towns have already been wiped out! Disease is spreading across the world! I need to ask you again... Would you really end your own daughter's life to save the world, if it came down to it?!"

The General would still not answer her.

"You said that my mother was unsuitable... It's nice to know that I wasn't your first option!" she said with sarcasm.

She stormed towards Cruz who was sitting on the floor going over the file, and then turned back to her father. "I'm going to my room... and because I'm a grown woman... Cruz is coming with me."

Cruz looked up, unsure as to whether it was a good idea to go with her or not. He looked over at the General, who shook his head in defeat. "It's called a stateroom or a cabin... and I guess that I can't stop you."

Cruz got to his feet and followed Astrid. "What was that argument about?" he asked her, as they made their way through the ship.

"About how we're supposed to end the curse. Let me say it has to do with blood."

"Blood? Are we talking about a blood oath, or something a little more sinister? Because I haven't reached that part yet."

"People believe that I might need to die to end the curse."

"Hmm... and your dad...?"

"Couldn't answer if he would be willing to sacrifice his own daughter to save the world."

"Yeah... I can see how that would destroy a father-daughter reunion."

#

They entered her quarters and closed the door behind them. "Wow, this is nice!" Cruz said in awe of her cabin. "I guess being the General's daughter does have its advantages, aside from the whole needing to be sacrificed thing..."

"But he did say that he wanted to find another way first." She sat on her bed and pulled out the phone that Dr. Reynolds had given her earlier. It had already gone flat, so she sat it down on the bed beside her.

Cruz sat down next to her. "I think that's what Reynolds was getting at back in the car.

Would I be willing to sacrifice you to save the world?"

"Well, would you?"

Cruz shook his head. "I don't think I could... and I don't think that you father could, either. Let's just try to find another way."

Astrid prayed that by working with her father, they could do just that. She got to her feet and took a few deep breaths to calm herself down. At that moment, she knew what it was like to be truly afraid.

Cruz stood in front of her and wrapped his arms around her. "Why don't we just stop thinking about all of this. We'll have a good night, and tomorrow we can start anew... get to training, kick some ass and relocate Pandora's Box... along with an alternate way to save the world that doesn't involve you dying or something just as grim. But tonight... we'll take a break and be normal."

Astrid smiled as she pressed herself firmly against him. She kissed him as she spoke. "Alright. You're right... Already forgotten... but do you want to know something that I do remember? That I heard what you said today... back at Alcatraz... 'Querida'... it took me a little while to figure out what it meant, because I only know a little bit of Spanish... but... it was very, very cute."

"Oh, I can continue saying cute things... under one condition," he replied, taking a break from his sentence to kiss her back.

"Oh yeah? And what's that?" She smiled at him.

"Continue kissing me?" he suggested.

"I can do that."

"You can?"

"Mm hmm..." She nodded, when suddenly, there was a knock at the door. Cruz pulled away from her nervously, afraid that it could be her father. But she pulled him close again.

"Shh, stay quiet and they might just go away," she whispered.

They started kissing again, and then there was another knock, this time louder. They separated again. Cruz sat back down on the bed and waited, as Astrid let out a loud sigh and opened the door.

"Sergeant Davids? My dad's second in command. What can I do for you?" Astrid asked smugly.

"Can we talk for a moment?"

"That's what we're doing, isn't it? Now talk."

"I get the impression that you don't like me..."

"No... I just don't know you... okay, now that's cleared up... We'll talk soon." She went to close the door on him, but he stopped her.

"Look, I heard you and your father arguing out there and I just want you to know that he loves you, despite how he comes off. In fact, when he and I left the military to start this whole new branch, his biggest regret was knowing that you had to go on thinking that he was dead and that he would never get to see you again. So, I know that he will do anything in his power to ensure that you don't have to die... Why do you think he wants you and your friend to train with the rest of us?"

Astrid pursed her lips together before she spoke. "I appreciate you telling me that... Thank you. But it doesn't make me feel any better knowing that you know my father better than I do."

"Look, I'm sorry... I'm not trying to upset you..."

Astrid sighed. "I'm sorry. I didn't mean to come off as a bitch. I'm just trying to deal with a lot right now, okay?"

"Okay... that's all I needed to say." Sergeant Davids replied. He nodded over Astrid's shoulder and said, "Hey, Cruz!"

"Hey!" Cruz hadn't moved from his spot.

Astrid closed the door again and made her way back to Cruz. "Now, where were we?"

"We were having a really nice moment of normalcy before Sergeant Buzzkill killed the buzz and started flirting with you," Cruz said, very frustrated.

"He wasn't flirting... Now, let's get back to our 'nice moment of normalcy' before someone else decides to interrupt us." She kissed him, and he ran his fingers through her hair.

"Alright, back to taking a break, because tomorrow will be interesting... and yes, he was flirting... You just don't see it... because you're clueless as to how beautiful you really are," he replied, kissing her again.

#

Meanwhile, back in San Francisco, soldiers raided Astrid and Cruz's motel room. They managed to log onto Cruz's computer to search for their whereabouts.

"They were here... Quite recently in fact... but it seems that someone manually wiped the computer from a remote location. There's no way of accessing what they were looking for," one of the soldiers said to his Sergeant.

"Find me Davids," the Sergeant demanded of his men.

"He's gone missing, sir!"

"What do you mean 'missing'?"

"I mean we can't find him!"

"Well then, bring me the doctor. We'll make him talk!"

Dr. Reynolds had done it. He had managed to synthesize a treatment to ensure that he did not die the same way that Tara and Ashley had. But before he could administer it to himself, soldiers began pouring into his laboratory. "Dr. Reynolds... you're coming with us!"

Chapter 8

Before the sun rose, there was a loud banging on Astrid's cabin door. She hid under her blanket to ignore it.

"I don't think they're going to go away," Cruz said, already showered, dressed and ready. His hair had been pulled back into a pony tail at the back of his head and the site of him in a military uniform made her gush. "Someone came in here earlier and slipped some clothes at the end of the bed for us. Training is going to happen whether we like it or not... I'll meet you in the galley," he said.

"The galley? That's the cafeteria, right?" Astrid asked, sitting up.

Cruz smirked at her. "Yes, now go and take a shower! Come on! Vámonos!"

"Okay, okay! Just have the coffee waiting for me when I get down there," she yawned.

Cruz nodded and left her to get ready in peace.

#

When she finally arrived in the galley with the other soldiers, she collected her breakfast and went to sit with Cruz, but Sergeant Davids stood in her path. "Sutherland, your father requests that I see to your training personally. He believes that it will be of great benefit to you."

"Davids... It's good to see you, too. What's with the special treatment?"

"You're being hunted by the military. While we are sworn to protect you that means teaching you how to defend yourself against the other soldiers. I happened to be the best under your father, so he asked that I see to it personally."

"What about Cruz?"

"I was tasked to train you, not Cruz. So, eat your breakfast and I'll see you in ten minutes."

Astrid rolled her eyes and stormed to Cruz's table. "What did Sergeant Buzzkill want?" he asked, pushing her coffee towards her.

Astrid laughed as she sipped her coffee. "To be a Sergeant Buzzkill, what else? No, my father tasked him 'personally to see to my training'. Apparently I get special treatment, while you have to train with the rest of the guys."

"Damn... I was looking forward to watching you in action. But I guess it makes sense. They need the best of the best to train you... It probably doesn't help that your dad has it out for me and that Sergeant Buzzkill is really into you... but, I'm not jealous. Not in the slightest."

"You don't sound so sure of yourself."

"Maybe because I'm not. Last night when you fell asleep, I went over that file. There is no love spell. So no supernatural forces binding us together... and I guess I'm just expecting you to find someone better than me... because hey, that's bound to happen! Now I'm wishing that there was a love spell... sorry..."

"So, no love spell?" Astrid started eating her breakfast.

"Nope... but while the artifact did bring us together, it doesn't explain anything about why I feel the way I do about you. I used to think that love at first sight was bullshit. But what I do know is that I do find you beautiful and I love being around you. Yeah, it's a little early to say the L word... and that's not what I'm doing here. But, now I get where Joey was coming from."

"I would love to meet this Joey guy," Astrid said staring into her coffee. "So what are you trying to tell me?"

"That you drive me crazy... and the thought of the world ending scares me... but, if you training with Sergeant Buzzkill means us succeeding in saving the world and you not dying, well, so be it. I'm all for it. But I'm still very insecure about myself and, there I go... rambling... again... this is why I prefer to be by myself."

Astrid blushed. "You're cute when you ramble. But I think that the reason I said there was some love spell was because..."

"Sutherland... it's time to train." They looked up to see Sergeant Davids standing at their table.

"But I've barely touched my breakfast," Astrid argued.

"Are you disobeying me, recruit?"

"No, I'm not."

"No what?"

"I said that I'm not disobeying you?" Astrid asked him puzzled.

Sergeant Davids glared at her. "Excuse me, recruit?"

Cruz gave her a look, telling her to say 'no, sir.'

Astrid listened to him. "Alright, no, sir!"

"What was that?"

"No, sir!" Astrid said much louder this time.

"Then get up and follow me, now!"

She got to her feet and as he turned to lead her out of the galley she rolled her eyes in Cruz's direction. She followed Sergeant Davids out of the galley and in to a private combat room.

#

Within half an hour he had already demanded her to run three laps, to give him thirty push-ups and submitted her to numerous sparring attempts, where he did not go easy on her. She sat up angrily on the floor, wiping the blood from her lip.

"Get up and we'll do that again!" he demanded.

"You've got to be kidding me!" Astrid snapped. "If this is about that attitude that I have been gi..."

"Don't be stupid. This is strictly about survival, now get up and let's go again! You don't like me, and I sense that. Let it fuel you!"

Astrid sighed in frustration and spat blood. She threw a punch at the man. He instantly blocked it and threw her to the floor again.

"You're beginning to be a real pain in the ass," she snapped at him as she got to her feet again.

"So fight me! The men who have the artifact want you dead. Your father is willing to die to protect you. I'm even betting to think that your boyfriend is willing to protect you. Do them both a favor and prove that you're willing to fight for yourself. That if they do die... it won't be in vain."

Astrid threw another punch at him. This time he blocked it, twisted her around so that she had her back to him, and restrained her. "So, my father made his whole family believe that he was dead... and for what? To adopt you as his son and turn his back on the military?"

"He did... and I bet that eats you up, doesn't it? Daddy's little girl loses her daddy."

"You're an asshole!" She snapped her head back, cracking him in the face.

It distracted him enough to let go of her. She turned and brought her foot up, instantly kicking him in the groin. But before she could make contact, he grabbed her ankle, twisted her leg and threw her to the floor again.

"Well, at least I'm an asshole that can protect myself."

Astrid got to her feet angrily and stormed out of the combat room slamming the door behind her and making her way to her father's cabin.

#

The moment that she had charged into her father's cabin, finding him at his desk, she began her tirade. "I hate you! I hate you for pretending to be dead. For leaving the military. For making me spar with your asshole replacement for a child... For everything!"

"I'm not surprised," he addressed her calmly, "...but I need you to know that everything I did, I did for a reason."

"Why? Because you felt like it?"

"No, because the men that I was working under were traitors to our country, so I had no choice. The only way to prove it was to go undercover. To fake my own death."

General Sutherland stood up from his desk. He knew that his daughter was waiting for a full explanation. She would not leave without one. "The divisions higher up offered me anonymity, resources and funding to expose them. It wasn't until a little over a year ago that I found the evidence that I needed to expose them. I planted infiltrators who found out that my former division had ceased Pandora's Box. But I wasn't aware that I had a traitor in my midst who was loyal to them. They heard me discussing your mother's ancestry to a trusted scientist. They released that information and went hunting for you. That's where Davids comes in."

"What does that pain in the ass have to do with any of this?"

"Well, six months ago, when I heard the news, I sent him out to keep a watchful eye on you. He was there the night that those men broke into your apartment. He fought some off, but before he could reach you, you had already left. He continued to lead them off your trail and then convinced me to bring you in, to keep you safe. Believe it or not, he's been trying to look out for you for a long time... because he knows what it's like to lose a father."

Astrid was speechless. "I... I'm sorry... I didn't know."

"Now, do you understand why I tasked him to train you? Not to mention, he's one of my best men. He knows what he's doing."

Astrid sat down on the chair beside him. She could feel the ship moving below her, and hearing this news was making her feel a little dizzy. She took a few deep breaths.

For someone who was supposed to be a psychologist, she was having a lot of trouble giving herself advice, especially in relation to her own feelings in regards to the oncoming apocalypse as well as her father being back from the dead. It was certainly a lot to take on.

She sighed. "Okay... maybe I should find him and apologize."

"That might be best."

Astrid got to her feet, but before she opened the door she turned to him and said, "I'll apologize to him... but I'm not ready to forgive you."

#

Dr. Reynolds had been dragged and left tied to a chair in a very dim room. He had been badly beaten and the sickness had begun to set in. The sores were forming all over his body.

He felt the need to scratch them, but with his hands bound, it wasn't possible. He had vomited multiple times on the floor beside him. Some had even gotten on his pants.

The soldiers had brought him there the night before, without giving a reason as to why. But he knew that it had something to do with Pandora's Box.

He was committed to not give up any information, but with exhaustion and the illness sinking in, he was unsure as to whether he could hold out or not. Besides, it was only a matter of time until the rage in him re-emerged.

When the door opened, it startled him. He hadn't been expecting it. The light was switched on. Dr. Reynolds was sitting in an operating room inside a hospital. A man dressed in a surgical mask, gown and gloves approached him, picking up the scalpel from the table beside them.

"Well, aren't you a mess to see. Look at you, sitting in your own vomit. Side effects from your new treatments, I'm presuming... fortunately, it's not contagious."

Dr. Reynolds' head bobbled around. He was feeling dizzy and could barely comprehend anything that the man was saying.

"I have been studying your treatments, Dr. Reynolds. You have not yet come up with a cure, just a mild treatment... just as I have been studying your cure for the sickness you are currently experiencing. I'm guessing that you're aching for me to give you your medicine... aren't you?"

Dr. Reynolds could barely speak. His whole body was in agony. His breathing was deep and his stomach had that nauseous tension once again.

"Maybe we could cut a deal," the man continued. "We have your family. We can give them treatments with no side effects... We can also cure you from the current state that you are in. Unfortunately, you will still have to deal with your rage, just until we end the Seven Sins Virus. All we need from you is your information regarding the artifact and the whereabouts of your most recent companions... that's all... then you can walk away from all of this. We can save the world and you and your family can live happily ever after... What do you say?"

Dr. Reynolds stared at the man, but before he could answer he gave in to the vomit that spewed from his mouth and onto the floor, some dripping onto the man's shoe. He was getting very weak, and that was a very enticing offer, indeed.

#

"How was training, Cruz?" Astrid asked as he joined her at the bow of the ship, late in the afternoon, overlooking the ocean. "You look exhausted."

"That's because I am. I thought that I was going to die." He leaned on the railing beside her and rested his chin in his hands. "I was ready to throw myself overboard... I'm not a fighter! I'm just the witty archaeologist with the obsession for research. If this is an apocalypse, why the hell are we wasting our time with these brute soldiers? Why don't we just find the stupid artifact, work on how to fix everything and then that's it... we'll be done!"

"But you are fighter! You have been fighting to put an end to all of this for a year now. You went on the Diane show and you were totally ridiculed... and for what? To fight to get your point across...

But it's working! People are dying due to Pandora's Box being more than just some stupid myth... and things are going to get a hell of a lot worse. So, you and I are going to have to do whatever it takes to end it. It's just not going to be easy."

"I know it's not going to be easy... It's just... it sucks! That's all."

"Yeah, it does. But knowing that we're both in this together... it makes it a hell of a lot easier."

Cruz nodded. "True. Which reminds me... I'm pretty sure that you were about to tell me something very important back at breakfast this morning. Do you remember?"

Astrid smiled at him, she did remember. But before she could speak, Cruz glanced over her shoulder. "Raincheck?" he asked, "because, don't look now, but that dick... Sergeant Buzzkill, is about to report for duty... to kill the buzz yet again... right on time as usual... I should go and get back to my research before I get the urge to push him overboard." He gave her a kiss on the cheek and left, leaving her wishing that he had stayed.

"I'm sorry for being so harsh on you, earlier," Sergeant Davids said making Astrid turn to face him.

"No, I think I should apologize. When I left, I went to speak with my father. He explained everything. Did you really come to my apartment looking for me that night?"

"Yes, I did... but by the time I got there, some guy was raiding your apartment and you had left out the window... but, I actually managed to retrieve something for you. Your laptop, I gave it to your dad."

"Wow, really? Thank you."

"It looked pretty important and very expensive, so I wasn't going to leave those men to have it."

"I don't know what to say. I'll have to get it from my dad later. Thank you, I really do appreciate it."

"You're welcome." He stared out over the ocean. "You know we're not marines... so we won't always be on a ship."

"Yeah... but do we really want to be on land when we have seen what humanity has become? Yesterday, I saw a proud café owner who had fed his greedy food critic to death."

"Hmm. It's scary isn't it? I mean, I saw a woman who lusted over a man so much that she needed him inside her... I don't mean that sexually... I mean, she ate him."

"Eww... Gross! I don't know what to say... That's just eww!"

"Yeah... Then I saw the tragedy of a father who was so jealous of his protégé son... It didn't have a pretty ending. That cut your father deep to see that one..."

"Why doesn't the military just give their treatments to the public? It would save a lot of lives."

"While it would... their supplies are running low... and it gets worse... the Seven Sins virus, if what our scientists are saying is correct... well, it's getting stronger... it's evolving past the treatments... We've had to go from taking it once a day, to three times a day... It certainly was not manmade... but clearly an act of God... Zeus, in fact."

"Ha, you sound like Cruz."

"Well, at least he's not a halfwit."

"I'm sorry?"

"Sorry, but... if it wasn't for him, we wouldn't be in this mess to begin with... and he's certainly no soldier, that's for damn sure," Sergeant Davids said with a laugh.

"Why's that so funny? He's been working his ass off to put an end to all of this. He regrets his actions more than anyone else does. So stay the hell off his case!"

"Alright, I apologize. I'll tell the men to lay off him, too... If that's what you want me to do."

"Why? What's your angle? Are you just trying to score brownie points from my father? Because I don't think doing favors for his daughter is going to work!"

"I have no angle. But right now it'd be better for us to work together than it would be for us to tear each other down. I have your back, Sutherland, and if Cruz needs it... I'll have his, too." Sergeant Davids turned and left.

#

After hours of reading over the research file of Pandora's Box, Cruz mustered up his courage to approach General Sutherland in his office.

He felt his palms sweating in nervousness as he held the folder close to his chest and knocked on the door. General Sutherland opened it. "Yes, Cruz? What can I do for you?"

Cruz looked around the office. "Can I have a word? You know, from one man to another? In private?" he managed to stammer.

General Sutherland opened the door wide, inviting him in and then closed it behind them. "You have five minutes," he said as he took his seat at the desk.

Cruz nodded and walked over to the chair. "Can I sit here?" he asked nervously.

"Four minutes, Cruz."

Cruz sighed and rested the file on the desk but continued to stand nervously. "Okay... I get that you don't like me much, sir. But I really like your daughter... and I have been going over everything in these files and I can't seem to find anything that means that she has to die to break the curse... These notes say nothing about the whispers that I heard... not that I could understand them, anyway... I mean, they had to let hope out of the jar... but that's it, there was nothing left inside when the lid wouldn't close... But, I have a theory... that those whispers that I heard were actually the spirits..."

"Cruz... you have two minutes left, and you're telling me nothing new."

"Sorry, sir... What I'm trying to ask... is... well, what if the reason that I am also immune is because I altered the curse by opening it... What if she isn't the only one whose blood can put a stop to it..."

General Sutherland stared at him. "Are you suggesting that your blood could also end the curse? We both know what ending the curse might entail, but what are you implying?"

"I'm implying that... hmm... I guess that I'm saying that if we can't find any other less morbid ways to end the curse, that...well, I don't want Astrid to have to die... I'm willing to put myself first... if I need to. I don't mean to say that I don't want to find another way... because I really do want to find another way... I really don't want to die... in fact, I'm rather scared of dying... But, if the pithos requests a blood sacrifice... let me be that sacrifice."

The General stood up and stared at him for a long time. "Are you saying that you would be willing to risk your life for my daughter?"

"Yes, sir... I think that's exactly what I'm saying. I mean, she is really amazing and... I'm not the kind of guy to just fall for the first girl that comes my way... and we haven't known each other for that long... but wow... yeah... that's what I'm saying."

Cruz forced himself to stop talking. He sighed and sat down on the chair at the desk, as the General's eyes continued to rest on him.

"Please say something..." Cruz pleaded, as he rested his face on his arms at the desk, in shock at his own realization.

General Sutherland sat down and continued to stare at the man before him. "Let's find another way to end this curse... shall we?"

Cruz raised his head up in confusion. "I'm sorry, what?"

"Well, I might not like it... but my daughter deserves someone who is willing to put her life before their own. If we can find another way to end the curse, then I would like for her to experience what it's like to be with someone who truly loves her."

"Whoa, it's only been a couple of weeks... we're not dropping the L bomb just yet... that's a bit early," Cruz said quickly.

"Are you saying that you don't love my daughter? That you're not the man who is willing to sacrifice his own life for her? Because that's the impression that you're giving me."

Cruz went silent. Whatever this was, it sure felt like love... or pretty damn close. He wasn't sure, as it was certainly something that he had never felt before. Sure, he had been with women in the past, and he had thought that it had been real. But, the way he felt for Astrid, he just couldn't explain it.

"That's what I thought. So, why don't we find another way to end the curse," the General said, accepting his silence as an answer. "Now, I have some information that I believe that you should hear. When Pandora's Box was ceased by my old division, they also took hostage a few members of the excavation team... your excavation team. While I have been led to believe that someone else has possession of the artifact now, we have a location of the hostages. They were given mood stabilizers to deal with the Seven Deadly Sins virus... but they were also tortured. While your old boss did give up your name, two of your friends remained tight lipped. We will be rescuing them, and I would like you to be in on that rescue."

Cruz's mouth gaped wide open. "Are you talking about...?"

"A Mr. Joey Prescott and a Miss Hannah Jacobson? Yes," the General said, checking his notes.

"They're alive?" Cruz asked in amazement.

"They are, but they haven't been treated very well... So until we can locate the artifact, they will be our top priority."

Cruz got to his feet in excitement. "Wow! Gracias! Thank you! I really don't know what to say!"

"You can say that you're going to keep up your training. We need more soldiers... and right now, your knowledge and your immunity is an asset to us. We need both you and my daughter to stay alive."

"Yes, sir!" Cruz picked up the folder from the desk and ran out of the office in search for Astrid to tell her the amazing news.

Chapter 9
One Year Later

A year passed by and Astrid and Cruz continued to train under the authority of General Sutherland in an undisclosed location.

Outside the walls, the Seven Deadly Sins curse had led to populations dying out, due to the widespread of disease and the mental instability of mankind. Even the supply of electricity, internet and network service eventually had ceased.

Medical treatments for the curse were becoming scarce, as the search for ingredients and capable scientists to synthesize them was proving to become next to impossible, not to mention the severity of the curse would continue to evolve faster against the treatments.

Fortunately, the scientists under General Sutherland had been well hidden, so the organization's supply was not at risk. Astrid had continued to grow closer to her father, spending the year to catch up on all the time that they had lost, when she had believed him to be dead.

The General even began to develop a soft spot for Cruz, and kept good on his word to not force him to cut off all his hair.

General Sutherland continued to send out infiltration teams to gather intel on the location of the missing excavation team, as well as the location of Pandora's Box.

Unfortunately, due to infiltrators amongst his own ranks, the news was always delayed or unreliable. This led to a major clean out of his troops, cutting loose everyone who had proven disloyal, until one day, when the intel proved to be accurate and he requested for Cruz to meet with him in his office.

"We finally have a precise location on the excavation team, and if we can find them, we believe that we will be one step closer to relocating Pandora's Box," the General told him. "I understand that my daughter will not be too thrilled that I am giving you the opportunity to go. But you requested this task personally, and I think that you're finally ready. It will also prove to be a brilliant test for you, for the future."

"Yes, sir. Thank you... sir!" Cruz said. "Should you tell her, or should I?"

"I'll leave that to you. Sometimes, I regret forcing her to train as hard as I have. She's become a real weapon now."

"Yeah, Sergeant Davids has done a good job with her. Yep... credit where it's due!" Cruz said lowering his eyes to the floor.

To anyone, it was clearly obvious that Sergeant Davids' affections for Astrid were anything more than friendly, even if they weren't returned. She loved Cruz and they all knew it.

"Don't fear Sergeant Buzzkill. He may be my second in command, but you will always come first to my daughter," General Sutherland said.

"Sergeant Buzzkill? I don't understand what you're talking about!" Cruz said nervously.

The General let slip a slight smile. "My daughter tells me everything. She's even called it to his face once or twice. Regardless, this mission, while it will prove to be a challenge, if you follow instructions and you use your head, I have faith that you will succeed, and that you will bring your friends back in once piece. But you'll be away for a few months, at least. Are you okay with that?"

"Yes, sir, I am."

"Good! Now go. You will be leaving tonight... and Cruz? Stay safe! We will need you when we find the artifact."

Cruz nodded and then left the General's office.

Cruz made his way to the sparring rooms, where he found Astrid and Sergeant Samuel Davids in heavy hand to hand contact.

Astrid currently had the Sergeant pinned to the floor and was holding him down. They turned to see Cruz enter their sparring room.

"...and you call me a buzzkill," the Sergeant joked to Astrid.

She punched him and got to her feet to embrace Cruz. Her face and arms were bloody, and her hair was falling loose from its pony tail.

Cruz used his thumb to wipe the blood from her lip and handed her a water bottle. "Oh, mami, you know I hate seeing you look so sore," he said pouting at her flirtatiously.

"I know, but we do what we need to do to survive, right?" She kissed him and drank her water bottle thirstily.

"Damn, girl. When was your last drink break?" he asked her.

"Don't blame me, she can get one whenever she wants," Sergeant Davids chimed in picking up his own drink bottle. "It's not my fault that she would rather spar with me than keep herself hydrated." He was trying to get under Cruz's skin.

"Oh, buzz off, Buzzkill," Astrid snapped. "Training with you was never my choice and you know it." The Sergeant shrugged and left her and Cruz to talk in peace.

"I hate that guy," Cruz said.

"I know you do. But unfortunately, we're stuck until we find the artifact. Speaking of, how did your chat with my father go?"

"Rather well, actually... but there's still no word on Pandora's Box. There was, however, news on Joey and Hannah's location... This time he believes that the news was accurate."

"That's great! Are they okay?" she asked, ecstatic for him.

"That's... kind of the thing..." he said, not wanting to look at her. She understood immediately but waited for him to continue. "Your father's giving me the opportunity to go and help with their rescue."

"Oh no, he's not! I'll clear this up, immediately!" Astrid said, ready to storm past him in the direction of her father's office.

He grabbed her by the waist and held her in his arms. "No, Astrid. I want to go. I want to be there when they find them. Please! Don't be mad!"

"Are you sure? That's coming from the guy who said he wasn't a soldier and wanted to jump overboard after his first day of training."

He smiled at her. "I said that a year ago. You know just how much I've been training for this... and your dad believes that we'll be fine. So, let's just trust him. Okay?"

"Alright, fine. But if you don't come back..."

"I will come back! I promise."

"How much time do we get before you go?" she asked as they left the sparring room and closed the door behind them. Sergeant Davids had been waiting outside for them.

"We leave tonight. So we have enough time to spend together before I need to pack."

"Good. At least I get a bit of time with you, first," Astrid replied.

"Don't worry, Cruz. I'll keep her warm, for you," the Sergeant joked.

"That's not funny." She gave the sergeant an icy stare.

"I think it is." He smirked back.

Astrid took Cruz's hand and led him back to their quarters. "I wish I could go with you. How long do you expect to be away for?" she asked.

"I'm not sure. Maybe a few months, at least."

"Wow, this will be the longest we've been away from each other... and it's changed a lot outside these grounds. The world's becoming nothing more than a wasteland. It reminds me of those old post-apocalyptic TV shows that I used to watch."

They were now standing in the middle of their room and he was holding her hands trying to win her over to his side. "I know, Astrid. Please stop trying to make me change my mind. I'm going."

"I'm sorry... Yes, you are going! And you're going to find Joey and Hannah, and if they are hurt in any way, we will help them. And we will find Pandora's Box and the world will be saved."

"Yeah... and then everyone that's left will need to rebuild and repopulate... which means..."

"Whoa... give us a chance to save the world first before we start with the baby talk again," she interrupted him with a smile.

"Deal. See? Something to look forward to," Cruz said, wrapping his arms around her. "I'll be back... For the moment... just kiss me."

Astrid did as he instructed, knowing that she was going to miss him more than she ever thought possible. They made the most of their time together enraptured in each other's arms, not knowing the next time that they would be together that way again.

After the rescue teams had disbanded, along with Cruz, Astrid found her father out in the training field speaking with his newest recruits.

They had made it a regular thing, taking in skillful individuals struggling with the curse and recruiting them up as soldiers, offering them medical treatment, food and accommodation for their families.

She waited until he had finished addressing the men and women soldiers and pulled him aside to speak in private.

"I understand that you have some disagreements with me sending out your boyfriend, but I should remind you that he volunteered to go. He has also come quite a long way with his training," the General said, before his daughter could begin another one of her tirades.

"I get that, but why couldn't you send me out with him? Thanks to you saddling me up with Buzzkill, I have come a long way, too. In fact, I could take on many of your soldiers with one hand tied behind my back!"

"You know why I can't. Besides, he asked me not to send you."

"And since when do you listen to Cruz?"

"I value his opinion when it comes to the safety of my daughter."

"Seriously? You'd listen to him but..."

Before Astrid could finish her sentence, Sergeant Samuel Davids interrupted them with an important message. "General! Our reconnaissance team just informed me that there's a battalion fast approaching our base! We need to be ready to strike. They've already taken down some of our men."

The General didn't need to think twice. "Sergeant, rally the troops. Astrid, come with me, now!"

Sergeant Davids did as he had been ordered, and the General led his daughter throughout their base collecting weapons.

"Astrid, did I ever tell you what happened the night that you were born?" he asked as he handed her a loaded rifle and a bandolier. They could hear the soldiers calling out, preparing for battle.

"Dad, this is hardly the time for one of our father-daughter chats. We're quite literally being attacked."

"I beg to differ. It's the perfect time. We don't do this quite as much as we should."

"Dad, the battle's that way! Why are we going this way?" she asked pointing towards the gates where soldiers were pushing to get through.

The General ignored her and continued talking as he led her away from the fight. "When your mother was pregnant, she refused to tell me if you were going to be a boy or a girl. She wanted it to be a surprise. So, I found out the night that you were born. Finding out that I had a daughter was the greatest feeling that I had ever felt. But you weren't breathing... and as the doctors were working on you, I remember saying that I would give my last breath for you to live..." They had reached his office, he opened the door and tried to push her in.

"Dad... what are you doing?"

"What I promised. I'm giving my last breath for you..." he said, trying to close the door to lock her inside.

"Dad! No, you're not! You're not sacrificing yourself for me! What's the point when it's my blood that will end the curse, anyway?"

"Astrid! When you asked if I would end my daughter's life to save the world. This is what I was afraid to tell you. No father wants to outlive their child! I know that I'm being selfish, but I cannot watch you die! Both you and Cruz are going to find a way to end the curse without either one of you dying. I know you will!"

Astrid tried to hold the door open to squeeze past him. Tears were running down both their faces.

"Astrid, there's a trap door under my desk. Take it and go!" he demanded of her.

"Dad! I can't leave without you! Don't make me, please!"

"Go, now!"

She wanted to argue again, but she knew for once that this was one moment that she needed to obey him. She hugged him tight. "I love you, dad," she sobbed.

"I love you more, baby. Now go! Be safe!" the General demanded of her. He closed the door and locked it behind him, pocketing the key.

He readied his assault rifle as he could hear the soldiers fighting. The men had gotten through. He stormed through his base, looking for his second in command.

Sergeant Davids was currently standing behind a building, taking full advantage of the moments to get his shots in, taking down multiple enemies instantly. The General dodged out of the line of fire to join him. "What's the situation, Davids?" he asked.

"These soldiers took us in by surprise. Most of our men didn't stand a chance. They didn't have enough time to prepare. They have the artifact back at their base! They're looking for her."

"Any word on the location of their base?"

"Negative, sir."

General Sutherland stood on the other side of the wall and peered around, taking down enemies instantly.

"There's a key in my pocket, Davids... You know what to do if I don't survive this one."

"Yes, sir. But you will survive. She needs her father," Sergeant Davids said. He peered past the side of his wall where he saw an enemy crouching behind a water tank. Sergeant Davids took the shot.

General Sutherland ran to take the fire off some of his other soldiers who were currently in over their heads. He took a bullet to the stomach, though continued.

He staggered back to the Sergeant's side again, where he had moved to the middle of the battlefield, behind the water tank where the man had been standing earlier.

"You're bleeding, sir!" Sergeant Davids gasped.

"It's just a flesh wound!"

"No, it's not. You know it's not."

The General removed the key from his pocket and handed it to his second in command.

"You know what to do! If I know her, she'll be waiting in my office for me to return. Go!"

"I'm not going to leave you to die here, sir!"

"Are you disobeying my direct order, Sergeant?"

"I guess that I'm taking a page out of her book!"

"Don't be stupid! I'm telling you as your General. Take the key and go! Now! Before the whole world falls apart!"

Sergeant Davids pocketed the key. "I'm not leaving you, sir!" He threw the General over his shoulder and dragged him out of the battlefield, heading for the man's office, and dodging rapid fire.

"Put me down, Sergeant! I'm only slowing you down!"

"Shut up, you tough old bastard! I'm not leaving you to die out there! Your daughter will kill me."

Sergeant Davids managed to drag him up to the office, but unfortunately, by the time he had made it, his superior had lost a lot of blood. He sat the General on the floor as he unlocked the door. He pushed it open and was instantly met by a rifle being aimed at his face.

"Seriously, Buzzkill! I almost shot you!" Astrid snapped at him.

"It's a good thing you didn't because I have your father. He doesn't have much time left. Help me!"

Astrid immediately helped him maneuver her father into the office and he locked the door behind them.

"You need to leave me. I've lost too much blood," the General gasped.

They could hear the men coming down the hall. "You both have to go now!"

"Dad... we can't leave you," Astrid gasped.

Sergeant Davids was trying to bandage his wound. "Astrid, he's right... he's lost a lot."

"Good, at least one of you is talking sense. Now leave... don't let my death be in vain! Go and find Cruz, and that's an order!" the General demanded.

Astrid knew that she had no choice. She had waited for her father in case he had returned, not wanting to lose him again. But he was right, they couldn't wait any longer.

She kissed him on the forehead. "I love you, dad!"

"I love you too, baby! And Davids, take the backpack and keep my baby safe!" They could hear the pounding on the door. Soldiers were trying to force their way in.

"I will, sir!" Sergeant Davids grabbed her by the arm and picked up the backpack from under the desk while Astrid pulled the rug up which revealed the trap door to the secret underground tunneling systems below. She and Sergeant Davids both climbed through.

Sergeant Davids pulled up the rug and closed the trap door over them, allowing them to make their escape.

#

For the past year, Dr. Reynolds had been tortured immensely for any information in regards to Astrid and Cruz. He had not known their whereabouts, and while he knew that it was possible to track his old phone to find them, he had refused to deliver up this information.

However, the news that the soldiers revealed to him one night made him fear the worst. The military had received word that Astrid and Cruz had met with her father.

General Sutherland was indeed alive and well and was trying to research an alternate way to break the curse. It was the news that their base had been stormed, that the soldiers had killed thousands of people, men, women and children, including the General himself that shattered him.

They were still going through the bodies to determine if Astrid and Cruz were indeed among the dead. If they were, then that would mean that losing his friends had been for nothing, and that the curse would not be broken.

Chapter 10

Days passed by as Cruz rode in the military truck along with his Sergeant and the rest of his team, passing through towns that had crumbled over the past year. They reminded him of the towns that he and Astrid had seen when they had been on the road together.

He sighed, he certainly missed those first few days when it had been just the two of them. But, while it had been fun, he knew that he needed to look forward to the future.

This mission would be the one that would save his friends, Joey and Hannah. He knew that they would love his girlfriend. He tried to envision what they would say when they met her.

Joey would instantly tell her every little embarrassing thing, in detail, that Cruz had done in his entire lifetime. Hannah would welcome the opportunity of no longer being the only woman of the three.

But even if that day came, how much longer would they have left to be together? They hadn't determined an exact way to break the Seven Deadly Sins curse yet, and humanity was certainly dying out. The treatments would not work forever.

He had meant what he had said to General Sutherland a year ago. If it came to it, he would be willing to die for the woman he loved.

That, in part, was why he wanted her to consider being the mother of his children, so he would have a legacy to leave in the world, if the worse should come to pass.

"Penny for your thoughts, Cruz?" a brunette soldier by the name of Natasha Martinez, who was sitting beside him, asked. "It can't be easy knowing that your hot girlfriend is back at base with Sergeant Davids. You know he makes all the girls swoon, right?"

While he was a little uncomfortable by the notion, he trusted Astrid. He also knew that she could kick Sergeant Buzzkill's ass if she had to. "All the girls but her... I'm not concerned about that, Tash. He's not her type," he replied.

"That's right, she loves the smart men! They're a real rare breed," Tash joked. "Such a shame, really, because she's hot!"

"That's right, I forgot you're into women, Tash... No wonder you're not in line to drop your panties for what do you call him, Cruz? Buzzkill?" Jake, who was sitting across from him asked. Cruz smirked. That name had really caught on.

"You have a problem with that, Jake – the rake?" Tash asked. "I've probably been with more women than you have in your lifetime... and I'm guessing that's because I know exactly what they want."

"No problem, Tash. I just think the whole 'girl on girl' thing is kind of hot."

"Yeah... like you'd ever be invited to that party," she replied, rolling her eyes, and then looking back over at Cruz, said, "You have a good girl on your hands. So what's the problem?"

"General Sutherland said that some good friends of mine are among the hostages that we're going to be rescuing."

"Friends? Cruz has friends?" Jake asked. "Any hotties? I mean, a beautiful girl always gives rescue missions a little something extra... wouldn't you agree, Tash?"

"While I would normally agree, it's a rescue mission... let's do what we can, because it's the right thing to do... not just to get some ass at the end of the day, shall we?" Tash laughed. "Right, Cruz?"

"Absolutely... and sorry to disappoint you, Jake... but the one girl that I do know, she's taken... My man, Joey was really into her before they changed."

Jake and Tash stared at the floor. They too had experienced the change of their own friends and families.

Suddenly, the truck came to a stop. "Are we there already, sir?" Jake asked their superior, Sergeant Jackson.

Their superior received an incoming transmission on his walkie-talkie. "Sergeant. We've heard some distressing news from back at base."

Cruz, Tash and Jake listened as Sergeant Jackson told them to stay in the vehicle. He climbed out and they waited until he had returned. His face held the expression of someone who had just received heartbreaking news.

"Is everything okay, sir?" Tash asked him.

The Sergeant took a breath and spoke. "Our home base has been attacked. We suffered quite a few casualties, very few soldiers made it out. General Sutherland was found dead in his office."

Cruz's entire world stopped. "Where's Astrid? Do we know?"

"They haven't been able to locate her body, nor have they been able to locate Sergeant Davids. With General Sutherland dead, this means Davids is our new General. They could have been taken hostage."

"Any survivors at all, sir?" Tash asked him.

Sergeant Jackson shook his head. "They came with multiple battalions, and after our luck with traitors in the past... we didn't stand a chance. We might have had some, but if so, they would have dispersed by now."

Cruz rested his face in his hands and pursed his lips together to keep his composure.

"Does this change our mission, sir? Should we go looking for them?" Jake asked, noticing Cruz's expression.

"I apologize, but we can't search for them just yet. This excavation team might have secrets on where to find the artifact... and we can't risk losing Cruz. With the General's daughter's location unknown, he is the only key we have in ending the curse."

"You say that like I'm nothing more than an object, sir," Cruz mumbled.

"I'm sorry, but in this war, you are. If it eases your tension, Sergeant Brown's men are searching for them. It's war, son. We need to continue on with the mission. I'll give you a day to come to terms with this and then we'll carry on."

Cruz remembered the first time that he had met Astrid. That message that she had sent him that night had been a desperate plea for help. He remembered how he had convinced the men to leave without any hassle.

The moment that he saw her emerge from the storage cupboard, he had been mesmerized, even though he found her a real pain in the ass to be around. He had been so cocky, calling himself a hero, only for her to knock him backwards on his ass and out of the line of fire.

She was his hero. She had saved him from himself a long time ago and if there was a way to save her, he would stop at nothing.

He also knew that she would not go down without a fight, and as much as he hated Sergeant... no, General Davids now... he knew the guy would not let anything happen to her. He just hoped that the two of them would make it out alive.

They travelled the rest of the way in silence. They would need to set up camp in a day, and then his first rescue mission would begin, provided his Sergeant would deem it safe enough for him to participate.

#

Astrid and Sergeant Samuel Davids finally made it above ground. They had been walking through the sewers for days now, and the sunlight, although it was hiding behind a cloud, hurt their eyes.

They found themselves standing in a ghost town. "You're exhausted. We should find somewhere to rest," Sergeant Davids told her.

"Get off my case, Buzzkill. We need to find Cruz," Astrid snapped tiredly.

"We've been walking for days. We stand no chance in finding him if we die from exhaustion in the process."

They were standing in the middle of a street, and while the Sergeant was inspecting a house, Astrid was going over a few of the cars in the street.

"Fine, if you want to go... go! I'm done worrying about you!" he snapped at her. "But think of it this way... we stand a better chance going together, and if you drive in the shape that you're in now... you'll only end up falling asleep at the wheel."

Astrid sighed. He was right and she hated to admit it. She thought back to the time when Cruz had fallen asleep in the car and they had almost crashed. If she wanted to stand a chance to find him, it would mean agreeing to get some rest.

She stared at Samuel and shook her head angrily. She stormed past him, towards the door and attempted to rattle it open. It was locked.

Sergeant Samuel Davids managed to find a window and opened it. He peered inside. A family had once lived there. It was evident that they didn't anymore.

He closed the window behind him and unlocked the door for Astrid, inviting her in. He locked the door behind them and evaluated the security of the house. It seemed pretty fortified. It would do for the night. Astrid stormed towards the master bedroom and locked herself in. She placed her rifle on the bed beside her, as she laid down.

She and the Sergeant had barely spoken a word to each other since they had left her father to die in his own office. That had been three days ago. She had only wished that it had been her father that had made it out alive, or that Cruz had been with her and had not gone on his stupid mission.

Travelling with Sergeant Davids, she felt more alone than ever. She sobbed softly, and gradually drifted off to asleep.

She eventually awoke to a loud knock at the bedroom door, which startled her. She instantly sat up and raised her rifle, aiming it at the door.

"Astrid? It's just me... Sergeant Buzzkill. Sorry if I woke you, but you've been asleep for eighteen hours. I wanted to check up on you."

She sighed. She hadn't slept for eighteen hours exactly. She had been up a few times to use the bathroom, but he hadn't known that.

"Well, I'm still alive...if that's what you want to know."

"While that is a relief, I went to the grocery store earlier... bought some food that hadn't expired. I made breakfast."

Astrid's stomach rumbled at the mere mention of food. "Alright. I'll come out," she said, "but then we're packing and leaving."

"You have my word. Scout's honor!"

She opened the door to see him standing outside. He gave her a polite smile and showed her the way to the kitchen table where coffee and cereal were waiting.

"Cheerios?" Astrid asked, glancing at the box for an expiration date as she sat in her seat.

"Would you believe it? They must have had a shipment in just before the store went out of business. There was a milk supply in the cupboard," he replied as he sat in his own seat and started eating.

"Thanks. My dad used to love Cheerios," she said softly as she picked up her spoon and started eating.

"I know, it's all he would eat. When I first met him, he would crack this joke. He'd be like..." Sergeant Davids heart softened at the mere mention of his mentor.

"... Oh my God! The Cheerio joke?" Astrid interrupted with a laugh. "Yeah, I remember that. He was such a dad."

For the first time in a while, the Sergeant was beginning to relax, just a little. "He was, wasn't he? I'm sorry if you felt like I kind of took him from you. It was never that way."

"Don't apologize," Astrid said quietly, knowing how much her resentment had left an impression on the man. "I know it wasn't that way. I'd hate to admit it, but he saw you as the son he never had."

"And you were his perfect daughter. He spoke about you all the time. He was so proud when you got into psychology," Sergeant Davids replied.

"Really? How much about me did he tell you?" she asked, very curious by the notion that he knew more about her than she had revealed to him herself.

"There were a few things, but really only the stuff he was proud about... which was actually a lot," he said honestly.

"It explains your fascination with me."

"Fascination? Hey, I only ever joke..."

Astrid stared at him. She knew that he was lying, but she continued to eat her cereal.

He understood her silence and sighed. "Okay, you're right. I like you... more than I should. I used to see the photo of you on your father's desk and I remember thinking how beautiful you were. Not to mention hearing about you from your father, you seemed absolutely perfect. But you don't need to worry. I won't overstep my line as you're with Cruz and I know that. But I do wonder how it would have gone if I had met you first, I mean... We actually could have met first..."

Astrid was unsure what to say. Instead, she shook her head and remained silent. She decided that it would be safer to change the subject. "So, when do we leave? And where are we headed?"

He picked up the heavy backpack from the floor beside him and rummaged around inside. He pulled out a file and placed it on the table, opening it. There was a map and a red dot over a location. "They've turned this town here into their own military base... that's where they believe the excavation hostages are being kept. If we can meet up with our own men, which includes your boyfriend, we should have the chance to regroup and decide on our next course of action."

"I thought you said that the men who stormed our settlement had it at their own base," Astrid said.

"Yes, I did... but do you really think that the two of us together can retrieve it by ourselves, without them capturing you?" he asked her. Astrid didn't respond, she knew that it would be suicide. "That's what I thought," he added, putting the file back into the backpack.

"Samuel, do you realize... that with my father, well... you know... do you know what that means for you?" she asked him, as she had come to the realization.

"As surprised as I am that you just called me by my actual name and not Buzzkill, yes... I do realize what it means... That when we regroup with the rest of them... well, they're going to see me as their General, and I don't even think that I'm ready for that just yet... Let's just go and find a car and be on our way," he sighed as he spoke.

As Sergeant Davids packed their things, Astrid showered and 'borrowed' some clothes from the woman who had once lived at the house. When it was time to go, she packed the box of Cheerios and they took the keys to the car outside and left.

#

Cruz sat with Jake and Tash at their camp, thirty minutes outside of town with the rest of the soldiers. Night time was approaching and this was their only chance to get in and find the hostages.

"Are you sure you're doing okay, Cruz?" Jake asked. "The Sergeant threw a lot at you yesterday."

"I am as good as I can be considering the situation I'm in. I just need to keep my mind on the mission. I can deal with the rest later," Cruz replied.

"You know that if you even look like you're struggling, Jackson will pull your ass out of there as fast as he can," Tash said.

"Look, guys... just stop worrying about me. We'll get in there, get the hostages and get out! I know what's at stake."

"Now that sounds like the words of a soldier." Sergeant Jackson said, approaching them. "Dust yourselves off and get out there. It's time. I've spoken with the rest of the men, they will be the distraction team, which should clear the path for you. Take the storm drain that we saw on the road earlier. That will lead directly to where they are keeping the hostages. I'm predicting it will have a few men, but you know what to do."

"Just like the ninja turtles," Cruz commented as he, Tash and Jake stood up and followed their Sergeant towards the storm drain with their gear and weaponry.

"Ninja Turtles?" Tash asked.

"At least your humor's back intact," Jake remarked.

"Like I said, we focus on the mission first. Joey and Hannah are in there, and right now their lives are at stake," Cruz said.

"Not to mention the rest of the hostages," Tash replied.

They reached the storm drain and their Sergeant pulled up the lid. Tash and Jake were the first to sneak down, but before Cruz could depart, Sergeant Jackson questioned him. "Are you sure you're ready for this?"

"As ready as I'll ever be, sir," he replied as he departed down the storm drain and his superior closed it over him. It was now or never.

The three of them reached the bottom, holding their noses and watching their feet as they stepped along the wet concrete. The stream of water ran alongside them like a river.

"Does anyone else feel the sudden urge to go to the bathroom right now?" Jake asked, as he flashed his torch over the running water.

"Shut up, Jake," Tash whispered. "You don't want us to get caught on our first rescue mission, do you?"

"Shh, guys!" Cruz whispered, as he stepped in front of them, shining his torch as they followed the water flow. He was listening out for voices. He switched off his torch as he heard some.

His friends followed suit, leaving them in total darkness as they all realized that there was certainly someone else down there.

The voices were coming closer. Cruz laid down flat on the wet concrete, as did his friends, making them harder to spot to whoever was fast approaching.

They had to squint, but they managed to see two silhouettes in the distance. "I thought I heard someone down here, earlier," one of the voices said.

Jake shuffled forward, bringing himself next to Cruz, who held his hand out for him to stop. But Jake didn't listen. He readied his sniper rifle and stared through the scope to get a better look.

The men looked like they were approaching. Cruz and Tash both managed to hold their breaths, but Jake was getting nervous. He brought his finger to the trigger, lining up his target.

The silhouettes seemed to be staring out at them. Jake panicked and took the shot. He killed one of the men. He gasped and immediately got to his feet ready to take another. He had to reload his gun.

"Jake!" Cruz gasped. Just as the remaining man took aim at their friend, Cruz and Tash both got to their feet and raised their guns at the silhouette.

There was a sudden bang, and the silhouette went down, but not before he had shot Jake. Tash had been the one who had killed the other man. She was in a state of shock at what she had just done. She had just taken her first kill on their very first mission.

Cruz turned on his torch and shun it on Jake. The shot had been a direct kill.

"Ay dios mio!" he exclaimed, trying to stop his friends bleeding, knowing full well that there was no point. Jake was well and truly dead.

"Oh no, Jake," Tash said. She was so scared that she could barely focus. She began to cry. Cruz knew that he needed to be the one to take charge.

"Tash, bring him back to Sergeant Jackson."

"No, what are you doing? I can't just leave you down here."

"Yes, you can. You're scared, I know. I've been there. Jake needs to be taken back to the camp. I'll be fine. Don't worry about me."

Tash nodded. She knew that she could jeopardize their mission, being in the state of panic that she was in. She obeyed Cruz's demand and carried Jake's body back to the storm drain entrance, as Cruz continued deeper underground.

Fortunately, he didn't come into any more trouble, and he eventually found the end of the tunnel. There was a light shining from the entrance above, so he pulled the map out from his pocket. This was the right way.

He climbed up the ladder and opened the cover a little, peering through. He had been led to the back road behind the police department. The distraction team was already in full swing. He could hear them fighting with the men at the base.

It was now or never. Cruz climbed out of the storm drain at full pace, holding his gun close to him as he made a run for the door, approximately twenty feet in front of him. He rattled the door handle.

"Gracias a dios!" he muttered under his breath as it opened in his hand. With the gun close to him, he peered inside. He had found the hostages. There were roughly thirty of them, men and women all in one cell. He closed the door behind him and looked around.

They had clearly been given treatment as none of them seemed unstable. Fortunately, there was no one in there guarding them, but seeing him dressed in his military uniform and his weapon at the ready, they assumed that he was one of their captors.

He looked around for a key. His hair was falling loose from his pony tail and he swept it back behind his ear as he spotted the key on the desk and went to retrieve it.

"Cruz? Cruz? Is that you? I don't understand!" The voice of Joey was very recognizable even after the two years of being apart.

"Yeah, bro! It's me," Cruz said, teary at seeing his friend clinging to the bars, as he brought the key to the door.

"Why are you with the military, man? You're a soldier now? What are you doing?"

"I've come to rescue all of you. But we need to be quick. My men are out there creating a distraction! Where's Han?" Cruz asked as he unlocked the door, looking for their friend.

The door swung open and Hannah was the first to run out. "Cruz!" she cried as she hugged him.

"Quick, everybody! Go out that door and run for the storm drain! Vámonos!" Cruz demanded of all the prisoners.

They obeyed, and Joey was the last to leave the cell. He gave his friend a high five that ended in a teary hug, with Hannah in the middle.

"Man, you saved us!" Joey cried.

"Of course, I saved you. I'm just sorry I took so long. But we need to get out of here!" Cruz said leading them both outside.

He ran behind Joey and Hannah. "Man, I met this amazing woman. We need to save her next. Her name is Astrid!" Cruz bragged as he ran with them to the open storm drain.

Hannah climbed through first. "If she's won your heart... she must be something," Joey said as he turned and faced his friend, ready to depart down the storm drain.

But as Cruz was about to follow his friend down, he was shot from behind. It crippled him. "Take my gun, Joe," he said handing it to him.

"No!" Joey said, as he watched the men fast approaching. "You gotta introduce me to your girlfriend. I'm not leaving you here!"

Cruz was severely wounded. He flung his gun down the hole and closed the lid so that Joey couldn't argue anymore. Cruz was risking his neck so that his friends could escape.

Chapter 11

Astrid rested her head on the glass window of the old pickup truck that Sergeant Samuel Davids had picked up at the last gas station. They had been driving for a day now and had passed through what had become of Chicago.

The beautiful city was now destroyed. Its buildings had been smashed, with rotting carcasses lining the floor, and the only people who remained were lone individuals who were clearly experiencing the full effects of the curse.

They were now in the middle of nowhere.

"Oh, shit!" Samuel said, smacking down on the steering wheel in frustration.

"What's the problem?" Astrid asked him, raising her head. Before he could reply, he steered the truck onto the side of the road only for it to break down.

"What's wrong with it?" she asked, as Sergeant Davids unbuckled his seatbelt in frustration and got out, leaving his door open.

"Hey, can you pop the hood for me?" he asked. He was standing at the front of the vehicle. She did as he asked of her and crawled over to the driver's seat.

"Try turning the key," he called out. She turned the key and the truck made a jerking sound. "And again?"

She turned the key again and it made the same jerking sound as before, but still, it did not start up.

"Shit!" he said angrily, banging down the bonnet and punching it with his fist.

"Something tells me beating it up won't work!" Astrid said half-assed, not moving from her seat.

Samuel approached the open door and leaned his elbow on top of the window.

"It's dead. I think we're walking," he told her.

"I thought as much." She climbed out of the truck and in the brief moment that she did, his expression had changed. His look of frustration turned into a lingering smile that held her in his gaze. He was also blocking her exit. "Buzzkill, out of my way, please," she said.

"You know... we're out here all alone... we could have a little fun, just you and I," he said.

"Another one of your jokes? Very funny!" she said sarcastically. She turned to the car to reach for the knapsack and then turned back to hand it to him. He took it from her, and at the same time, took a hold of both her hands.

The backpack dropped to the ground and he brought his face in closer to hers. "Let's stop fighting this thing between us. When we spar there's this amazing chemistry... when you pin me to the floor... well, it always leaves me wondering what else you could do to me... What's Cruz getting that I'm missing out on?"

"Buzzkill, I need you to back off, now! You need to take your medication. You're letting lust take over." She tried to free her wrists from his hands, but he wouldn't let go.

He brought his lips to her own. "Maybe we shouldn't fight it and just let it take over. Be with me, right here."

"Sergeant! Back off, now! You're out of line!" she snapped angrily at him again. He still had a hold of her wrists and she was trying to struggle free. "I'm with Cruz, and you know that!"

"He'll never know," he whispered to her. "I want you, Astrid. I always have... I won't tell him."

"Let go of me!" she snapped. The minute she said it, she brought her knee up between his legs. His lust had distracted him from her attack.

He buckled over and groaned, giving her the chance to pick up the bag and run a small distance away to unzip it. Before she could pull the bag open, he was close on her heels.

He threw the bag down again and brought her back over to the truck, grabbing her arms and holding them behind her as he pressed himself against her.

"I love when you fight me, all that energy and your body on mine..." he whispered to her.

"Well, you won't mind if I did this, then." Once again she brought her leg up, first in the groin and then as he stumbled back, she kicked him again, though this time in the stomach.

She ran to retrieve the bag again and went straight for the open door of the truck. She climbed in, closed the door and applied the central locking as she unzipped the bag. She was breathing heavily and trying to keep calm.

This was the first time that she had opened the backpack since they had left. She was surprised as to what she found inside; her old white laptop.

She had completely forgotten all about him telling her that he had retrieved it from her apartment. It reminded her that Sergeant Davids was in fact a decent person after all.

"Astrid, come on, stop playing and let me in, please... Have you ever done it inside a truck? It could be fun." She was starting to panic. She managed to find the medication vials. His supply was running low.

It was no wonder he was acting so unstable. She brought the serum up into the syringe. The last person that she had injected with medication was Dr. Reynolds. She was certain that he would have died by now. She prayed that this would not have the same impact on Samuel.

He continued to knock on the door. "Astrid... just let me in, or I will smash the window to get to you... Don't make me do it!" She had one attempt to inject him with the serum. She could not fail.

She was still sitting in the driver's side. She hid the syringe in her right hand and with her left, she unlocked the door for him to open it.

Sergeant Davids opened the door, and she swung her legs around to face him, concealing the needle. "Thanks babe, I knew you would change your mind. Don't worry, I won't tell Cruz... if you don't," he said.

He leaned forward pressing himself onto her. He started kissing her neck. She clutched the syringe in her hand, bringing it up towards his arm. But before she could jab it into him, he ran one hand up her leg and the other hand up her back. She needed him to stop moving. "We could be good together," he whispered into her ear, "and you know it."

She continued to remind herself that it was the lust taking over him. It calmed her down remembering this fact. He brought his lips to her own and kissed her, closing his eyes for just a moment.

But as he did, she injected the serum into his arm and dropped the empty needle on to the floor of the truck.

It must have worked, as his eyes fluttered open again and he froze in realization at what he had just tried to do.

"Astrid!" he gasped, immediately pulling himself away from her. "I'm sorry. Please, forgive me. I'm so sorry!"

She breathed in and out softly, and looked at him. "Are you okay now?"

"I think so. Please, forgive me. You know that's not really me... I would never..."

She ignored his apology. "Why didn't you tell me that you were running low on your treatments? We need to find a doctor as soon as possible."

He stared at her in remorse and then looked away. "I didn't think it would be a problem. I had a two-week supply... but the virus... curse... whatever it is, it keeps... it keeps taking over. It's getting stronger. I really didn't want to burden you. You have enough to deal with. I'm so damn sorry."

"Alright. I know you're sorry. Just as I know you wouldn't normally do that..." She reached back into the bag to count his supply. "You barely have enough for a week."

"I know... I guess I've been trying to see how long I could stretch them out for... but it's hard... especially being so close to you. Look, maybe we should just walk it to the next town. I'll give you the map and we should go our separate ways. It's too dangerous for us to travel together!"

The thought of him trying that on Astrid again angered Samuel. As much as he cared for her, he would never intentionally hurt her that way, as much as he might joke about it.

"No, Samuel. You promised my dad that you would look out for me. I'm not letting you break that promise. Besides, if you get out of line, I can always kick your ass again."

"You shouldn't have to... you shouldn't need to... Yes, I promised your father that I would look out for you... not the other way around. I mean, look at me. I was quite literally about to smash the window to..."

"...I mean it. We're in this together. I'm not turning my back on you. I was a psychologist before all of this. I've dealt with mentally unstable people before. This thing, it makes people go crazy, and you were affected by lust. We've seen worse, remember? So just drop it, okay? We're not separating. We'll regroup with the rescue team as soon as we can. They should have enough supplies. Then we'll go from there."

"Look at you taking charge. You'd make your dad proud. I promise I'll get you back to your boyfriend. We should leave now, or we'll be stranded here over night," he replied, glad that she was willing to continue with him. Unfortunately, it made him want her all the more.

Regardless, he took the bag. They both collected their weapons, he assisted her out of the truck and they walked along the side of the road together.

"If we're going to continue working together," Astrid added, "I need you to be honest with me. If you're running low on your medication... I need to know about it. Okay?"

"From here on out, you have my word as a soldier."

"Good."

#

Joey and Hannah sat away from the rest of the camp which was filled with soldiers and the other rescued hostages. They had been bandaged up and fussed over by the military doctors after having been relocated to another camp three hours from where they had been kept.

As far as Joey and Hannah knew, the soldiers were working on a way to rescue Cruz, but they would not let either of them in on the rescue.

"Don't worry, Joe. They'll find him," Hannah said. "I just can't believe that he joined the military. The thought of him trading his laptop and books in for guns and working with these guys..."

"Yeah, me too... But a lot has changed in two years... this world is about survival now... if only he didn't find that damn pithos..."

"Well then, we probably wouldn't be together now, would we?" Hannah asked. "Everything that's happened has brought us to where we are now. I know that it's been hard... We've been through a lot... but at least we've been through it together."

Joey kissed her on the forehead. "I still would have kept on wooing you..." As he spoke, his expression did not change from the deep-set frown. From behind her, Joey could see the Sergeant chatting with a dark-haired female soldier that had lost her friend in the mission.

"Hey, Han. I'll be back in a minute... I need to talk to somebody." He kissed Hannah on the cheek and stood up to speak to Tash.

She had given up speaking to the Sergeant and was attempting to take her leave.

"Hey! Tash, was it?" he asked.

"Yeah... You're Joey, right? Your girlfriend is Hannah? Cruz mentioned you both."

"You know my man, Cruz?"

"Yeah! We were all trained together... were sent on this mission together... but then, we lost Jake and he sent me back... and now... Shit, I should have just stayed with him!" Tash mustered up her strength, trying to prevent herself from crying.

"So, when are they going back for him?"

"We've got soldiers keeping a lookout on the remaining men at the base. We're just trying to determine the right time to strike."

"I want in!" Joey said.

"We can't do that. You're not trained, besides... we just rescued you."

"...and Cruz was captured for trying to rescue me," Joey argued, feeling very much at fault.

"And we're not going to let that be in vain... We're not letting Jake's death be in vain either. You will stay here even if I have to hold you here myself. I'm sorry..."

"Fine... just get him back for me."

"We will. Now go look after your girlfriend. She looks a little out of sorts over there, all by herself."

"Thanks," Joey sighed, as he took his leave.

Tash slumped down next to a group mixed with soldiers and the rescued hostages. "I can't believe we lost Jake and Cruz," she said to a male soldier by the name of Alex.

"Yeah... it certainly feels like we're losing this thing. We've lost too many people. You don't think they'd kill Cruz or Astrid, do you? I mean, they would need them alive, right?" Alex asked her.

"I'm not sure. But don't worry, we'll get them back!" Tash replied.

"I'm sorry... did you just say Astrid? Her last name wouldn't have been Sutherland, by any chance, would it?" the blonde woman who was sitting beside Tash asked.

"Yeah, she was the General's daughter. She and her boyfriend Cruz were supposed to be the answer to ending this whole damn thing. Why do you ask?" Tash replied.

"Oh my god! Astrid!" the blonde woman gasped. "I was her housemate... those guys kidnapped me because she was my best friend before all of this. God, I hope she's alive! Do you think she is?"

"We're not actually sure. We're guessing that if she didn't escape with Sergeant Davids, then they're keeping her alive until they figure out a way to end the curse. My name's Tash, by the way." She held out her hand for the girl to shake. The blonde woman accepted and shook her hand.

"I'm Stacey. God, I really hope she's still alive. I have so much I need to apologize to her for!"

"Yeah, I think we all do. That curse has messed with all our heads! Everybody except for them."

"They're immune? I didn't think that was possible."

"Didn't you know?"

"No... the last time I saw Astrid... we had a big fight... I was taken over by greed and I had to shop... I even stole her purse... I was arrested and captured by the military... and..." Stacey looked as if she was ready to break down and cry at any moment. But she kept her composure.

Tash put her arm around her. "Hey, it's okay. You're safe now."

There was a moment between the two as they both smiled subtly at each other, but Tash brushed it off. "I should probably go and speak with my Sergeant. We'll talk later, okay?"

"Of course." Stacey glanced over to where she saw Hannah and Joey sitting. They had spoken to her a few times in the past two years of being held hostage together.
But the irony that their friend Cruz and her friend Astrid were both immune and dating was astonishing.

She stood up and made her way towards them. "Hey, Hannah. Hey, Joey," she said as she approached.

"Hey, Stacey. Is everything okay?" Hannah asked her.

"Did you know that our friends were both immune to this curse thing?"

"I knew Cruz was, he opened it..." Joey replied, "but who was your friend?"

"Her name's Astrid... but God... I just hope she's okay."

For the first time in a while, a side smile lit up Joey's face. "Huh... so that's Cruz's girlfriend. Sit down, Stacey. We should talk." Hannah gave a surprised smile and Stacey sat beside her.

As they got to talking, the soldiers discussed their plans from inside Sergeant Jackson's tent.

"Have they left their base?" he asked.

"Negative, sir. We believe that they're waiting for reinforcements," one of the scouts said.

"So, we don't have much time. It needs to be tonight. They wouldn't be holding him in the same place as the hostages, and we've lost a few men. This could be suicide."

"Send me, sir! I know the risks. Cruz is my friend," Tash offered.

"I'm sorry, but that will not be an option, Lieutenant Smith. You and your men can go. In the meantime, we will need to find a new location, it will only be a matter of time until their reinforcements find us."

"Yes, sir," Lieutenant Smith replied.

Sergeant Jackson looked over at Tash who had a look of frustration on her face. "Is that clear, soldier?"

"Yes, sir," she said softly.

Sergeant Jackson drew out a map of where their new base would be and then dismissed them all. The soldiers left his tent to carry out their jobs, as Tash stormed across the camp angrily, though trying to keep calm.

She was pissed off that she couldn't go. She went searching for her knapsack and sat down beside it.

"Hey, Tash. Are you okay?" Joey asked, approaching her.

"I'm fine. I just really wanted to go out on this mission. The Sergeant requested that I stay here," she said standing to face him.

"That sucks!"

"Yeah, it does. No offense."

"None taken. Do you think they can get him back?

"Yeah, I do... but I can't just sit here and do nothing while my friend..." She stopped talking as she saw Joey smirk.

"Yeah... I get where you're coming from... I'm in the same boat as you."

"Yeah, and if they fail to get him back... I don't care what these soldiers say... I'm going back in there, myself. And you're going to help me!"

"Are you stupid? Cruz literally just risked his ass for you. They held you prisoner for two years and you want to go back in there?"

"I know my way around there... I might also know where they're hiding him... I've given that information to your Sergeant already..."

"Look, we're being relocated to another base before their reinforcements find us. I suggest you leave the rescue work up to the soldiers. Let them do their jobs."

They were joined by Hannah and Stacey. Tash looked over at Stacey and shook her head.

"It's funny that the three of you would join forces... Look, if Sergeant Buzzkill managed to get Astrid to safety, he would be looking for our camp. I get that you hate our options but it's best for everybody to just obey orders... Cruz is important to us. We will get him back... and I doubt that General Sutherland would have allowed anyone to capture his daughter."

"Sergeant Buzzkill?" Joey asked.

"I mean Sergeant Davids. Damn it, Cruz!"

Stacey smiled over at Tash. "Alright. We'll take your word... because after everything I know about Astrid's dad... he would stop at nothing to risk his life for her. I still can't believe he was alive. She would have flipped."

"Oh, she did," Tash smiled back.

"No... What about Cruz? We can't just turn our backs on him," Joey argued.

"Joe... we need to listen to them. Whether we like it or not. He'll be okay," Hannah argued. "Besides, it looks like they want to round us up to go to the next base... it's our safest option."

Joey looked at her and took in her soft face, her red brown hair and beautiful smile. "Okay... but only because I can't risk you getting captured again." He had given in to defeat.

Chapter 12

Cruz had been chained up and was hanging by his hands from the roof of an abandoned house. The men had removed his top clothing and his bullet wound had been patched up, but only to keep him alive to torture him some more throughout the night.

His whole body ached all over. He had been beaten in the time that he had been kept there. It had been enough to torture him, but not enough to kill him. They needed him alive. He was covered in blood all over his face and body and he could taste it in his mouth.

But now he was alone. His hair hung freely passed his face as he stared down at the ground. The soldiers had continued to interrogate him in relation to the whereabouts of Astrid. In doing so, they had given up the news that she had not been captured. She had made her escape with Sergeant Davids.

Cruz had never been prouder of the Sergeant, knowing that he had taken her to safety. Nonetheless, he still hated him... and he was still a buzzkill. But the thought that Astrid was out there looking for him gave him hope.

His next plan of action was to take them off her trail entirely, and to prolong his own life. He needed to find out what they knew in regards to the location of Pandora's Box.

He heard the door swing open, they were coming in with their next line of approach. He kept his head down, staring through his hair at the soldier who had come to interrogate him next.

"Look at you. You almost look like a Hispanic Jesus with all that hair," the man said to him. Cruz remained silent.

The man picked up a metal poker and inserted it into the fireplace. He held it there as he continued to speak. "Now, you know what is to come next... So, make this easier on yourself. Where's the girl?"

Cruz refused to answer. The soldier slowly brought the flamed metal to his back. "Tell us where she is!" he demanded.

Cruz yelled out in pain as the hot metal pressed into the skin on his back. This man could kill him, and even if he knew of Astrid's whereabouts, he would still not breathe a word.

"Wouldn't you love for the world to go back to normal? We can do that, Mario Cruz... Just tell us where she is!" The man removed the metal from Cruz's back. Tears had welled up in his eyes from the pain.

"Stop protecting her... make this easy on yourself. We know where Pandora's Box is. We know that she is the descendant of Pandora and we know that her blood will end the curse. Don't be so selfish and tell us."

"Her blood? What's her blood got to do with any of this? I've done as much research as you have, if not more. If you really want to end this curse, work with us. Drop the hunt for her. We'll think of another way," Cruz demanded.

The man was standing back at the fireplace. "Do you think I'm stupid? Of course it's her blood! She is the descendant!" The man brought the poker back to the flame as he spoke.

"No... I'm just as immune as she is. I'm not on any treatment at all. You don't need her. I opened the pithos. I've done my research... hell, I have all the information that you need... the information that was never released to the public! It's all in my head... So let's face it... I'm the key. Not her!"

The man stared at him long and hard. He was clearly weighing up his options. He put the poker down and silently left the room.

Cruz waited alone in the room, grimacing at the pain that he was in. He rattled the chains and pulled on them a little, praying that they would come loose. But they didn't. He prayed that wherever Astrid was, that she would be safe.

He revisited the moment that her father had made him realize just how much he loved her, when he had told him that he would be willing to give up his life for her.

Then he thought back to the moment when he finally dropped the L bomb on her. She had smiled, kissed him and said it back. She always had to have the last say. They certainly were a match made by the gods. He would always feel that way.

He only prayed that she would forgive the lengths that he was willing to go through, to spare her the burden.

The man finally returned. "Okay, we're moving... you're coming with us... Let's see just how useful you really are..."

Cruz sighed in relief. Thank god his plan had worked.

#

He remained shackled as they quickly led him towards a truck. He could hear the sounds of gunshots and fighting. His fellow soldiers had come to save him, and from his peripheral vision he could see it all happening around them.

In his mind, he cursed his comrades for coming to his rescue. They were ruining his plans. But at the same time, he was relieved. He stopped walking, and a rifle was held at his head. "Keep walking," the man demanded.

Cruz smirked as some of his fellow soldiers ran towards him. "Cruz, get down!" one of them said. He obeyed and flew to the floor, just missing the line of fire.

Three men were shot and Cruz got back to his feet quickly, only to be held up at gunpoint. He wanted to disarm the man of his weapon, but with his hands in chains, he needed to rely on the help of his team.

One of them was a man who usually worked as a scout. He went by the name of John Banks, but the men back at base referred to him only as Banks.

Banks held his rifle aimed in the direction of Cruz's captor. One wrong move and Cruz could be dead. But then Banks had a rifle held on him.

"Hey, Banks... it's okay..." Cruz said. "I'm going to go with them. I'm going to comply."

"Are you kidding me, Cruz?" he demanded. Cruz gave him a look. But before Banks could agree to his plan, Cruz's captor had been shot from behind as well as the other men.

More soldiers had arrived onto the scene. Sergeant Jackson and Lieutenant Smith were amongst them. They had taken down a great deal of men in the assault and had taken over the base.

Lieutenant Smith unshackled Cruz. "They know where the artifact is," Cruz said. "They were going to take me with them."

"No need, Cruz. They're sending in reinforcements," Sergeant Jackson said. "We'll leave our scouts to watch where they go... You need medical attention, asap."

Cruz did not argue further. He was led to one of their own trucks with his Sergeant and the rest of the soldiers. They travelled for the rest of the day until they had finally reached their new settlement.

Once there, Cruz received the medical treatment he needed in the tent and as he was resting up, he received some visitors who immediately made him smile.

"Joey! Hannah!" Cruz cried out in delight.

He went to get up, but they bombarded him with hugs, making him silently flinch from the pain to his back.

"It's good to see you in one piece, man!" Joey exclaimed, letting him go.

"You, too. It's been so long! I mean... I did see you guys when I was pullin' your asses out of there last night... but still," Cruz said with a smirk.

"Those dressings are so... so... military, aren't they?" Hannah asked eyeing the bandages on his back.

"Well, this is the military, Hannah," Cruz replied with a grin.

"You haven't changed a bit. It's a wonder how you managed to meet a girl who can put up with you," she said with a laugh.

Cruz smiled at the mere thought of Astrid and wondered just what she was doing at that moment, but Hannah continued. "...so this girl, I'm anxious to meet her... we met her friend Stacey, in fact."

"Stacey? No way!" Cruz was astonished.

"Yeah, man. She's outside with that soldier girl, Tash."

Cruz laughed. "With Tash? That's just typical... damn fate. Astrid's going to flip when she knows that Stacey's alive. We've lost too many good people."

He thought back to Dr. Reynolds, Jake and a few others that they had known over the time.

#

"They've been here!" Sergeant Davids exclaimed, as he and Astrid scoured the site of what had once been the rescue team's camp site.

"Seriously? So, what? We've lost them?" Astrid asked in frustration.

"Yeah, and that's not the worst of it, either."

"Why, what's the problem?" she asked as she leaned up against the blue Honda sedan that they had picked up in the last town.

"I have three more vials left... That'll give us another day at the most."

"Always with the bad news, Buzzkill. But that map said that there should be a town close by...

that's where the hostages were being kept... Maybe they have something to restrain you if you get too hard to deal with."

"You're thinking handcuffs, that could be good..." A smirk crossed his face, but then he stopped. "...Sorry, I should lay off the flirtation, hey?"

"Yes, you should." She rolled her eyes at him and went to hop into the driver's side of the car, but he grabbed her and brought his finger to his lips, asking her to keep quiet.

He removed his hand from her arm, and she listened to the noises that had grasped his attention; the distant sounds of trucks approaching.

"They're military trucks... Get in the car, quick. I'll drive."

She did as he said and he drove out of the clearing as fast as he could to hide their car. He drove them to a secluded area just outside of the town and they climbed out again, carrying their weapons and knapsacks until they found a few trees to hide behind to get a good look at the trucks.

Sergeant Davids looked through the scope of his gun to see that they were the reinforcements of the men who had once occupied the town, using it as their own base.

"They're not our men," he told her. He invited her to look through the scope.

"So where are our men?" she asked looking back at him.

Sergeant Davids looked back through the scope as he continued to speak. "They clearly saved the hostages, ransacked the hell out of this place and left."

"God, I hope so!" Astrid exclaimed. "We need to find them."

"Get behind me," he snapped, immediately holding her close to his chest as he stood behind a thick tree. Two trucks drove right past the trees that they were hiding behind.

He was holding her far too close to himself for her own comfort, while he continued to keep an eye out, ensuring that the trucks disappeared.

He let go of her once he knew that it was safe to. "Sorry, but it was important. We could have been seen," he said.

"I'm getting the impression that you're loving this," she said in frustration.

"Maybe just a little bit..." he said, with another grin.

She rolled her eyes at him again and looked back in the direction of the trucks. "I wonder where those trucks are heading."

Sergeant Davids pointed his rifle back into the direction of the town and watched through the scope. "We're not going to stand a chance if we go into that town just yet. If we can see them, who's to say that they can't see us?"

"What are you suggesting?" she asked him cautiously.

He lowered his gun to address her. "If my knowledge serves me correctly, those reinforcements came for a reason. So we find a place to hide out for a little longer, and when they leave, we sneak into the town, collect what we need and follow them from a distance."

"But you need your treatments. I'm not risking travelling with you any longer without them. If there is any chance of us meeting up with the rescue team, I'm taking it. I'm not taking any risks, and you shouldn't be, either."

"Are you disobeying my order?"

"You bet your ass I am....You know what? Screw this!" She went to storm away, but he grabbed her again.
"Let go of me!" she snapped. But he turned her to face the direction of some soldiers who were walking towards their direction.

"Get to the ground," he whispered in her ear.

As she laid down on the ground, he rested his rifle on the rock close by and crouched down to peer through again. He hadn't yet seen their faces. He was ready to take a shot until one of the men turned around.

"Astrid, they're our men. They're scouts from the rescue team," he said with a smile that lit up his face.

But the excitement was gone when one of the men had been shot in front of him. The scouts had been spotted. The second scout got to the ground and readied his weapon, looking for his partner's attacker.

Sergeant Davids spotted the attacker and shot him and his accomplice, killing them both on impact.

Surprised at his sudden rescue, John Banks ran towards Sergeant Davids, and joined him and Astrid in their hiding spot.

As Sergeant Davids continued to examine their location for more men, Banks and Astrid both readied their weapons, also surveying the area.

"General Davids! It's good to see you and Sutherland both alive and well," Banks said, with his eye focused through his scope.

"You too, Banks. Where's the rest of the crew?" Astrid asked.

"New base." He took a shot at an oncoming soldier in his scope.

"Where's your truck, Banks?" Sergeant Davids asked him. "We'll make a run for it."

"It's ten minutes away, sir!" Banks replied.

"Good! On my say, take one last shot and then we leave... we need to run. Are you ready, Sutherland?"

"Yes, Buzzkill... er... sir," she replied.

He smirked at her and then on his count of three, they all took a shot, got to their feet and ran, following Banks back to his truck.

With the sounds of gunshots behind them, they continued to run as fast as they could. First Banks, then Astrid and then Sergeant Davids following behind.

They made it to the truck. Banks and Astrid climbed in, then they heard the sound of a gunshot and Sergeant Davids swore out in pain.

As Astrid climbed into the truck, she turned back to see that he had fallen to the ground. There were soldiers following behind.

"Banks! Astrid! Go now!" he ordered.

"That ain't happening, Buzzkill!" Astrid exclaimed. She jumped back out of the truck, knowing full well that she was risking her life for him.

She dragged him, crippling and wounded, but they managed to climb into the truck as Banks sped off down the road. The bullet had been lodged into the back of Sergeant Davids leg, and as he sat in the middle of them, Banks glanced over.

"That's bleeding bad, sir," Banks said as he continued driving.

"... I just need something to compress it," the Sergeant replied.

Astrid rummaged through the bag and pulled out some bandages, some rubbing alcohol and ordered that he show her his leg, so he did. It was lodged in his lower calf muscle but it was still visible from the skin. It wasn't fatal.

She poured the alcohol over the bandages, and then pulled the bullet out slowly with her fingers. With the remainder of the bandages she dressed his wound. She handed him the bullet.

"Here's a souvenir, Buzzkill."

He took it and shook his head with a smile. "Has anyone ever told you just how much you're like your father? Only he would joke about something like that."

"Yeah, you have! One too many times," she said smugly.

Banks looked over at them. "I'm surprised the two of you haven't killed each other yet," he remarked. "We should be at camp in a few hours. You both look tired, maybe you should get some rest. We seem to be out of the line of fire."

"Sounds good to me," Sergeant Davids replied.

Astrid rested her head on the window of the truck. She was exhausted and very much relieved by the fact that she would be in Cruz's arms in only a matter of hours.

She knew that she had been spending far too much time with Sergeant Buzzkill, so much in fact, that he was starting to get under her skin in a way that she couldn't quite shake him.

He still irritated her, but in a way that she hadn't quite expected. It began to anger her. Even though her heart belonged to Cruz, she felt as if this man brought out another side of her, a side that she really didn't want to release, as it would mean that she would need to admit to herself that she had feelings for him, something that she was not willing to do.

She continued to tell herself that there was nothing between her and Sergeant Samuel Davids, but her mind brought her back to the moment when his lust had taken over, before she had struck him in the arm with the syringe.

That moment that his lips were rested on her own, when he had placed his hands on her, there had been the briefest of moments that she had to resist the temptation to kiss him back.

She loved Cruz and she was not willing to lose him, so she vowed at that moment that when they caught up with the rest of the team, she would do everything in her power to avoid spending any more time with Sergeant Davids.

#

She awoke to the sound of Buzzkill's voice, along with the sound of the rain on the truck. "Hey,

Sutherland... wake up... I told you I'd get you back to Cruz. We're just reaching camp now."

Astrid opened her eyes and gave him a brief smile, to say 'thank you,' before she looked around outside. Sure enough, they were surrounded by the green tents and numerous soldiers holding up their weapons in the rain.

They checked over Banks' truck and saluted as they saw their new General.

When Banks parked the truck, Astrid climbed out and supported General Davids as he, too, climbed out of the truck.

"Astrid! Astrid!" The sound of Cruz's voice made her heart stop. She looked around, as General Davids supported his leg by leaning up against the door of the truck and gave her a friendly smile.

Astrid could barely breathe as Cruz ran to her, picked her up and spun her around. "I missed you! I was so worried about you!" he said with tears in his eyes.

She wrapped her arms around him tightly and kissed him, relieved to be in the arms of the man that she loved. He continued to kiss her lovingly as they stood together in the rain.

When he brought his lips away from hers, they were surrounded by a group of soldier, who were addressing their new General.

Cruz saluted General Davids. "Thanks for bringing her back to me," he said.

General Davids gave a polite smile and nodded. "Always." He then turned back to his soldiers who led him out of the rain to have his leg checked out.

Cruz turned back to Astrid and embraced her tighter than ever before. "I have a surprise for you, mi amor. But first, let's get you out of the rain."

Chapter 13

Astrid was wrapped in a blanket and brought out of the rain and over to the medical tent by Cruz, where she was fussed over by the medical crew. "You guys! I'm fine! No injuries!" she said tiredly. After a check over, the staff left her and Cruz alone to speak in private for a little while. "How was your first mission?" she asked him.

He smirked. "I got kidnapped and tortured. You know, the usual..."

"What? Are you okay?"

"Relax, I'm fine... see?" He did a little dance on the spot to prove it.

She smiled at him. "God, I missed you... and it's only been a few days!"

"How are you coping? I heard about your father... and then, it can't have helped being stuck with Sergeant Buzzkill all that time... er, correction... General Buzzkill."

Astrid went silent, as the mere mention of her father made her want to tear up.

"I'm sorry... still a sore subject," he said as he sat down beside her.

"It's okay. So, where are these friends of yours that I've been hearing all about? And where's my surprise?" she asked him.

Cruz smiled at her and turned to the entrance of the tent. Astrid followed his gaze to see their visitors that had been waiting for the right time to approach.

They got to their feet as Joey, Hannah, Tash and Stacey joined them.

"Oh my God! Stacey! I had no idea that you were one of the hostages!" Astrid gasped. She immediately ran to her blonde friend and they hugged each other tightly.

"I missed you, Astrid... I'm so sorry... sorry for everything!" Stacey said through tears.

"I am, too. I'm sorry you got roped in to all of this."

"You have nothing to be sorry about... I'll admit, it was tough... but we managed to pull through, and look... we both made it..." As Stacey spoke, they let go off each other and laughed to hide back their tears of joy.

"God, girl. I missed you... How are you coping after everything that's happened?"

"I'm fine, actually... I'm just glad to be out of there... And this whole military 'getup' that you've got going on... I never would have pictured it in a million years..."

Astrid hugged her again. "You and me both. I'm just so glad you're safe." She turned back to see Joey and Hannah standing alongside Cruz. "Let me guess, Joey and Hannah? I've heard so much about the pair of you. It's great to finally meet you."

"When Cruz said he had a girlfriend, I actually thought he was kidding," Joey joked. "It's really good to meet you. You're actually really pretty, you might be a little out of his league."

"Hey, that's my girlfriend you're talking about," Cruz chimed in.

"It's really good to meet you, Astrid," Hannah said as she gave her a hug. "I just wish that it were under better circumstances."

"Yeah... but hey, at least it's finally happening. I'm curious to hear about all the skeletons that he's been hiding... I'm betting that there's a few!" she smirked as she looked over at Cruz.

"I'll be glad to share..." Joey joked.

"Whoa, whoa, whoa! No! That's not happening!" Cruz said adamantly, as Astrid turned to face Tash. "Hey, Tash, glad to see you made it through your first mission. Where's Jake?"

Tash and Cruz both took a deep breath.

"Oh," Astrid sighed. "Okay... well, that's to be expected."

"It's good that you made it here safe, Sutherland," Tash said giving her a hug. "It can't have been easy dealing with Buzzkill the whole time."

Astrid hugged Tash. "I have to admit, he's not the first person I'd choose to make my escape with... but..."

"...I'd be careful how you address your new General, Martinez..." The sound of General Davids' voice interrupted their conversation.

"Sorry, sir!" Tash apologized, saluting him immediately. Cruz followed suit and saluted, too.

"Do we have to salute?" Joey asked Cruz in a mere whisper.

"You're a part of the excavation team, am I correct?" General Davids asked him.

"Yes, sir," Joey replied.

"Then no, you don't need to salute me. I'm just glad that you all made it out safely."

"That was Cruz's doing, sir," Tash chimed in. "He risked his necks for all of us."

General Davids looked over at Cruz. "I heard how tough it was out there... You've done well, soldier."

"Thank you, sir," Cruz said. There was an unspoken conversation between the two, a tension that all those present could feel, so thick that it could be cut with a knife; two men in love with the same woman.

General Davids looked over at Astrid. It was evident that he had just received some bad news and needed her opinion. Normally, he would go to her father but she was the closest thing that he had right now. "Sutherland, can we have a word, in private?"

"Seriously?" she scoffed. "I mean... yes, sir." She followed him to the other end of the tent, frustrating Cruz.

"I guess that's why you call him Buzzkill," Joey said under his breath.

Cruz nodded in response.

"What's the problem, sir?" Astrid asked.

"Why are you calling me, sir?"

"Because it's a formality... why else?"

He sighed. "I get that... but I don't want this... any of this... they're all looking at me for advice, for orders... I don't even know what to tell them..."

"I wish I could help... but I'm not exactly a solider... I was just the General's daughter who you were forced to train, remember?"

"I get that... but... right now you're the only person I trust talking to..."

"What about higher up? Admirals? Chiefs? You must have someone to report to? Who did my father report to?"

"That's just it... He never told you this, but we lost contact a while back. We're on our own... I don't even know where we can send the hostages. Not to mention, I was just told that we have lost communication with our medical base. Astrid, we're losing too many men... we're falling apart. Why do you think your father was so insistent in recruiting more soldiers?"

"Wow... okay... Well, you shouldn't be talking to me... We have Sergeants out there. Jackson, Brown, Sanders. They're your men, you should be collaborating with them... working with them... not coming to me. I'm not even an officer."

He looked over at Cruz and then back at Astrid. She sighed as she realized just why he was coming to her.
"No... I'm not doing this with you..." She turned to leave, but he grabbed her arm.

"Please... You were a psychologist before all of this... Right now I just need someone to talk to."

"Okay, fine... you can vent... but our priority should be retrieving Pandora's Box. It's the way to end the curse and be done with everything."

"Which we can't do without men... and without our medical team... we're low on medical supplies..."

"Are there any towns nearby that we can fortify? Create a new base? I'm sure we have enough people with enough trades to help out... Hannah over there was the site doctor for the excavation team... then we can send out some of our men to locate the medical teams, to look for medical treatments, and Cruz and I would be more than willing to go in search for the artifact as soon as we can... We'll just need a whole bunch of firepower behind us."

General Davids seemed satisfied with the answer. "Thank you, Sutherland."

"It's the obvious solution. You're just overwhelmed. Just go and take some down time... and leave me to my own." He nodded and left the tent as Astrid returned back to Cruz and the rest of the group.

"What did Buzzkill want?" Cruz asked her.

"I'll tell you later... right now, let's just enjoy the time we have... tomorrow's going to be busy."

"Anyone up for a round of poker?" Tash asked trying to break the tension. "I have some cards."

"Sounds good, Tash!" Astrid said changing her tone.

#

The group sat by the fire for hours catching up on the past few years, playing cards and allowing themselves to laugh for a little while.

It was evident that there was an attraction between Stacey and Tash, although it was clear that neither of them were willing to admit it.

Another thing that was clear was Cruz's frustration for General Davids' obvious affection for Astrid.

As she was lost in a fit of laughter with the rest of the group, Cruz noticed the General looking over at her from across the fire. He looked away when he realized that Cruz had seen.

Cruz whispered into Astrid's ear if he could have a moment of her time to speak in private.

"Sure." She took his hand in hers and allowed him to lead her away from the camp site. They sat down on the grass with the dim light of the camp fire behind them, looking into the wilderness.

"Every time I see that guy, he's always staring at you," Cruz said in frustration. "He's seriously into you... don't tell me that you don't see it!"

Astrid hesitated before she spoke again. "Yeah... he is... He even had the balls to admit it."

"What? So I'm right?" Cruz asked, unsure how to feel. "How'd that go?"

"He told me straight out. He's been holding onto it for a while now. What makes it worse is that he was hit by lust, and even though he's been taking his treatments... I don't think they're working."

"Why? Did he try something while you were travelling?"

Astrid sighed. "Our truck broke down in the middle of nowhere, and he had been trying to increase the time between his medications... trying to make it last... He tried to come on to me... he wasn't in control of himself... I managed to inject the treatment into him before anything happened."

Cruz felt the anger building up inside of him. "I'm just glad that you were able to stop him... but argh! It still pisses me off!"

"Cruz, it's okay... I'm okay, see? We're both here together and you know that I love you... and at least we both know that I can kick his ass if I need to," she said with a smile that relaxed him.

She took Cruz's hand in her own and rested her head on his shoulder. "I get that this is getting to you... but I want you to remember that it doesn't matter how he feels, because the feelings aren't mutual. I only want you."

"You want me, huh?" Cruz asked, his frown turning into a side smile.

"Yeah, I do... You know I do."

He kissed her passionately and ran his hand up her back, but she pulled away for a moment. "Really? Right here?" she asked.

He shrugged. "No one can see us... we're behind the tents."

She raised her eyebrows at him, but he made a face that made her give in and kiss him back.

"Cruz, Sutherland... I'd hate to be a buzzkill yet again... but that's not very professional." They rolled their eyes to see General Davids standing behind them.

"Right on time," Cruz said as he and Astrid both got to their feet to leave.

"How long were you standing there?" Astrid asked.

"Long enough... Maybe you should return back to camp, Sutherland," the General said, dismissing her.

She and Cruz knew that he had overheard their conversation, so they both went to leave, to avoid further embarrassment, but General Davids continued. "Cruz... before you go... Can I have a word?" Cruz looked at Astrid in surprise, but stayed there nonetheless, as she left to join the others.

As Astrid bypassed Sergeant Brown speaking with some of his soldiers behind his tent, she overheard a conversation amongst them that caught her attention. She thought that she had misheard, so she continued to listen in without them realizing.

"Our soldiers will be here before the night is through, sir. I saw them follow our truck in when we arrived," Banks said.

"Good, we've done well eliminating their men... at least we have Cruz and Astrid in the same location this time. It won't be long. We just need to take down that poor excuse of a General that Sutherland appointed in charge."

"Yes, sir."

Without hesitation, Astrid ran back to General Davids and Cruz, who seemed to be in the middle of a heated argument.

"Whatever pissing contest the two of you have going on right now, I need you to save it!" she demanded.

"Why? What's going on?" Cruz asked, noting her concern.

"Sergeant Brown and Banks! They're both traitors! They led the reinforcements to our camp... They're planning an attack tonight!"

"Are you sure? This is not something that you joke about!" General Davids said.

Astrid stared at him. "Why the hell would I lie about this? I know what I heard! We need to mo..." Suddenly, they were alerted to the sounds of gun shots.

"Get your weapons ready!" Sergeant Davids told them.

Sergeant Jackson approached them. "Our own men have turned against us. We're under attack from the inside, sir!" he announced.

General Davids looked over at Astrid. "Sutherland, Cruz... gather your supplies, take the truck and get the hell out of here, now!" he demanded of them.

Astrid went to disobey him. She wanted to stay and fight, but he gave her a look for her to obey. Cruz took her hand and they both ran back to the group who were currently unsure as to what was going on around them.

"We're going!" Cruz demanded as he gathered the weapons.

"I'll get the supplies and the keys to the truck!" Astrid said.

She ran into the tent to retrieve the keys and the knapsack that she and General Davids had brought with them. She placed the keys down on the table so she could fill up the bag.

Astrid raided the medical cupboard with as many treatments and first aid kits as she could fit into the bag and fled the tent again, accidently leaving the keys behind.

She ran through the camp site with Cruz, Joey, Hannah, Stacey and Tash, towards one of the nearby trucks.

"Who's got the keys?" she asked, remembering that she had left them on the table back in the tent. "Oh, shit! Tash, take the bag! I need to get the keys!" she said, throwing the bag over to the soldier.

"Don't be stupid!" Tash yelled. "Come back!" But she had already left.

Astrid ran back to the tent, and as she picked up the keys, she could hear gun fire right outside. "Crap!" she exclaimed. She found a rifle sitting by one of the chairs and prepared it ready for her run back to the truck.

She watched as General Davids was under heavy fire. It was obvious by the bodies that lined the ground and the soldiers storming their base that they had lost many of their men and the excavation team already.

General Davids was holding his own, but not well enough for her liking. She pulled up her weapon and instantly started firing, providing him with cover fire. He turned to see her from the tent, clearly angry that she had disobeyed his orders.

Astrid ran towards him and ducked behind a large rock. She continued to shoot as General Davids managed to run towards her.

"Are you crazy!" he yelled at her. "I told you to go! I wish that for just once, you would obey one simple order!"

She ignored him and continued to shoot the last of the men coming their way. Once it was evident that they had a clear path back to the truck she got up to run.

"Come with me!" she demanded.

"I can't! I need to know if there are any survivors!" he argued. "There has to be at least some who made it!"

"Whatever... Suit yourself, but I'm getting the hell out of here!" she snapped at him. Astrid took her weapon and ran back to the small armored truck. The rest of the group were hiding behind it, out of view, until Cruz saw her approaching.

"What the hell took you so long! We need to go, now!" he demanded. She held the keys in her hands and threw them over to him.

"Oh, sorry! My bad!" he apologized, and unlocked the doors, inviting everyone into the back of the truck. "Vámonos!" he yelled.

She climbed into the front passenger side as he started up the truck.

Cruz took off as fast as he could, leaving the campsite behind, when Astrid saw someone limping in her rearview mirror.

"Cruz, wait!" she exclaimed.

"What? Why?" He stopped the truck in frustration, and he saw just who they were waiting for.

Astrid opened her door and invited General Davids into the truck with them. He had packed a backpack before he had left the camp.

"Any survivors, sir?" she asked as she shifted into the middle of the cabin, between both the men. General Davids closed his door and stared angrily at the road in front of them while they waited for him to answer.

"How could we be so stupid!" he finally snapped. Cruz continued to drive silently as he and Astrid listened to him vent. "We trusted them... Brown and Banks. I watched as they gunned down Jackson right in front of me. So many that we trusted... that your father trusted... Why would they do this? They're all dead!"

Cruz sighed. "Let's just end this thing, shall we?" He was clearly upset that his Sergeant had been killed.

They continued to drive in silence down the road, and travelled until they could no longer see anyone trailing behind them and the scenery changed into nothing but clear landscapes.

Eventually, Astrid climbed into the back of the truck, joining the rest of the group, leaving Cruz and General Davids alone in the cabin.

"I guess this means that we have no choice but to get along," Cruz said under his breath, not taking his eyes off the road.

"I guess it does... Until we end the curse, that is..." the General said, knowing that he was referring to their conversation from before the battle.

"Correction, until I end the curse. But, in the meantime... you stay well away from her!" Cruz replied.

Chapter 14

Astrid sat in the back of the truck with Joey, Hannah, Stacey and Tash, as Cruz and Samuel tended to the driving. It was late and the only ones who were still awake were her, Tash and Joey.

"So, what's the deal with Buzzkill?" Joey asked after a long silence.

"Where do we start?" Tash asked.

"He was my father's second in command and one of the best fighters under him when they first brought us in... My dad recommended that he tended to my training..."

"...and he's in love with you," Joey replied.

"That, too..." Astrid said with frustration. "Don't get me wrong, he's a good guy... and he's been through a lot..."

"...Being promoted as General and losing all his men in one week is a little more than a lot, Sutherland," Tash chimed in.

"Yeah, it can't be easy..." Joey added, "but it's not every day that Cruz meets a girl that he's really into... and I know you're into him, too... Just don't let anything get in between that."

Astrid sighed. "I understand where you're going with this, Joey... I really do. But there's really no need. Cruz is... well... I love him. From the way he gets all corny, to the way he pulls that expression when he finds something seriously funny... Even that intense expression when he doesn't want to be bothered... He's become very important to me... that's why I'm in a rush to find a way to end this damn curse so we no longer need to live on the run..."

"Good... I'm glad to hear, 'cos he's never been that way with anyone before and it's my job to keep an eye on him."

"Look," Tash cut in, "you have nothing to worry about. I've been friends with Sutherland and Cruz for what? A year now? They're solid as a rock!"

"Okay, I hope so. Because that man deserves to be happy..." Joey replied, clearly satisfied with her response. He smiled down at Hannah who was asleep, resting on his shoulder.

Tash looked over at Stacey who was sleeping across from her beside Astrid and then looked away again.

Astrid noticed Tash's glance at her friend, and shook her head with a smile but said nothing about it. "I can't believe we lost everyone," she sighed.

"Yeah... it's a lot to take in. How's Buzzkill handling it?" Tash asked.

"He could be better. He went through all the tents looking for survivors. There wasn't any, so I think he feels responsible."

Tash nodded. "I'm not surprised. We should ease up on him a little."

Astrid agreed, feeling empathy for the man.

#

The sun was coming up and Cruz had been driving for a while now. General Davids awoke in his seat and looked around at their surroundings. "San Francisco?" he asked out loud.

"Yes, sir. You guys will need treatments if we're to keep on going... and a year ago there were so many doctors here... it's a long shot, but it's a risk that I'm willing to take."

"While that's a good idea... you don't need to keep calling me sir, or General anymore for that matter."

"You're just letting the misery get to you, man... "

"No, I'm not, Cruz. You, Tash... even Astrid calling me 'General'... well, it means that I'm of some higher rank than you... which, I'm not... not anymore. I lost all my men last night. So, technically I'm of no rank. Call me Davids, Samuel, Sam... Hell, even call me Buzzkill... Just don't call me General anymore."

"Alright, if that's what you want... Buzzkill." Cruz smiled as Samuel turned away. "Wow! So much has changed in a year..." Cruz continued, referring to the ruins and boarded up buildings that had become San Francisco.

It was clear that they wouldn't be able to continue driving the truck much further along the direct road due to the sea of cars that were scattered about. They would need to find another route.

He turned off until he found an abandoned truck depo to hide their vehicle in and parked out of sight.

"Last time we met with anyone outside the military, Reynolds was afraid that disease was spreading throughout mankind... it was all over the news," Cruz said as he looked around at their location from in his seat.

"I heard about that. We'll use our masks before we search the city, but we may need someone to stay here and watch the truck," Samuel said.

"We should break into groups..." Just as Cruz had spoken, Astrid had made her way towards them from the back. She kissed Cruz on the temple from behind his seat, making Samuel flinch.

"Good morning, guys. What are we doing in San Francisco?" she asked.

"Gathering medical supplies," Cruz replied. "We'll need a team to stay here and a team to go and collect them."

"I'm aching to stretch my legs. Hannah and Joey are, too. But Stacey's still asleep... and something tells me that Tash wouldn't mind staying here until she wakes up," Astrid said.

"I think that I might stay here too, then," Samuel said with a smile. "At least I can drive it out of here if we need to. You guys should pack the tranquilizer rifles. At least if you meet any shady characters you'll be prepared."

"...And you no longer want to be called, General, anymore..." Cruz said with a cheesy grin. He was referring to the fact that the man couldn't help but give orders.

"Well that's settled, then," Astrid said. "I'll go get the others organized."

Cruz and Samuel both watched as she left to tell the others. Cruz felt bad for Samuel. It couldn't be easy to lose everything in such a short amount of time and to know that the one thing he wanted most of all was entirely out of his grasp.

Nonetheless, he shook his head and hopped out of the truck with his tranquilizer rifle.

He opened the back of the truck and supported Astrid, Joey and Hannah as they climbed out the back.

"Wow, daylight!" Hannah exclaimed at the bright sun.

"Where are he headed, Cruz?"

"San Francisco Laboratory."

Hannah's eyes lit up. "Really? Oh my god! It was always my dream to work there..."

"Too bad it will all be in ruins, Han... We need to salvage what we can," Cruz said as he readied his weapon and scoured the street ahead. Fortunately, the city seemed empty, despite the bodies that lined the floor.

"I don't think I remember this place smelling so bad the last time we were here," Astrid said as she and Cruz led Joey and Hannah down the street lined with destruction.

Cruz put his arm around her. "That's because it was at least still functioning... and not so... dead? But I have to admit... I've been excited about the four of us actually spending some quality time together."

"I don't think that walking through a city lined with dead bodies to collect medical supplies was quite what you had in mind," Joey joked.

"It's close enough... We make do with the hand that we're dealt. Don't we?" He planted a kiss on Astrid's cheek as he spoke.

"You two are actually very cute together," Hannah replied. "Do you think that the rest of the group will be okay back at the truck?"

"They'll be fine," Astrid said. "Tash can handle herself... and Davids... well, I think he needs a break right now."

"Agreed. He's not taking things very well," Cruz replied. "We had a good chat last night... I hate to say it... but he's actually a good guy."

The group stared at him. "Er... I think that's the nicest thing that you've said about Buzzkill since the moment you met him, Cruz... are you feeling okay?" Astrid asked, putting her hand to his forehead.

"You know... that isn't an accurate way of reading someone's temperature..." Hannah joked.

"See, such a doctor!" Joey replied, laughing.

"That's why we need her for this mission," Cruz replied. "We're going to our friend's old floor to find out if we can rummage up his old notes... if we can... Hannah, we'll need you to figure out how to synthesize some more treatments."

"Wow, Cruz... 'mission'? You really are a soldier now," Joey said.

"Oh, only on the outside, Joe. I'm still a nerd where it counts..."

When they finally reached the laboratory, they were surprised to see just how fortified that it had become.

"Okay... so, something tells me that getting in isn't going to be as easy as we had first anticipated," Cruz said.

"Actually... that's a good sign ..." Astrid replied. "If it's fortified, that means there's people inside! We just need to convince them to let us in!"

#

Once Stacey finally awoke, she and Tash joined Samuel in the cabin of the truck.

"How are you coping, sir?" Tash asked him.

"If you don't mind... I've already asked Cruz not to keep calling me 'sir'. Our division has fallen which means we're all of equal rank, Tash."

"So, what do we call you then, sir... I mean... Davids?" Tash asked him.

Samuel smiled. "Whatever you want... Something tells me that Astrid and Cruz will both continue to call me 'Buzzkill' whether I like it or not."

"You have to admit that it does have a nice ring to it."

Samuel sighed. "Yes, sadly... it does." He continued to stare out the window.

There was an awkward silence and he turned back to them after a while. "I never expected Astrid to come back for me... you know, back at the camp."

"She didn't... she forgot the keys..." Tash replied.

"She provided me with a hell of a lot of cover fire on the way back... and she made Cruz stop the truck when she saw me coming."

"I get what you're getting at..." Stacey said after a while, "but Astrid's the kind of girl who has to help everybody. It's her way and it always has been. She sees you as her friend... she couldn't just leave you there to die."

Samuel nodded. "I know, she's a good person."

"And you love her..." Tash added.

"Tash!" Stacey said, embarrassed that Tash had spoken it out loud.

"It's true, I do. I shouldn't, but I do, although I'm not going to ruin what she has with Cruz. Especially while we need to work together to end this curse... They deserve this time together, at least."

"What do you mean by 'this time together'?" Tash wondered.

"Cruz hasn't been able to find another way to break the curse that doesn't involve either one of them dying. He's willing to die to end the curse. I can't believe that I even said that he wasn't a real soldier, once."

Stacey and Tash were speechless. "Astrid would never allow that!" Stacey said, astonished.

"That's because she doesn't know. I only found out last night, but he told the General a year ago."

"Whoa!" Tash gasped. "Why did he tell you? Why you and nobody else?"

Samuel shrugged. "I'm not so sure."

"He told you because he doesn't think that you will tell her," Stacey said. "Because he knows that you would rather her survive than him... That was clever of him. If Astrid knows, she will stop at nothing to prevent it from happening. But with you knowing..."

"...You'll be able to stop her from ruining his plans," Tash finished. "Man, that guy's clever. Don't tell me that you will allow for him to risk his own life!"

"I've lost too many men to allow him to do something so reckless... Of course I won't! But what other option do we have?"

"We'll find another way!" Stacey snapped. "I'm not losing my best friend again... and I'm not letting her lose anyone that she loves! That girl's been through a lot... even before all of this!"

"A lot? Yeah... with her father and all," Samuel said.

"Er...That's not even the half of it."

Samuel was going to say something else when they saw someone approaching the truck. He nodded in the direction. With the truck's tinted windows, they knew that they couldn't be seen from outside, unless they were standing right next to the door.

They studied the man. He had a rifle in his arms and he was examining their truck.

"Do you think he's been affected by anything?" Tash asked.

"I'm not sure. He doesn't seem angry. It could be fear. Something else, maybe?" Samuel said. "Stay in here. Tash, lock the doors... I'm going to find out." He readied his tranquilizer rifle.

"Are you sure?" Stacey asked him.

He nodded and stepped out of the truck. He started walking towards the man. "Hey, are you okay, sir?" he asked the stranger.

The man stared at Samuel. "I'm fine... I'm great, in fact! Is this your truck?" he asked.

"It sure is," Samuel said. "Maybe you should just be on your way."

"Is that what you think? Get him boys!" As the man spoke, at least twenty men began to surround them. Some even climbed onto the roof of the truck.

"What do we do?" Stacey exclaimed.

"We wait for his cue," Tash said calmly. She had already locked the doors and was currently readying her rifle.

Suddenly, someone knocked on Stacey's door, making her scream. The man licked his lips to see both the girls sitting in there. He was teasing them and it was clear he was suffering from the lust curse. There was a sudden loud bang and they turned to see Samuel shooting at the men as he ran back towards the truck.

Tash quickly unlocked his door, opened it and took a shot at the man who was currently standing there, giving Samuel the advantage to climb back into the vehicle

He locked the door behind him as Tash traded seats with Stacey and turned the engine on. She drove as fast as she could out of the parking lot. The sound of men falling off the top of the truck startled them all.

#

As Astrid's group stood at the entrance of the San Francisco Laboratory, she continued to ring the buzzer until they heard someone speak to them through the speaker.

"Yeah? What do you want?" the man on the intercom asked her.

"We're old friends of Dr. Reynolds," she said.

"Dr. Reynolds hasn't been here in a year!" the man replied.

"No, but before he left we were working with him..." Cruz continued. "...He believed that we might have been the cure to stopping the cur... er the virus."

The speaker had clearly been turned off after hearing Cruz speak. "They probably don't know if he died or not, he could still be alive," Cruz suggested.

"Your optimism astounds me, my love," Astrid replied with a smile.

Cruz was about to say something as equally sweet when the door opened before them. An older gentleman, seemingly the man who had spoken through the speaker, was standing there.

"You're the ones who are immune?" he asked them.

"Well, these two are..." Joey said, pointing at Cruz and Astrid. "But we're doctors who might have a theory in relation to ending the curse."

Hannah raised her eyebrows at Joey. He clearly doubted that the man would let him pass if he knew that Joey was not really a doctor.

"Alright... Dr. Reynolds' lab's a mess... but you should know the way... hey... I remember you two..." he said looking at Astrid and Cruz. Any sign of Reynolds?"

"Not in a while, I'm afraid," Astrid said casually.

The man stepped out of the way and closed the door behind them as he invited them in.

As they made their way into the laboratory, it was clear that the employees had reinforced the place to invite their families to live there. There were currently numerous people standing around the entrance watching them.
It was also a relief to see that the entire facility was booming with electricity thanks to the generators.

"We'll just make our way to Reynold's labs, shall we?" Cruz said as he headed towards the elevator.

They made their way up to Dr. Reynolds floor, where Astrid and Cruz immediately began searching for his notes.

"Wow... this man Reynolds was such a slob!" Joey said noticing the mess all over the floor.

"He had a freak out before I left..." Astrid said sadly. "I had to inject him with a serum that he had been working on."

Cruz put his arm around her shoulder. "He would have found a treatment for the illness... I'm sure of it."

They continued to scour the floor for any research notes in relation to the treatments, to no avail. Just then, Cruz noticed the computer sitting on the desk and remembered the generators that were providing electricity to the facility.

"Oh, baby!" he said rubbing his hands together as he took his seat at the computer. "What have you got for me?" He switched on the computer and to his delight it lit up. It was password encrypted.

"Now what will you do?" Astrid asked him, referring to the login screen.

"Give him a moment," Joey said as they watched as Cruz began trying different passwords.

"This guy once managed to hack the dean's computer to up his own grade."

Astrid looked shock. "No way! Really? That's almost as surprising as the Indiana Jones movies," she smiled.

"Okay, I've done it!" Cruz said excitedly. He had logged into the computer and had pulled up the desktop. He immediately began searching for any data coinciding with The Seven Deadly Sins curse and any treatments. "Man... seriously? Even the backups have been wiped!" he said angrily.

"Looking for these?" the man that had invited them into the facility earlier, asked. He was standing in the doorway holding up a stack of notes. He was joined by two other men, both holding up weapons.

"Yeah... there they are." Cruz got to his feet and approached him.

"The military took Dr. Reynolds! What makes you think that we would just hand these notes over to you? You betrayed him when he was only trying to help!"

"Excuse me?" Astrid asked puzzled.

"Don't lie to me. You're dressed in military uniforms. There's currently a military truck outside, and just over a year ago a whole bunch of you guys came in and took him against his will! Fortunately, we have the only copy of his notes!"

"Wait, Dr. Reynolds is alive? Was alive?" Astrid gasped.

"Don't play cute! How could you betray him like that!"

"We never betrayed him in any way! The men that took him were enemies of ours! If there's any way that we can get him back, we will! We want to end this thing, and even though the guy came off as a real jerk, we would do anything to help him if we could!"

"Astrid..." Cruz began, "do you think it's possible that whoever took him, also has the artifact?"

"It's possible! I think we now have an extra motive!" Astrid replied. "Look, if we can get Dr. Reynolds back safely we will... but please, we won't be able to make it without his work. My friend here is a doctor. Cruz and I are the only people who are immune and all we ask is for the notes so we can synthesize a treatment... the same treatment that has been keeping all of you alive for so long. Please... we aim to end this curse for good!"

It was clear that the doctor was a fair man. He approached them slowly and placed the notes beside the computer. "You can create them here, as many as you need... but then you must leave... You would also be glad to know that this is an altered strain and not the one he was working on before he was taken. I managed to alter it a little to make it last longer... Please, just get him back!"

Cruz nodded at the man. "We will," he promised.

"Thank you, sir. You won't regret this," Hannah said politely looking over the notes. He smiled at her and then left them in peace.

Chapter 15

"Are you sure that's where they went?" Stacey asked Samuel, as they looked up at the boarded-up building that was once San Francisco Laboratory.

"That's where Cruz said he was headed... I guess we just need to wait. Any sign of those men from earlier, Tash?"

Tash checked the rear-view mirrors. "No, sir... I mean, Buzzkill." She glanced over at him from the corner of her eye and grinned, knowing that 'Buzzkill' was sure to get a rise out of him.

But he shook his head and glanced out of the window, ignoring her. "Hmm... those stores have lights on! They must be working with backup generators!" he said, putting on his mask and some gloves. He loaded up his rifle and picked up his backpack, ready to head outside.

"What are you doing? Why would you want to go back out there? What if those men come back?" Stacey asked, amazed that he was willing to venture back outside.

"I'm hungry, so I'm getting breakfast that doesn't come under the category of rations... plus, we're going to need food and other supplies. I've been a soldier for a very long time, Stacey... so I'll be fine. Just watch the truck, okay?" Tash shrugged her shoulders and Stacey locked his door as he left.

Tash tapped her fingers rhythmically onto the steering wheel as she glanced around outside the truck nervously.

"And then there were two," Stacey joked.

"Yep..." Tash said under her breath.

There was an awkward silence again, and then Stacey asked, "Do you think he's buying breakfast for the rest of us? Because I'm really hungry."

"I guess so. He's normally the first to buy us food and drinks... He's actually a pretty good guy... if you're into that sort of thing."

"Not my type." Stacey said, looking away.

"Really? I think Astrid and I were the only girls in our unit that he couldn't sleep with."

"Oh, I'm not surprised when it comes to Astrid... She only ever dated one handsome jock type of guy back at school... it didn't go down very well. So, I'm not surprised she went for someone who's the complete opposite."

"What do you mean?" Tash wondered.

Stacey shook her head. "Never mind... Why doesn't he have your eye? You're very pretty... and you look like you'd be his type."

"What's that supposed to mean?" Tash asked, slightly offended.

"I don't mean that in a mean way... just... hmm... don't worry about it."

"Stop saying that. You can't keep saying something and then just end the conversation with 'never mind'... It would be like if someone brought a chocolate cake, waved it in front of you... offered you a slice and then said 'nah, never mind'."

"Such a hurtful metaphor, why would you even say that? I love chocolate cake!"

"Yeah... so do I, that's why I used it... Actually, I could really go for some right now..."

"Yeah... me, too. And maybe some chocolate... and some wine... and a mani-pedi... oh, and one of those massages," Stacey sighed. "If I keep going this way, I might need to take my medication."

Tash laughed at Stacey, but then continued speaking "But what were you getting at? Why do I look like Buzzkill's type?"

Stacey went quiet again. "Look, don't pay me any notice. I have this problem where I tend to put my foot in my mouth a whole lot. I can come off as insensitive... I always have. Astrid does the same thing... ha! And she's a psychologist, well... was!"

"Look, I'm not Samuel's type, and he's not mine... He likes women who have an interest in... well, men! And... well, I'm not exactly into men. I'm into women and I always have been."

"That's good to know..." Stacey said, looking away.

Tash blushed. "Why's that good to know? You're not going to pay me out about it later, are you? I've copped a lot of crap in the past and I'm glad to have finally found some friends who don't treat me any differently over who I'm into."

Stacey smiled. "Of course, I won't pay you out about it! I'm just surprised that Astrid never told you about me..."

"Told me what about you? She's not exactly one to gossip... unless it's about Buzzkill... or about how good Cruz is in bed... which is something I really don't need to know..."

"Yeah... she does like to share... but no. I'm not into men, either... but on that subject... Cruz has really pretty hair for a guy..." Stacey remarked.

"He does, doesn't he? It's very shiny... Just don't tell him that, or he won't shut up about it!" Tash said with a smile. "Maybe we should just drop this conversation for now. I mean, wherever we're headed after this, something tells me we'll have enough time on the road..."

#

Hannah studied the information in Dr. Reynolds' research notes, along with the updated work from the doctor. She was currently mixing chemicals and knew exactly what she was doing.

"This is actually a lot simpler than I first thought... provided we don't use your blood, Astrid... because your blood mixed in with that other ingredient is a real toxin... But if we substitute it with this ingredient here... just like this man, Dr. Andrews did... well, that's what prolongs the process... making the treatment a little longer lasting... It seems that Dr. Reynolds was just clutching at straws."

Astrid, Cruz and Joey all stared at her, entirely baffled as to what she had been talking about. "Sorry... I'll tell you straight... this new treatment will only need to be taken once a day... instead of every few hours."

"That's great, Hannah!" Astrid exclaimed.

"See why we brought her here?" Cruz said with a large grin painted to his face. "But now we have the hard part..."

"Finding the guinea pig..." Astrid was just as doubtful as Cruz was.

Hannah looked over at Joey. "Hey, babe... come here!"

"Er... Hannah!" Astrid cut in. "The last time I saw someone test a treatment on someone... I'm pretty sure they died... Are you sure that you're willing to try it out on Joey?"

"...Astrid, it's okay... I know what I'm doing!" Hannah replied.

"Woah..." Cruz broke in. "That was the last thing that Dr. Reynolds said last time, too... You'd understand our hesitation..."

"Hey, Cruz... it's okay," Joey cut in. Hannah gave him a look to let him know that she could handle the conversation herself.

Hannah gave Cruz a comforting smile. "Do you really think that I would trial something on Joey that I wasn't sure would work... I mean, the last time you saw us 'stable'... yeah, he was chasing me around like a love sick puppy dog... but, since then... after everything that we were forced to go through over the past two years of our life together... Joey and I have been keeping each other grounded. I love him. I wouldn't risk his life for anything, unless I was one-hundred percent sure that I was right about it."

Cruz nodded. "Okay... I trust you... just, please... don't poison him!"

Hannah nodded and injected the serum into Joey's arm. "Okay, here goes nothing."

#

Samuel walked along the streets passing the bodies that had decayed over time and were laying rotten in the streets. There was a stench of the dead in the air around him. The bodies were all in positions which depicted the exact activity that they had been undertaking at the moment of their deaths.

There were some bodies who had died of some kind of disease, which is why he was glad to be wearing his mask and gloves.

There was the body of a man lying on the floor, by an outside café table. The table was filled with plates of expired food. He had clearly died from overeating.

There were the corpses of bodies who had died making love to each other in the streets. They would have starved themselves from food, drink and would have been exhausted.

Some people had even been the victims of homicide, though the scenes that horrified him the most were those that had died by committing suicide.

He thought back to when he had been on the road with Astrid. He could remember every moment that his lust had taken over him. He hated himself for trying to force himself onto her.

None of these people had any control of their actions, just as he could not control himself at the time. For something to be able to screw with your head in such a way, to make you do things that you would never dream of doing... it was the scariest thing any man or woman could deal with. Yet that was now the new reality unless Astrid and Cruz could find a cure.

The stores around him had all been boarded up, just as the laboratory had been. But he managed to find a small grocery store that had a small gap in between two planks of wood that were covering the door. He knocked on one of the planks loudly and waited.

There was no answer, but he knew that someone was in there watching him. He caught a glimpse of an older gentleman of African American descent, standing at the counter. "Go away! We're not in business!" he said.

"Please! I only need supplies!" Samuel called back to him. But the man just shook his head. Samuel pulled his bag off his back and pulled out a black marker, some paper and a single vial of his treatment.

He wrote down a list of the items that he needed, and at the end of his list he wrote the words: 'Will barter with one vial of my treatments. Please!'

He slid the note under the door and showed the man that he was willing to put his rifle down. He did not mean to harm him in any way. He stepped back from the door and waited.

The elderly man approached the door, studying him. He picked up the note and read as Samuel held up the vial, showing him its contents and placed it onto the floor. Samuel took another step backwards.

The man took the note and stepped out of Samuel's line of sight. He had to go on faith that the man would help him.

Samuel stood outside in the middle of the street, watching his surroundings. He was dealing with a lot and he knew that his own grief was catching up with him.

There was a large part of him that wished that he had died the night before. He had been willing to go down fighting. He had watched all his men turn their backs on one another, gunning each other down in cold blood, men that he had known for years.

He had been ready. His life had been forfeit from the moment that he had signed the paperwork to join the military in the first place. There wasn't a doubt in his mind he had been willing to die at that campsite.

But that stubborn woman hadn't let him. She just had to come in with all guns blazing and save his ass. Furthermore, she had made Cruz stop the truck when they had the opportunity to escape.

He hated that she couldn't be simple like every other woman that he had ever met in his life. She challenged him far too much for him to be able to stand, and she would always be out of his reach. But, at the same time, Astrid could just smile and he could feel his whole world stop.

It had been that way since before he had even met her. He had fallen in love with her picture many years ago, and after every story her father had told him about her.

He had never thought that he would get the chance to meet her in person. However, that had all changed when that damn pithos had been opened.

He had been made to watch her from afar... to love her from afar, and to ensure her safety. But that night when she had been attacked in her apartment had changed everything.

He had been given the order to rescue her. There was chaos everywhere, which he had to fight through to get to her. Seventeen floors to travel up by elevator. But by the time he had made it, she had already escaped from her bedroom window.

He had fought with the man in her apartment for her laptop, then he had chased and fought the man on the window ledge. He had smashed the window to the stairwell and he must have lost her there, because she had been nowhere to be seen. She had disappeared entirely.

It wasn't until he had used her computer to track her most recent messages that he found that she had been in contact with Cruz. Using his military resources, Samuel had managed to investigate Cruz and track his internet activity, which had led him to Dr. Gregory Reynolds.

Samuel had requested to be planted in with their enemy's division, to lead them off her trail. At the same time, he had been sending her messages, hoping that she would track him down herself. He had used a name that her father had given him, which he was certain would have grasped her attention; that name being Roger Charlie.

He had followed them to the motel in San Francisco, writing down the name in the guest book, hoping that she would see. He had hidden out in the motel to lose the men that he had infiltrated, as well as used it as an opportunity to reach out to her.

He had only recited Hesiod as he had been reading her father's file on Pandora at the time. It seemed fitting.

Then, he had managed to lure out Cruz. He had been the perfect bait to lure out Astrid. But still, Samuel wondered how things would have been if he had succeeded in finding her first. If he had met her before Cruz had come to her rescue.

The click of the door unlocking distracted him from his thoughts. The shopkeeper was standing there holding a box filled with food and supplies. He had not only collected the items on the list, but had also packed a few extra resources.

He stared at Samuel, unsure as to whether he could trust the soldier or not. But seeing the rifle resting beside the building gave him faith.

"Thank you!" Samuel said, stepping forward to take the box which seemed too heavy for the old man to carry. Samuel took the box and stepped backwards. The man picked up the treatment vial from the floor.

"It's military grade," Samuel said. "It only lasts for a few hours, but it does work. Please... in this world I believe stability is more important than money."

"Where's the rest of your crew?" the man asked him. Samuel stared at the floor. He really didn't want to talk about it.

The older man nodded. "I fought in World War II... We lost a lot of men, too... It can't be easy with the way times are changing, with all this mental instability."

Samuel shook his head. "No... it's not. Our whole base was massacred. Only a few of us made it out alive."

The older gentleman handed Samuel back the vial. "Here, take this... I have an agreement with the scientists around the corner. I supply them with food, they supply me with treatments."

"Are you sure?" Samuel asked him.

"Absolutely. Besides... something tells me that you'll need it far more than I will." He placed the vial neatly into the box of supplies.

The man picked up Samuel's rifle. "It's a tranquilizer?" he wondered out loud.

"Yeah. Most of the civilians that have been affected cannot help how they're acting. It was mixed with a dosage of the treatments... It provides them with a little temporary sanity when they awake. It was my General's idea."

"Smart man!" He went to place the weapon on top of the box of supplies that Samuel was carrying but stopped mid action.

"Get into my shop, quick!" he exclaimed, as they were suddenly surrounded by a large group of about twenty men, riding in on motor bikes, holding weapons aimed at them.

Samuel fled into the store with the man, who closed the door and locked it from behind him. "We met with those men earlier! Who are those guys?" Samuel asked.

"Trouble! They've tried ransacking every store down this street."

The chaotic sounds of motorbikes continued to roar from outside. "Come out, Jenkins! We know you're in there! Give us what we've come for and we'll make it easy on you!" one of the men called out. His voice was followed by the loud bang of a shotgun.

"My friends are around the corner!" Samuel exclaimed.

"Let's just hope they haven't been found," Jenkins replied.

#

Astrid, Cruz and Hannah anxiously watched Joey as they waited to see if the treatment had worked. "How do you feel?" Hannah asked him.

"I feel fine..." Joey said. "No rage... nothing..."

"That could be good..." Cruz said. Joey got to his feet and they continued to watch him, expecting something. Anything at all.

"You guys... I'm fine!" he said looking at them uneasily.

"Well then, provided this holds up, it looks like we have our treatment supply!" Astrid said excitedly.

Hannah begun packing vials and chemicals away into the old silver briefcase that Dr. Reynolds had once used, removing the vaccines that had already been in there.

Cruz looked a little disheartened as he saw the briefcase.

"We'll rescue him," Astrid assured him. "I know we will."

"Providing me with hope once again, mi amor..." he said with a smile.

"That's my job, my love," Astrid said smiling back. She then looked over at Hannah. "How much of a supply do we have?"

Hannah counted the vials and the syringes. "There's enough to last the rest of us for a few months... provided we take them daily. There's enough for Joey, Stacey, Tash, Davids and myself... I also packed the chemicals to create a few more batches, just in case."

"Brilliant! Let's take them and go!" Astrid replied.

The group left San Francisco Laboratory with their treatment supplies and promised the scientists who resided there of their intentions to search for Dr. Reynolds.

They found the military truck out on the road and were surprised to find that only Tash and Stacey were inside. Cruz, Joey and Hannah climbed into the back.

"Where's Buzzkill?" Astrid asked Tash as she climbed into the cabin with the girls.

"He went searching for food and supplies an hour ago. I think he went around the corner. We heard motorbikes earlier and a few gunshots... it didn't sound good."

Astrid sighed. "Alright, let's go find him!"

Chapter 16

Tash drove the armored truck to a deserted area just up the street from where she had heard motor bikes roaring and weapons being fired. From a distance, they saw a large crowd of bikers swarming the entrance of a general store.

"I bet twenty bucks that that's where Buzzkill's hiding out," Astrid said.

"You're on, Sutherland!" Tash replied, as she parked a little up the road and out of the way from the biker's line of sight.

Astrid reapplied her mask and gloves and loaded her assault rifle. "Get Cruz, I'll meet you out there!" she told Tash. With her rifle in hand, Astrid opened her door and climbed out, closing the door behind her.

"They're the same guys as earlier!" Stacey exclaimed. "Are you all seriously going to take them on?"

Tash called out to Cruz and then turned back to Stacey, as she applied her own mask and gloves and readied her rifle. "This is what we do... One of our men's in there. We won't turn our backs on him... Lock the doors after me."

Tash, Cruz and Astrid ran down the street and stood behind a pile of abandoned cars with their weapons at the ready. They hadn't yet been spotted by the gang who were calling out to whoever was in the store.

"On your cue, Sutherland," Tash whispered as they stared through their scopes.

Astrid lined up her target in her scope to get a closer look. "Cruz... that's Vince and his men... They're on mood stabilizers..." she whispered.

"Those guys attacked us earlier... they were unstable... they must have just found some treatments," Tash whispered.

"It looks like Vince's group has grown by seventeen men over the past year," Cruz replied in the same whisper. "Are we playing nice this time, Astrid?"

"I'm going eye for an eye... though in this case an arm for an arm..." Astrid replied. In one swift movement she shot a tranquilizer bullet into Vince's arm that was carrying his weapon.

It forced the man to drop his weapon. He cried out in pain and instantly knelt back down to pick it up. The first attack alerted the bikers to their presence, as they immediately went into the offense.

Cruz and Tash followed Astrid's suit and began shooting the rest of Vince's men with their own weapons. They began to charge for Astrid, Cruz and Tash, on their motorbikes.

"How long until these things work?" Cruz cried out to Astrid as he dodged an incoming bike after taking a shot.

"Two minutes, Cruz!" Astrid called back. They started running backwards, continuing to shoot tranquilizers in the process.

"Oh look!" Vince called out as he zeroed in on Astrid on his bike. "I remember you... You like to take charge."

"Yeah... That's me! It's been a while, Vince!" she called back. She had to dive out of the way and onto the ground as he shot a bullet in her direction.

"For a military bitch, your bullets suck!" Vince called out. He raised his shotgun aiming for her head. "This time, I won't miss!" he said as he stopped his bike. He shot a bullet and once again she dodged out of the way.

"You were saying?" she said with a smirk. But then before she could roll back out of the way, he went to shoot another bullet. Before he could, there was a loud bang and he instantly fell off his bike. He dropped his gun on impact.

At first glance, Astrid thought that the tranquilizers that she had shot earlier had worked. But, as she came to, she realized that he had been shot dead from another weapon.

She looked up to see Samuel standing beside an older man. Samuel had been the one that had shot Vince with a weapon that she had assumed he had been given from his shop keeper friend.

"Sorry, Sutherland... Payback for you coming to my rescue last night," Samuel said as he ran towards her and helped her to her feet.

"Aww, there you go... killing my buzz yet again, Buzzkill!" Astrid joked. "Let's go help the others!"

From their location they managed to take down more men. Within seconds Vince's followers began to fall from their bikes unconscious, thanks to the tranquilizers. However, their bikes began to run out of control.

"Head to my store!" the shopkeeper told them all. They obeyed him and ran towards the doors, with the sounds of the motorbikes going out of control behind them.

When the door was closed the older man introduced himself. "My name is Arthur Jenkins. Thank you for your help out there. They have been harassing us for just under a year. They've been after our supplies and our treatments."

"That might be our fault," Cruz said. "Astrid and I met them on the road a year ago. We told them that we were headed to San Francisco for treatments."

"Well, I was the one who told them. It was an attempt to escape," Astrid said. "But those tranquilizers won't last for long. Might I suggest that we lock them up somewhere?"

"Do you guys have a prison system here that hasn't been escaped from?" Cruz joked.

Arthur Jenkins laughed. "Yes, we do. I'm also pretty certain that I can get some help apprehending them. Samuel here tells me that you're looking to put an end to the curse."

"Yeah, that's true," Tash said. "Cruz here opened the box and we intend on putting the world back together... in a way that will not risk any more lives!" She stared at Cruz pointedly.

Cruz looked over at Samuel, wondering if he had told her about his plan, when suddenly, the group were joined by a woman in her mid-thirties and what were clearly her two children.

"Whoa!" the young boy who was roughly ten years old said. "We saw what you did from the windows! That was awesome!"

His younger sister, who looked barely any older than three, shied away behind her mother's legs, only appearing every so often.

"This is my granddaughter Alisha and her two children," Arthur said.

"You're with the military aren't you?" Alisha asked.

"We were," Tash said, "but things have been getting pretty tough, so we're kind of out on our own."

"Are you staying?" the little girl asked Astrid.

"No, I'm sorry. We can't," Astrid said, kneeling down at the young girl's level. "We're going to find a way to fix the world."

"Like superheroes?" the boy asked them.

"Yeah... like superheroes," Cruz replied with a grin.

"Wow! That's so cool!"

"We won't have much time left until those tranquilizers wear off," Astrid said addressing the group. "Four hours max, wasn't it?"

"Yes... four hours," Samuel replied.

"The motorbikes sound like they've stopped," Tash added.

"Feel free to take whatever you need from my store. I still have some suppliers who are very proud business owners," Arthur told them.

"You guys deserve it!" Alisha said. "If you're ever back in the city, you're more than welcome to return!"

"Thanks again," Samuel said. He took the box of groceries from earlier and Arthur supplied them with three more boxes as they took their leave back to their truck.

"Those kids back there..." Astrid said as they reached their truck. "We haven't seen very many in a while."

Cruz nodded. "Yeah... it's very sad to think what's actually happened to the children in this world."

"And to consider what the children who have survived have had to witness..." Samuel added.

"I hate to change the subject," Tash said, "...but who's driving?"

"Cruz and Samuel have been sharing the driving all night. Let them get some sleep. I can take over if you like," Astrid offered.

"I would love the chance to rest my eyes for a little while... I can't remember the last time I got my forty winks," Cruz said tiredly.

They opened the back of the truck and began to hand the boxes of food and supplies to Joey and Hannah.

"I have a map in my bag of where I think we should head to next, so I might sit up for a little while longer," Samuel said, looking over at Tash. He knew that Cruz would hate him, but he had every intention on filling Astrid in on Cruz's plan to end the curse. Tash clearly understood.

#

After a while, Samuel had directed Astrid out of the city and on route to Washington. They were sitting alone in the cabin, and amidst the strange tension that Samuel continued to put off whenever he was around her, Astrid attempted to break the ice.

"I'm surprised that Tash isn't in here," she said.

"I think that she and Stacey have something going on... or they're about to... They put off that vibe."

"I guess that I'm not surprised. I have to admit... Stacey and Tash finding each other, it's actually rather sweet!"

Samuel nodded in agreement as Astrid kept her eyes focused on the road before them. "Has Cruz told you about how he plans on ending the curse?" he asked her.

"No... I just know that he's pretty keen on finding a way that doesn't involve me dying."

"Okay..." Samuel said, not knowing what to say next.

"Why? Has he told you anything?" she asked, glancing over at him for a moment.

Samuel avoided her eye and glanced out the window.

"What is it?" Astrid asked him, puzzled.

"Nothing, don't worry," Samuel said.

"Buzzkill... I know when you're lying. What's going on?"

Samuel pursed his lips together, trying to decide the right words to use. He stared at her, knowing that he couldn't lie to her. "If Cruz can't find a way to break the curse... he's willing to die to prevent you from having to lay down your own life."

"I'm sorry... what?" she snapped at him.

"Focus on your driving, Sutherland... he didn't want me to tell you."

"Are you kidding me?!"

"No... this is why I shouldn't have said anything... but I am telling you because you have the right to know... I don't think that you should be kept in the dark. Apparently, your father knew a year ago... Cruz only told me last night."

"He's been planning on doing this for a year now, and he hasn't even told me? Seriously?! No wonder he's in such a rush..."

"A rush? A rush for what? To find Pandora's Box? Why would he be in a rush if he hasn't found another way to end the curse?"

"Never mind. Don't worry about it."

"Okay... but there was more to what he said..."

"Like what?" Astrid glanced over at him, a little impatient and very annoyed.

"Last night... he asked me to be there for you... afterwards."

Astrid parked the truck onto the side of the road and glared at Samuel. "Excuse me?"

"I'm guessing that he'd like to know that you'll have someone that will look out for you."

Astrid took a deep breath and then spoke with very little emotion in her tone. "Stay here for a minute!"

She unbuckled her seat belt and stormed into the back of the truck, making her way towards Cruz, who was still sleeping peacefully. She shook him lightly and when his eyes fluttered open she glared at him.

"Hey, what's happening?" he said with a smile, but then as he took note of the expression on her face, he added, "Uh oh."

"Uh oh is right, buddy!" she snapped. "What's this about you wanting to end your own life to end the curse?"

"Buzzkill told you? Seriously! You can't trust that guy with anything," Cruz said angrily.

"Well, we can clearly trust him with your life! Because there is no way in hell that I will allow you to play the martyr!"

Cruz sat up, and for the first time that they had known each other, he snapped at her angrily, surprising himself in the process. "Why, Astrid? Because that's your job? Because you're some damn descendent of Pandora? I told Davids because I felt that he would agree with me, that you ending your life for this stupid curse was the last thing that either one of us could ever let you do."

"So what? I have to just stand back and let you off yourself in a bid to save the world? Seriously, Cruz! One minute you're talking to me about having babies? And for what? You don't even plan on being around to raise them... but then again, why does that even matter? You even told Samuel to be there for me afterwards... clearly to play the daddy! For Christ's sake! I don't even..." Astrid stopped herself before she could finish her sentence.

"You don't even what? Astrid? What is it? Say it!" Cruz snapped at her.

She shook her head. "I don't even know why I bothered to consider it, Cruz! I don't even know why I bother at all!" She got to her feet and stormed towards the cabin of the truck.

Then, without turning around, she added, "Find another way to end the curse, Cruz... because otherwise... there's just no point!"

She sat back in the driver's seat, knowing full well that everyone had just witnessed their argument. Samuel glanced over at her. "I'm sorry, Astrid," he said.

"Sorry for what?" she replied dryly. "For being the only person that I trust to tell me what Cruz had planned? If that's the case... you have nothing to apologize for..."

Samuel wasn't sure what to say. He was sorry for being the one to tell her, knowing how angry it would make her feel, but he also couldn't allow her to go on not knowing and to feel defenseless if Cruz did die. Samuel was giving her the chance to fight for the man she loved, even if it was not in his own best interest.

"I know it makes you mad..." Samuel went on to say, "but he was only trying to look out for you. He loves you and you know it. No one wants to see the person that they love die."

She glanced back over at him, taking in what he was saying. She sat quietly for a moment. Then she started the engine back up and mumbled under her breath, "Some things are just unavoidable!" She pulled back on to road and continued on their way in silence.

#

Cruz could not fall back asleep after his argument with Astrid.

Joey, Hannah, Stacey and Tash all continued to stare at him in silence. By the looks on their faces, he knew that they agreed with her.

He glanced towards the cabin of the truck, where Astrid and Samuel were speaking quietly. Cruz was angry at Samuel for being the one to tell her, for him being the one that she was venting to now, and he was mad at himself for believing that Samuel would keep the secret from her.

As mad as Cruz was, and as much as he could understand things from Astrid's perspective, it still didn't change the way that he felt. He knew that in his heart, he couldn't watch the love of his life die. Just as he knew that Astrid felt the same way about him.

But his head continued to tell him that there was no other way. Zeus was a vengeful bastard. Most of the gods were. A blood sacrifice made of love was always the highest price to pay.

"She's right, you know," Joey said looking over at Cruz. "You might hate to hear it... but she's right."

"Yeah... I know. Please don't remind me," Cruz grumbled, staring into his lap.

"But at the same time, I understand why you wanted to do it," Joey continued.

Cruz looked back up at his friend as Joey got from his seat and sat beside him. "I just can't believe you never told me that you were wanting to have kids... That's pretty serious, man."

"Yeah it is."

"Just as serious as you wanting to lay down your life for her... She's really stolen your heart, hasn't she?" Joey asked, making Cruz nod silently. "So... You know what I suggest? I suggest that we do what we used to do. We research! Whatever city we find ourselves in next... we find the biggest library possible, we pour over books and old texts, anything to do with Ancient Greece, Pandora, the gods... anything that might have been forgotten or overlooked... We look for a loophole! So, that way, when you're holding that old brown jar in your hands again, you'll know exactly what to do to break the curse... and then you and your girl over there can live happily ever after! Don't leave her to the hands of soldier boy, because she loves you, man. Don't throw it all away."

Cruz smiled. It was very typical Joey wisdom. But then Joey said something that surprised Cruz. "Man, we both held that pithos... wouldn't it have been weird if I had opened it instead?"

Cruz raised his eyebrows and looked over at his friend. "That would be an interesting twist of fate," he replied.

Cruz thought to himself, if that had happened he would have never met Astrid. The world might still be cursed, but the rest... none of it would have ever happened.

For the first time in the past few years he was thankful that he had opened the pithos and that Joey hadn't.

#

"Why Washington?" Astrid asked Samuel. "What's your plan of action when we get there?"

"We're going to appeal to the president," he replied looking over at her.

Astrid smirked, and it was followed by a laugh. "...Oh, wait... you're serious?"

"Very serious, Sutherland."

"So, what? We hunt him down? I mean, we'd have a better chance of locating Pandora's Box before we find him. He'd be in hiding... and if we do find him, what then?"

"Well, we're bound to run out of bullets and supplies... Plus, who better to help us than the man who runs the entire country?"

Astrid shook her head. "Big dreams... Okay... I'll bite... if we miraculously meet him, what do we say? Hey, Cruz and I are both immune to the Seven Deadly Sins and we want to fix everything... can you help us locate it and give us bullets? Not to mention most of the military have betrayed us and they're bound to be under his reign..."

"Well, do you have a better idea?"

Astrid sighed. "No, I don't. I'm just screwed up right now, so I'm unleashing it on you, I'm sorry! I'm dealing with my dad, and then I just can't get my head around this whole thing with Cruz. Argh! Then there's the stress with everything that's been going on as of late... I don't mean to steal the limelight... because you're going through a whole lot, too."

"It's okay... I mean, I lost a mentor and my men... but you lost your father, the fate of the world is quite literally resting on yours and Cruz's shoulders and you just found out that the man you love had planned to sacrifice himself to spare you the burden... You have every right to be pissed off... I'm just glad that you're trusting me enough, to vent to me... But do you know what would be good right now?"

"What's that?"

"A good old sparring match to let off some steam," he said with a smile that lit up his face.

Astrid laughed. "Thanks, the humor works just as good, too."

"I'm serious. Put everything aside for one moment, including how I feel about you... and just think about every time that you were angry and you just let me have it. It always made you feel better. Gets those endorphins pumping!"

Astrid nodded. "You're right... very right... but things are... well, they're just different now. I mean, things are all up in the air and you quite literally told me how us sparring really makes you feel... I wish that I could say that it was just your lust speaking, but we both know that..."

"...That's how I really feel." Samuel nodded. "I know... I remember... speaking of... I'm due for my medication."

"No, you're not, you took it earlier. You take it more often than the rest of them," Astrid realized as he unzipped his backpack and administered his next dosage.

"Trust me... I need to. I always need to when I'm around you."

Astrid bit her lip. She needed to change the subject. "I'm hungry... Maybe we should stop and eat? I've been thinking back to those food supplies and just how much I could go for a coffee right now, even if we have to boil the water over campfire."

This time it was Samuel that laughed. "I think a meal break sounds perfect... there's a gas station coming up just down the road. I'm guessing the rest of the group would agree, too! And it will give you and Cruz a chance for a little heart to heart... and maybe a chance to get your endorphins pumping in another way... with him, I mean."

Astrid grinned. "Sure... like that would ever happen with a Buzzkill like you around," she joked.

Chapter 17

Astrid drove to an abandoned truck stop down the road, and while Samuel fueled up and attended to the maintenance of the truck, the rest of the group entered the store in search for food.

There was a distinct smell coming from the store which they all recognized, and as the group helped themselves to the shelves, Astrid and Cruz searched for any owners who may still occupy the facility.

To their dismay, they found the body of a man in his late sixties, who had left a suicide note. He had been dealing with fear, which had caused him to hang himself in the back room only a few months ago.

"This never gets any easier to deal with," Astrid mumbled under her breath as she handed the bag of cookies that she had been eating over to Cruz and stormed outside.

"Hey, Astrid!" Cruz called out, following after her.

She stopped and pressed her back against the brick wall of the building outside.

When he approached her, she snapped at him. "That man in there... how he died... it's pretty much what you're expecting me to deal with... but it won't be some lonely old stranger... it will be you,

Cruz! You! It will be the man that I love! The most important person in my life... is that really what you want to put me through?"

"I'm sorry. No, it's not," Cruz said in a mere whisper as he took her hands in one of his and stroked her hair lovingly with the other.

"Then what are you sorry for? Because I won't let you die for me..."

Cruz paused for a moment. "I'm sorry for getting mad at you earlier. You were right... hell, as much as it sucks, you're always right. I just... well, the thought of you having to die to end the curse... It's torture, because... I guess, that if it wasn't for me, we wouldn't even be in this mess... but at the same time I wouldn't even know you... and honestly, I'm glad that I met you! Sure, it took the whole world going to shit for it to happen... but this... you and me, it means everything to me. I want nothing more than the world to go back to normal, to wake up next to you every damn morning... to have children with you... hell, to even have to go to some boring nine to five job everyday just to come home to you. That's it... boring, but I want it. So no... I don't want to die... but at the same time, thinking that you might have to die to end a curse that I unleashed onto this world... well, it's not right. I am responsible! I should be the one made to suffer. Not you."

"But you don't get it! I don't want to live in a world without you! All that stuff that you said... I want it, too. But I'm not going to bother if I have to do it alone. Please... just promise me that you and I, together... that we will think of a way to end it... Please! You're not in this alone. We're a team!"

Cruz stared at her. He let a comforting smile spread across his face, for her benefit only. "Okay, fine!" he said, trying to convince himself. "...We'll do it your way."

"Oh, thank god!" Astrid said, wiping away the tears that had formed in her eyes. She wrapped her arms around him tightly and kissed him passionately, as they allowed themselves to be swept up in the moment.

#

"Well, it looks like Sutherland and Cruz have made up," Tash said to Stacey as the two of them made their way back towards the truck. They could see Cruz and Astrid escaping to find some privacy.

"Good... the whole silent treatment thing was starting to get a little hard to handle," Stacey replied digging into her bag of chips, hungrily. "Almost as bad as that smell in there."

Tash nodded. "That smell in there... I hate to break it to you, but that was the smell of a decomposing body."

"You really didn't need to tell me that. I thought that that's what it was, but I could have been fine without the confirmation."

"Sorry, Stacey... but that's the world that we're living in. We can't just ignore everything to make it easier on ourselves."

"Yeah, but sometimes sugar coating everything is by far the better option."

"Stacey, look around us... We can't exactly sugar coat an apocalypse now, can we?"

"I get that! But are you forgetting that for the past two years of my life that I... look, don't worry about it!" Stacey was having trouble controlling her tone of voice, as she thought about the past two years of her life.

Tash immediately regretted her words. "I'm sorry, Stacey... I didn't think..."

"No! You didn't think, Tash! Do you want to know what torture methods those bastards used on us? Let me just say, it makes me appreciate women so much more! Right now, the only thing that I have to be happy about is the fact that I didn't have to go through it alone!"

"I'm sorry... Stacey, do you want to talk about it?"

"No! I don't want to talk about it! I just want everything to go back to the way it was before... I want to go shopping, I want to feel good about myself and the world around me... I just... I can't keep seeing the world like it is right now. It's just too hard to deal with... so please, just let me see things through my own sugar coated point of view...

because right now, that's all that I have left to keep me from falling apart."

Stacey stormed away from Tash, passing Samuel angrily. She climbed into the back of the truck and drank a bottle of water and ate her chips alone.

Tash glanced over at Samuel, unsure what to say about Stacey. He had barely noticed her enter the truck, anyway, as he was too caught up in his own world.

The man wore a tired expression on his face that Tash couldn't help but feel pity for. "You did a good thing, Buzzkill," she said.

"A good thing? I just refueled the truck," he said raising his eyebrows at her, unsure as to what she was referring to.

Tash smiled. "You told the woman that you love the news that she needed to hear, so she wouldn't lose the one that she loves. Damn, love triangles are so confusing!"

Samuel leaned up against the truck and nodded. "Try being in one... Anyway, doing the right thing sucks. Do you know if Hannah's new treatment works? Because right now I need something that's going to last if I have to be around that damn woman so much."

"Have you ever thought that maybe it's not just the curse making you feel this way? That it's more to do with how you really feel? I mean, think about it... you only feel the need to use them when you're around her. Yet, do you feel the need to use them when you and I stand so close to one another?"

"No, I don't."

"That's my point... And remember, most people lust over anyone and everyone... do you feel the need to take it around Cruz?"

"Cruz? No way!"

"There you go! I'm not a scientist, but maybe your love for her just increases your lust for her, especially because you know that you can't have her... It makes a lot of sense, if you really think about it."

Samuel shook his head slowly. "Tash... I hate to admit it, but you could be right. Speaking of love interests... aren't you letting your curse dictate your own actions?"

"What do you mean?"

"Well, you clearly like Stacey, yet whenever it seems like the two of you are getting close, you move right away again, like a yoyo... like sitting on opposite sides in the back of the truck. You're afraid of getting close to her."

"I get it... I'm a soldier, I shouldn't be scared."

"On the contrary, you're allowed to be scared. But let your fears drive you to be brave, especially when it comes to how you really feel about someone."

"Like you did with telling Astrid Cruz's plans, knowing full well that it would push her all the more out of your reach?" Tash asked, while glancing over to see Astrid and Cruz emerge from behind the building.

Samuel sighed as he saw what she had been looking at. "As long as she's happy, I'm happy."

"I get that we're dealing with an apocalypse, but there's still people around... You shouldn't be afraid to meet someone new. I want to see you happy, too..."

"Oh, come on, Tash. If I wanted to be with someone else, I could have done it a long time ago... you know that. I've certainly had the opportunities..."

"Yeah, but you've been idolizing her so no one will ever compare to her in your eyes."

As Cruz and Astrid approached, Tash and Samuel stopped talking and Samuel got back to work checking the pressure of the tires to avoid Astrid's gaze.

"Where's Joey and Han?" Cruz asked.

"Last I saw, they were raiding shelves to provide us with a bigger supply for the trip," Tash replied. "Where are we going, anyway?"

"Washington!" Astrid said, glancing over at Samuel. "We're going in search for the president."

"The president?" Cruz and Tash asked in unison.

Samuel got to his feet. "If we can appeal to him, we might be able to convince him to help us, maybe supply us with the resources we need to locate Pandora's Box."

"I hate to be the buzzkill this time, Buzzkill..." Cruz said, "but how do you expect us to do that? The Whitehouse isn't exactly open for business."

"I figured it's worth a shot. We're bound to run out of supplies, and we're also looking for a needle in a haystack... So maybe the president will have some sort of links that we can exploit."

Cruz raised his eyebrows. "You do realize that it's also possible that he could turn on us like everyone else has, right? I mean, we're risking a lot getting anyone else involved."

"Just as we're risking a lot by standing around doing nothing," Astrid added. "Sorry, my love... but I have to agree with Samuel. We need resources, we need help... he's lost his country... we can use that to find some mutual ground... but we'll need to find him first..."

Cruz sighed. "Alright... I guess that I'll go and find the others, then." He turned and left in the direction of the store looking for Joey and Hannah.

"Thanks, Sutherland," Samuel said. "I appreciate having you in my corner."

"Don't thank me. It's the most logical option we have right now. But you look exhausted, so you're going to use this time to sleep... no exceptions."

Samuel smiled over at her. "Right, General Sutherland!" he joked, but the moment he said it, he, Tash and Astrid all regretted hearing it, after the death of their General and Astrid's father.

Samuel climbed into the back of the truck, and as Astrid went to leave, Tash took a hold of her arm and whispered, "I think that you should speak with Stacey. I don't think she's coping too well."

"I'll invite her to sit up the front with me. It might be good for us to spend some quality time together."

#

It wasn't long until the group were packed up with extra food and supplies and on route to Washington. "It feels like we haven't really spoken in a while," Astrid said to Stacey as they took in the sites, while driving along the road.

"What do you mean? We spoke earlier!" Stacey said, confused.

"I mean heart to heart."

"Oh... Tash, right?" Stacey asked, clearly understanding where she was coming from with the line of questioning.

"Yep... Tash. She happened to mention that she was a little worried about you."

"Of course, she did. Look, I get what you're going to say... That you're here if I need to talk about everything that's happened, when I was... when... well, you know... but hey, I'm coping. I wouldn't mind a little retail therapy, though."

Astrid laughed. "We might be able to make a small detour to a shopping mall at some point. Have you taken your medication?"

"Yeah, I did earlier when we were at that gas station. But it's funny... we're living in a world where shopping has quite literally become an addictive illness, and where I need to take medication to handle my cravings for shopping!"

"Yeah... it's like we bypassed the shopaholics anonymous stage... and went straight to medicating you... But it's not so much the shopping that's the problem, it's the..."

"...the greed. I know... But I just get these urges where I need anything and everything just because it's there... It's horrible, but after everything that I went through... It makes me want everything all the more, just to make me feel good about myself... Unfortunately, it doesn't last... I'm still me... and those things... they still happened to me... and I still feel miserable! They happened to Hannah, too... but she had Joey to turn to...so I would collect stones from one of the cells that we were kept in... Small little stones that no one else noticed. They were my mini security blankets... and then they would give us our treatments... And when that happened, I no longer felt the need to collect them... Because it forced me to face my real demons, because I was in control of my own mind... which is the way they wanted us to be when they tortured us."

"Stacey, what did they do to you exactly? You know that you can talk to me. It's me... You were there when I thought my father had died... the first time. And then, when my mother... well... you remember... you were there... But what happened to you?"

Stacey wiped away at the tears that had filled her eyes, trying to battle her own inner emotions. "I was raped, Astrid! And not just once... They allowed men... who weren't on any treatments at all, and who were filled with lust, to have their ways with us... while the male prisoners were beaten by anger-filled men... They even killed Hannah and Joey's old boss. They beat him to death, even after he had told them about Cruz... they just wanted more information on him. And when they interrogated me about you... Well, I didn't know where you were, so I couldn't tell them anything. I didn't know a thing. I thought that you could have been dead after all those messages that you had sent me, about it being too dangerous, to return home... And they didn't believe me... they found your purse in my possession and they felt that everything I said was a lie... and then they would... Well, the rest is history now, isn't it?" She was trying hard to wipe her tears away.

"Oh my god! Stacey! I wish I had known. I'm just so sorry! If I'd known..."

"If you had have known... you would have handed yourself in... I know you. There were times that I wish that I did have the answers that they wanted... I felt so selfish for wishing that... but I just wanted it all to stop."

Astrid took a deep breath. Her friend had given into her tears, so she pulled the truck over and parked on to the side of the road. She held Stacey tight, stroking her hair and comforting her.

"I'm so sorry, Stacey. I wish that I knew," she said. "God, we will end this curse... I promise you we will!"

Stacey sniffled as her head rested on Astrid's shoulder. "I hope we do," she said, "but please... don't die to end it... I really can't lose my best friend... We've been through everything together, and I would rather face the end of the world with you by my side then watch you die."

Astrid wiped her own tears away and faked a smile. "I'll try not to die... I promise!" She prayed that she could keep that promise.

"Good..." Stacey said wiping the last of her tears and trying desperately to change the subject. "Now, we should get back to driving... and I need to hear everything about Cruz and that soldier! And why do you keep calling him 'Buzzkill'?"

Astrid managed to stifle back her own tears with a laugh as she drove back on to the road. It was very typical of Stacey to deflect her own emotions by bringing up safer conversations. "Oh, I'll tell you everything..." Astrid promised, "...provided you promise to tell me what the 'sitch' with you and Tash is. She's a great girl, and a very good soldier, and she's become a really good friend, too!"

Stacey blushed. "Sure, I'll tell you... but you first... provided they can't hear us back there."

#

Cruz looked around in the back of the truck. Tash, Joey and Buzzkill had all fallen asleep and Hannah had just finished counting the medication supply and was currently administering her own dosage.

They were relieved that Joey had not suffered from any side effects from taking the medication; it gave them all a little hope.

Cruz couldn't imagine having to be under the compulsion of any of the sins. They were all very randomly affected. It surprised him as to how some people could be affected by something that summed up their own personality, while others, like Hannah, were affected by something that was totally out of character for them.

"Is there enough for everybody?" Cruz asked Hannah after she discarded her syringe into the injections bin.

"Yeah. There's plenty. I just hope that we can end it all soon and not have to rely on the medication."

Cruz nodded. "I do, too. Hannah, can I ask you something?"

"Sure, Cruz. What's on your mind?"

"It's a big question."

"A big question? Is it medical? Or personal?"

"Personal... What would you do if you were in my position?"

Hannah stared at him, trying to determine what he was trying to ask of her. "I don't follow... are we talking about if I had opened the pithos? Well, I guess that I would find a way to end the curse... like you're doing."

"But what if you had quite literally exhausted all of your options... I'm talking about already having read through every piece of information on Pandora that the military had kept since the times of the ancient Greeks... if the only way to end the curse was to either lose..."

"...Lose the one you love, or die for the one you love?" Hannah finished his sentence, making him nod. She looked over at Joey and then back at

Cruz. "You told Astrid that you would find another way, didn't you?"

Cruz nodded again and waited for her to give him the answer. "I'm sorry, Cruz... but I can't give you the answers that you want. I want to... but in the end the only one who can answer that is yourself. But what I will tell you is that no matter what you choose, Joey and I... well, we will stand by you... no matter what... given you have exhausted every opportunity first... But I will give you a little advice... Just a little bit. No matter what happens... make the most of the time that you have now. Humanity could die out and we might only have tomorrow left... We don't know... but whatever happens... make the most of it. Show Astrid just how much you really love her, because in the end... I believe that it's love that will break the curse."

"You and those damn Disney movies, Han!" Cruz said as he stifled a grin.

"Hey, there's nothing wrong with true love's kiss... Even Hercules was Disney!"

Cruz thought about this piece of information. Hercules was Disney... Hercules was also the son of Zeus. It occurred to him that maybe he was looking at everything the wrong way. He had researched everything on Pandora and everything on the pithos.

But the one thing that he hadn't researched the hell out of was Zeus. The god who had created the curse in the first place. Just maybe, exhausting this new line of research was the key to ending the curse.

Chapter 18

Astrid parked the truck on the side of the road in front of a hotel in Washington D.C. at ten a.m. She had been driving all night and drinking nothing but cold coffee. She was exhausted and wasn't feeling all that well. She was amazed that she had made it all that way in the condition that she felt that she was in.

Stacey had fallen asleep in the seat beside her, and Astrid knew that the rest of the group had also slept through the night.

She was amazed at how the streets around them were filled with people dressed in expensive work suits, who clearly had jobs to attend to and weren't phased in the slightest about the large military truck that had pulled up on the side of the road. It was as if the apocalypse wasn't even happening.

To Astrid's delight, the entire city was filled with electricity, making her feel as if she had driven to an alternate dimension.

"What the hell?" she wondered out loud as she took everything in.

"Is everything okay?" Cruz's voice made her jump as he snuck up behind her.

"Oh my god, Cruz... you scared me!"

"Sorry... what's with this city? Have they even noticed that we're in the middle of an apocalypse?" he asked.

"I don't know... but there's a hotel there... I am so tired, so I don't care what the rest of you do... I'm aching to have a shower and to sleep in a proper bed."

Cruz smiled as he wrapped his arms around her shoulders from behind. "Well, then maybe we should all check into that hotel, and you can go and get some rest."

"Mmm. I like that idea. Sleep sounds good."

Cruz kissed her on the top of her head and said, "Why don't you lead the rest of the group to check in and I'll find somewhere to park this thing."

"I think that sounds amazing," she said as she nudged Stacey awake. "Hey, Stacey... We're going to go check into that hotel. What do you say?" Astrid asked her friend.

"Wait... An actual hotel bed? Not a seat or the floor? Oh, thank god!"

Astrid and Cruz grinned. "Yes, Stacey, a beautiful soft hotel bed with your name on it..." Astrid replied, "with a shower, oh... and maybe a spa if we can afford one and a pool."

Stacey stared at them both. "See? That's why you're my best friend... You get me! You don't have to tell me twice!" She immediately opened her door and jumped out of the vehicle.

Astrid gave Cruz a kiss on the mouth and climbed out her door, making her way towards the rear of the truck. She opened it to allow for the others to climb out. They, too were stuck in awe at just how operational the city appeared to be.

"What's the go with this place?" Joey asked her, wiping sleep from his eye.

"I'm not sure, but there's a hotel right there that we're going to check into to rejuvenate ourselves," she replied.

As Samuel climbed out of the truck, he looked around at the men and women passing them by in the street, and then back at Astrid. "I think they've still been affected, only they've made the most of it. It looks like pride and greed for money," he explained.

"It's better than the chaos from rage, gluttony or sloth."

"It's good enough for me!" Tash chimed in. "Now, let's go check out this hotel! Last one in has to bring in the luggage and food supplies!"

"That'll be Cruz!" Astrid said. "He's going to hide the truck!"

"Sucked in!" Tash said to Cruz through the window, where he was now sitting in the driver's seat.

"Ah well... I'll catch up with ya's in a bit," he replied. Cruz glanced at the group to ensure that they were all safely out of the way. He waved and drove off to park the vehicle.

"Speaking of checking into the hotel, I should have enough cash to cover accommodation. Your father left us with funds in case we needed it for after the apocalypse, but I also saved a little money, too," Samuel said as they entered through the doors.

#

The beautiful main foyer was booming with guests and workers. Astrid approached the front desk and addressed the woman at the counter, who immediately looked at them all in distaste. She was clearly dealing with pride.

"Yes? How may I help you?" she asked staring down at them, disgusted at the way they were all dressed poorly.

"We would like five double rooms for the next few nights, please," Astrid asked politely.

The woman stared at them as if they were crazy. Samuel pulled out his wallet and took out enough money to cover the costs and attempted to hand it to her, but she would not accept it.

"I'm sorry, sir... but have any of you even showered in the past decade? We can't let you in here looking or smelling that way. This is a well-respected hotel!"

Astrid attempted to keep her peace, but found that she no longer could. "Are you kidding me? It is quite literally the apocalypse across the fucking country... no, across the fucking world! And while I get that Washington is filled with so many proud people, proud of their jobs... we still have a job to do. Have you even set foot out of Washington? Because if you had, you would see that this is the only city across the country that hasn't turned to shit! So many people are dead! So just take my friend's money and give us our fucking rooms so we can shower and sleep! Or you will have a whole lot more to worry about than a bunch of travelers entering your hotel in dirty clothes. Is that clear?"

"Wow!" Tash muttered under her breath. None of the group had been expecting that.

This time Hannah approached the desk. "Please... Just give us some rooms. We will wash up, look much more presentable and you won't have to deal with us again. I promise."

The woman at the counter stared at them all. She took Samuel's money and requested that the bellboy give them the rooms as far from the main entrance as possible.

The group followed the bellboy towards the rooms, and Samuel pulled Astrid aside. "Are you okay, Sutherland?"

"I'm fine. I'm just tired and I'm over it. I'll just go shower and get some sleep and I should be okay after that."

"You're sure? Because I know that Cruz wants to head to the library with Hannah and Joey for research, Tash wants to take Stacey shopping later and I was going to get washed up and try and request an audience with the president. But I can always stay here with you, if you like."

"No, go! And do me a favor... try and figure out what the hell is wrong with this city!"

"I will." He smiled down at her as he walked her to her door. She closed it behind her and slumped inside, leaving him to find his own room.

By the time Astrid had finished in the shower, Cruz had brought up the bags including a spare change of military wear, for her to change into. She dressed and laid down on the soft bed as he laid down beside her.

"So, Stacey told me about your little spill at the woman down there... I wish I had seen it," he told her.

"Not my finest hour, but she... well, I guess that she was dealing with pride... but still... I'm just so sleepy and I'm over the apocalypse... Wake me up when it's all over and done with."

Cruz wrapped his arm around her waist and smiled. "Joey, Hannah and I are going to go to the library to see what we can learn about Zeus. Why don't you go for a sleep, then take some time off? I heard Stacey and Tash say something about shopping. Maybe you should join them."

Astrid laughed. "Yeah, Buzzkill told me earlier... I actually think that that is the most normal thing I've ever heard you say..."

He smiled at her with his cocky grin. "Yeah... it was bound to happen sooner or later..."

She rolled closer and snuggled into him and said, "I understand that Washington is filled with lots of proud, stuck up people... but I can see myself wanting to stay here for a little while longer. Right now, I need this normalcy."

"Well then, maybe we should stay a little while longer then, just until we know where we're headed next,"
Astrid yawned. "I like that idea."

"Don't... you'll make me yawn, mi amor..." He yawned, kissed her on the lips and said, "Get some sleep, you'll feel better after. I'll see you tonight." With that he left to give her some privacy, knowing just how hard it would be to do what he was intending. But, at the same time, he knew that it was the best thing for them both.

#

A few hours later, Astrid was joined by Stacey and Tash, who woke her up by slumping down on the bed beside her. "Oh good! You're awake!" Stacey said excitedly.

"That's just because you woke her up!" Tash replied.

"It's okay, guys... what's up?" Astrid asked sitting up against her pillow.

"We're about to go shopping and I really need you to help me curb my cravings!" Stacey said smiling.

"Stacey, I'm exhausted and I'm really not feeling all the best... Please just..." Astrid began.

"...That's only because you're stuck in those ugly military clothes... I went past a window earlier... there was this beautiful purple top with your name on it...Well, not literally with your name on it... but, you get the reference," Stacey said.

Tash chimed in. "Astrid, you really don't look well... Are you alright?"

"Wait, Tash!" Astrid said. "Stacey, what did this top look like?"

"Oh... it was beautiful... it had a few nice buttons at the front, a small amount of cleavage and... there were these jeans, they were to die for... They also had this black jacket, it would have suited you... but, if you're not interested... and you want to continue to wear khaki... that's entirely up to you..." Stacey said. Her smile was the biggest that Astrid had seen in a while.

"Okay, fine... I'm going... argh!" she said in defeat.

She let her friends lead her out of the hotel room to go shopping.

#

Meanwhile, at the library, Cruz sat hunched over at the computer, beside Joey, Hannah and a pile of books.

"You find anything yet, Joe?" Cruz asked, taking his eyes off the screen for a moment.

"Nothing we don't already know..." Joey said putting his most current book down on the desk and picking up another. Hannah looked over at Cruz. It was evident that he was giving up.

"We'll think of something," Hannah said, trying to offer support.

Cruz sat up abruptly, he could no longer hold his temper. "There's no use! We have gone through everything!"

"Not entirely everything..." Joey lied. Yes, they had, and they knew it.

"We have looked at Pandora! We have looked at Zeus! We have looked at every fucking god under the sun... or above the sun or whatever!" Cruz snapped. "We've looked at so many different religions and tales that my brain hurts!"

"Cruz, calm down, we'll keep looking..." Joey said, looking around at the people in the library that were staring at them.

Cruz raised his voice angrily. "Last night I had this dream! It's led me to believe that all of this... all this right here..." he said waving his hands down at the books and at the computer screen, "...it's pointless! It's for nothing! All we're doing is procrastinating, while the entire world relies on medication to function... or they're killing each other and they're killing themselves! This is my fault! And all I'm doing is prolonging the inevitable! That dream last night... those whispers... I was able to understand them... My blood will work! I know it! And I am done! I can't do it anymore! I'm going to find that stupid artifact, I don't care what either one of you think... right now, I don't even care what Astrid thinks... because at least she will be alive to be mad at me... because I'm doing what I need to, to make sure that she survives!"

Cruz pushed the computer screen off the desk and sent it crashing onto the floor. He stormed out of the library with his friends following after him.

He reached the street, just as Joey and Hannah caught up to him.

"Cruz, are you okay?" Joey asked him.

"Please stop asking me if I'm okay," Cruz replied. He was no longer yelling. "... Because, no, I'm not. I haven't been okay in a long time. I caused the apocalypse. I know that it's really hard to see right now, as this whole city is nothing but a masquerade... but I caused it! At the same time, I met the most amazing woman. I can't keep up this charade. I really can't."

Hannah and Joey looked at him supportively. "Look, man... whatever you choose to do, we'll support you one hundred percent," Joey said after a while.

"Thanks! Because I'm about to do the hardest thing that I've ever had to do in my whole life... I'm going to need as much support as I can get."

#

Samuel had managed to purchase a presentable looking suit and shower before setting out. He was now standing in a posh-looking waiting room, waiting to speak with some associates of the president.

He had been reading notes on the bulletin board and had finally received the answers as to why Washington hadn't succumb to ruins like everywhere else.

It seemed that the president had men who would apprehend the unruly in the city, and had scientists to medicate the ones who weren't... All except for the prideful people. Clearly, they had their uses. It seemed that running a city was much easier than running a country.

Samuel could hear the television in the background: The Diane show was airing. He had once thought that television had ceased everywhere, but it was what she was saying that told him otherwise.

"...Good afternoon, good afternoon. Hold the applause. I must say that it is amazing to be on four times a day. Now, things have been rough, I know... but at least you can all rely on your favorite TV host to get you through. I should remind you, that for those who haven't been taking their medication... Please remember to take it... it's the one thing keeping you all alive right now. Otherwise, you know the consequences... We've lost far too many cities to let that happen now, haven't we?"

Samuel was alerted to a tall, skinny, dark haired man, wearing glasses, sitting cross-legged on one of the seats in the waiting room with him. The man cleared his throat. "At least the superficial benefit... the rest of them have to suffer!"

"Sorry?" Samuel asked him.

"It's the ones who have the money and can afford the treatments who get them. The poor are kicked from the cities to fend for themselves," the man said.

"That's the way it's always been, isn't it?" Samuel wondered.

"It was never this bad... Our president gave into pride, and he refuses to take the treatments... because he's too proud to do so... no one will riot against him, so he has what he wants."

"But the rest of the country is dying out. How could that be what he wants?" Samuel asked as he sat down beside the stranger.

"Oh, I've worked with him... it isn't what he wants... he doesn't have enough people under his thumb... but he's making do with what he's got. He has to. They haven't been able to locate a solution."

Samuel nodded. "I just hope that I can help."

"How can you help? You don't look like a scientist, nor do you look like that man that Diane once interviewed."

"Mario Cruz?" Samuel asked, raising his eyebrows.

"Yeah... you've been doing your research?"

"Somewhat."

"Wait... the show never gave his full name... What is your stake in this?" the man questioned him sternly as he adjusted his glasses.

"Mr Davids?" the receptionist called out to Samuel, interrupting their conversation. "They will see you now."

Samuel stood up, but before he left, he turned to the man and said, "I can't say because lives depend on it. But I might have an in with the ones who can help..."

Samuel turned and left to meet with the associates that he had come to meet with. He did not know that the whole time he had been speaking with the one man who had been supplying the president with the solutions for the medications, that man being Dr. Gregory Reynolds.

Dr. Reynolds watched as Samuel left the waiting room, wondering what had become of Cruz and Astrid. He prayed that they were not injured in anyway, and he knew that following this 'Mr. Davids' would be the key to finding his old companions.

#

Astrid stood in the dressing rooms and smiled in the mirror at herself in her new outfit. Just outside, she could hear Tash and Stacey laughing happily.

She considered everything that they had been through over the past few years. The temptation to stay here with the medication that they had was just too hard to resist. Things could be normal. They could turn their backs on the rest of the world so easily.

But her desire to help others was far too strong. She thought back to the children that they had met in San Francisco. They had saved them from Vince and his men, and there were many more out there facing these consequences.

She felt her misery setting in again, knowing that they would stay here until they could form a plan, then be on their way again. She just hoped that humanity wouldn't die out in the process.

As she was lost in her own thoughts, she felt nausea sinking in again. She vomited into the bin just outside the change rooms. She felt so weak and so nauseous.

Her heaving got the attention of her friends. "Sutherland, you don't look so good," Tash said.

Stacey immediately held back Astrid's hair and placed the back of her hand to her forehead. "You're burning up. I think we need to take you to see a doctor, immediately."

Astrid stopped vomiting and collapsed to the floor. A weakness that she had never felt had taken over her entire body. As Stacey ran to pay for the clothes, Tash supported Astrid out of the store, to find the closest doctor in their vicinity.

Chapter 19

Samuel left the White House with a proud sense of optimism. Things were beginning to look up for the group, and he was excited to tell the rest of them. He had appealed to the board's prideful side.

General Sutherland had once told him that it was about reading people. If you could do it properly, you could appeal to their egos. Especially in a world where prideful people existed.

Samuel thought that he had done quite well as per the result, and as the sun was setting he made his way back to the hotel.

But, something wasn't quite right. He stopped walking. He knew that he was being followed. Samuel looked around, and while there were crowds of people and cars in the streets, he couldn't identify just who was following him.

He picked up his pace, running down the street, until he found the right building to hide behind. He hid behind the wall and waited for his follower to run past him.

He focused his senses and managed to hear the rapid breathing of the man who had been chasing him. As the breathing got closer, Samuel picked the right time to swing out his arm. His chaser immediately smacked into his outstretched fist and was taken aback.

Samuel pulled out his pistol and aimed it at the man. It was the same tall slim man from the waiting room, earlier. "What do you want?" Samuel demanded.

"To know where you're hiding them!" he yelled, putting up both his hands.

"What gives you the impression that I'm hiding something?" Samuel asked lowering his weapon, seeing that the man wasn't a threat.

"You are ex-military! The military are always hiding things! I used to hold the utmost respect for soldiers, but this world has changed everything! What do you know about Mario Cruz!"

Samuel studied the man. It was clear that he was no threat. But then he realized that he did know who the stranger was. It was no wonder he was so afraid of the military.

Samuel had been amongst the team that had stormed his hometown searching for Cruz and Astrid just over a year ago, before they had gone to San Francisco.

"You're Dr. Reynolds," Samuel said softly, putting away his gun.

Dr. Reynolds instantly went into the offense. He angrily brought his hands to Samuel's throat and pushed him up against the wall in an attempt to choke the life from him.

"You took them! What have you done to them!" Dr. Reynolds demanded. "Please tell me that they haven't been treated the same way that I was!"

Samuel could barely speak. He could barely breathe as Dr. Reynolds' hands were blocking his windpipe. But Samuel would not fight him.

"They're... they're safe... I left the name... Roger Charlie..." he managed to blurt out.

"What's that supposed to mean?"

In an instant, Samuel grabbed Dr. Reynolds' hands from his throat, twisted his arms and restrained him from behind. He was no longer a threat, giving Samuel a chance to catch his breath.

"Roger Charlie was the... the name I left on your bunker," he gasped. "I'm a friend, not a foe. Cruz and Astrid are both safe. We kept them safe! See? We're not all that bad." Samuel threw Dr. Reynolds to the floor.

The doctor looked up at him. "They're safe?"

"They are... We recently went back to San Francisco and their friends were able to work on a treatment. Your treatment. They thought that you were dead."

"No thanks to you!" Dr. Reynolds said.

"That wasn't my doing... I had to save them from those men. I can take you to see them, provided you tell me how you made it out. I need to know that we can trust you after everything you've been through. I won't let anyone hurt them. What do you say?"

Dr. Reynolds stared at him. The past year of his life had been torture, all at the hands of military soldiers, yet he had still made it out. The question really was, could either one of them trust the other?

#

Astrid, Tash and Stacey made it back to the hotel room, straight from the doctors and sat down on the bed. There was a solemn atmosphere about them. All those present had a strong feeling that things were about to get a whole lot worse.

"Well, that changes things!" Tash exclaimed.

"Yeah... it does!" Astrid said softly. "I could seriously go for a shot of bourbon right now... Even vodka would be alright... But I get it... that would be the worst thing that I could do."

"Well, not exactly the worst thing!" Stacey said. "But it wouldn't be advisable!"

"So, what do we do?" Tash asked. "Remember, we're a team... so, it's a 'we' thing..."

"A 'we' thing, Tash?" Stacey asked. "I think it's more of a..."

Suddenly, there was a knock at the door, making Stacey stop mid-sentence.

"Astrid, are you in?" the voice on the other side of the door called to them.

"It's Buzzkill!" Tash said in a loud whisper. "What do we do?"

"You're acting likely we've been caught doing something illegal!" Stacey whispered back.

"You guys! Stop whispering!" Astrid demanded of them as she ran over to the door. "Just don't talk about it! No one talk about it! It's just between us, okay? At least then, it gives me a chance to come up with a plan!"

Tash and Stacey both got to their feet and nodded as Astrid found her composure and opened the door. "Hi, Buzzkill! Here to kill the buzz again?" she joked nervously as she greeted him at the door.

"Er... Astrid, as relieved as I am to see that you're in a much better mood... there's something that we need to discuss and it's important!" Samuel told her. He didn't move from the doorway.

"More important news?" Tash butted in. "Haven't we heard enough important news?"

"What's she talking about?" Samuel asked Astrid curiously.

Astrid gave Tash a stern look, while Stacey said, "Nothing. It just had something to do with the TV... did you know that the Diane show is back?"

Astrid looked back at Samuel. "What did you need to talk about?"

"Wow! Are you wearing makeup? You look beautiful!" he said, just noticing for the first time.

"Buzzkill? Did you get through to the president's men?" Astrid was still trying to keep her composure. His compliment threw her a little off guard.

Samuel could tell that she, Tash and Stacey were hiding something, but he chose to ignore it. "Sorry. Yes, I did... and they are willing to help us. They want you, me and Cruz to meet with them tomorrow... I tried to appeal to their egos... but then I met somebody who..."

Astrid felt the sudden desire to crack a joke. "Oh my god! You met someone? Is she cute?"

"What? No! I met this man who..."

"Wait, Buzzkill, are you trying to tell me that you're gay?" Astrid joked again. "Because, hey, I'm okay with that." Tash and Stacey both smirked.

"Sutherland, are you okay? You're acting really weird. What's going on with you?"

"I'm sorry... I'll behave... no more jokes! Scout's honor! What is it that you need to tell me?" She took a deep breath to regain her composure and Samuel cleared his throat, trying his best to conceal his smile that she had brought out of him.

"Dr. Reynolds is safe. I found him... well, he found me. He's been working for the president. Apparently, he was rescued by these men and was brought here to Washington. They've even been hunting down his family for him," Samuel said.

"Wait, Dr. Reynolds is alive?"

"Yes. He's currently waiting in the lobby. I don't think he trusts me just yet, so I said that I would come and get you."

"Who's Dr. Reynolds?" Stacey asked. Tash shrugged.

"Wow," Astrid said, practically speechless. "Buzzkill, can I meet you there? I'll be right down."

Samuel shrugged his shoulders. "Sure. I'll just go and let him know."

Astrid closed the door behind him and then looked back at Tash and Stacey. "I thought he was dead," she said, surprised by the notion, and still trying to come to terms with her other news.

"Clearly not," Tash replied. "But, the more doctors, the better our chances... especially now that..."

"...Don't say it, Tash! Just don't say it!" Astrid snapped.

Tash obeyed and she and Stacey followed Astrid down to the lobby to meet with Dr. Reynolds.

#

Night was fast approaching and Cruz paced outside the hotel in frustration in front of his friends Joey and Hannah.

"You really don't need to do this, man," Joey tried to tell him. "You love her, and this was the total opposite from what we discussed earlier in the truck."

Cruz stopped and stared at his friend. "Si amas a alguien, dejalo ir," he mumbled.

"Er... are you forgetting that I don't speak a word of Spanish?" Joey asked.

"Sorry... didn't you ever hear that saying, 'if you love somebody... set them free'?"

"I did, but I thought the guy who must have said it had no clue what he was talking about."

"Okay, picture it this way... the one thing that I want is to have a baby to this woman, and well... the last thing I want is to have a baby to this woman, in the world that we are currently living in. Do you get where I'm coming from? Back in San Francisco, those kids... well, god knows the things that they would have seen. There were dead bodies lined all over the city. I need to do this now, before I change my mind. I know that Buzzkill will treat her good, he'll protect her."

"Do you really want that?" Joey asked him.

"Hey, Astrid's the last woman in the world who needs protecting!" Hannah said at the same time. "She's pretty tough... Hasn't she saved both you and Buzzkill at some stage?"

"Yes, she did... and no, this isn't what I want... but my mind has been made up. Every time I look at her... every time that we're together, I hate myself, knowing that this is my fault. Maybe if the world was different... Things would be, well... they wouldn't be like this... but..." Cruz stopped pacing and leaned his back up against the wall.

Hannah and Joey stared at him. Their friend had become a broken man. There would be no talking him out of this one. He wiped away his tears.

Suddenly, Tash and Stacey exited the hotel, seeing them standing there.

"There you are!" Stacey exclaimed excitedly.

"Astrid has been looking all over for you... There's someone you need to see." Cruz, Hannah and Joey looked up at them silently.

"What's going on, you guys?" Tash asked. Her smile turned into a look of doubt.

"Nothing!" Cruz replied. He stormed past them all and made his way towards the room that he shared with Astrid.

She was standing there deep in conversation with not only Buzzkill but also... Dr. Gregory Reynolds.

"Reynolds!" Cruz gasped, stopping in his tracks.

"Cruz... It's been a while. It's good to see you safe and sound!" Dr. Reynolds said.

"You too... I'm sorry, I don't mean to be rude, but..." he looked back at Astrid. "Can we please talk?" he asked her nervously, with the look of desperation across his face.

"Sure, there's actually something that I need to speak with you about, too!" She seemed to be just as happy as Stacey and Tash had been earlier.

They were joined by the rest of the group, but Cruz led her close to the window where they couldn't be overheard. He nervously tried to come up with the right words to begin.

He took a deep breath as he managed to find them. "So, Joey, Hannah and I have been pouring over research all day and... hmm... well, we haven't turned up anything."

"That's okay, we can keep looking. I'll go with you tomorrow. I'm not exactly a history buff... but we can do it together, Cruz... we're a team, right? Which is exactly what I need to discuss with you..."

"...Astrid, that's kind of the thing. I won't be here tomorrow..."

"I'm sorry? I don't understand. Buzzkill managed to get us a sitting with the president's men tomorrow. They're willing to help us... and with Dr. Reynolds here... I think that we're finally on the right track to finding this thing."

"Astrid… Ay dios mio! This is so hard... I love you, you know that, right?"

"Okay, now you're starting to scare me..."

"I know, and I'm sorry... but look! I have a theory that I want to check out... I might know where they're keeping Pandora's Box and I am going to go after it... Me, Hannah and Joey... we have to go."

"Cruz... I don't like this... You're seriously bringing me back to that night that we first met, when I just wanted to help and you quite literally said that you had nothing for me to do, and you made me feel absolutely useless."

"I'm not trying to do that... but in a way, that's exactly it..." Cruz paused to take in Astrid's features; her green eyes, her light brown hair and her lips that he would miss most of all. She was beginning to get angry with him and he could see it.

"Astrid, don't be mad... but... I can't bring you with me... Last night, when I was asleep in the truck... I had a dream... I dreamt that I was back in Europe. I managed to understand the voices... It was like they were telling me exactly what I needed to do to end the curse, and my blood... it will work... I know it will. Please, Astrid! I need to do this alone. I know you're going to hate me, but please... I opened the pithos and I just know... I feel it in my gut... I know that my blood will change things..."

Astrid grabbed his hand, pleading with him. "Cruz, No! You can't! I won't let you!" There were tears streaming down her face.

He tried to shake her hand off his arm as he, too, began to cry. "Please, Astrid. I can do this. I want you to be happy... To live a happy life in a world that isn't crumbling! I know that Buzzkill will do that for you... he can give you everything that I can't... and he can be there after everything... I know he will... He loves you... just as I ..." He stopped talking to kiss her passionately, to show her just how much he loved her. "...love you!" he finished his words.

"Please, Cruz... don't go... Don't! We will find a way to do this together! Please!"

Cruz let go of her and shook his head. "Hannah will be leaving the treatment supply for the others. She can make up more for her and Joey after we hit the road. But there should be enough to last the others for nearly a year... Please, stay safe."

"Cruz! No! Cruz! Don't go!" Astrid pleaded. By now everyone in the room was watching them.

"I have to mi amor... Te amo!" With that he turned and joined Joey and Hannah as they said goodbye and left the room.

"Wait, Cruz! I need to tell you something!" Astrid called out behind him. He turned back to her, the tears falling down his face freely. She had every intention on telling him the news that she had found out earlier, the news that she, Tash and Stacey had been keeping. But she knew that it would not change his mind. In fact, it would make him choose to leave all the more. "I love you," she chose to say instead.

He nodded and left with Hannah and Joey, making her heart crumble into a million pieces. She felt sick to her stomach, and as she knew that the world around them was nothing more than an apocalypse, she felt that the end had surely come.

She continued to watch as he disappeared from her sight. After a moment, Tash and Stacey approached her.

"Why didn't you tell him?" Tash asked quietly.

"Because, a baby wouldn't make him change his mind about being the hero... about risking his own life to save the world. Besides, something tells me that he already knows."

Chapter 20
6 Months Later

"Can you remember the last time that we were here?" Joey asked, as he and Cruz sat inside the tent, under the hot sun in Olympia.

Cruz sat at the table going over the books. He stared at Joey giving him a look that meant 'don't remind me' and went back to his reading.

"Sorry, man... I forgot... you're focusing. Hey, here comes Hannah and the Amelia Earhart of our time, Jessie Maxwell... and don't look now, but she's looking your way."

Jessica 'Jessie' Maxwell was a pretty, dark-haired pilot who had joined their expedition a few months ago. In the past few years she had chosen to write about the apocalypse and had jumped at the chance to work with the US excavation team to put an end to the curse. She had also become good friends with Hannah.

It was also clearly obvious that she had a strong fascination for men with dark hair and dark eyes, seemingly Cruz.

"Yeah... I get it, Joe. I'm not interested... and you know I'm not. We're here to work, not mess around," Cruz snapped.

"Man, you used to be fun," Joey frowned. Hannah and Jessie entered the tent and plonked down bottles of water for Cruz and Joey.

"I just had some serious déjà vu, guys," Hannah said, looking over at Joey.

"Only this time, I'm no longer inviting you out for drinks, Han... I'm giving you the whole course," Joey said smugly.

"Somewhere a younger version of myself is saying don't do it, Han, it's a trap!"

"I wish that you guys would be serious for just once! The world is still ending, we still... I still... Argh!" Cruz snapped. He was not able to finish his own sentence.

"Is he always like this?" Jessie asked Hannah.

"More often than not, but we consider what he's been through," She replied. "Speaking of... It's medication time."

She opened her briefcase and handed them all their epi-pen vaccines. "I'm so glad we invested in these things, it makes it so much easier."

Cruz shook his head, took his research and headed into the ruins. Joey followed in after him. "I get that the past few months have been hard for you, man. But you broke up with her... So, you need to stop acting like a spoiled brat all the damn time. We're trying to help you, and you're not making it easy."

"So don't bother, Joey. I never asked for you and Hannah to return with me..."

"No, you didn't, but we did because we're your friends... and you might have pushed away the one woman that you loved more than yourself... but you can't push us away. So stop trying. It just gets annoying after a while."

Cruz stared at his friend and then down at the ground. Deep down, he was thankful that his friends had returned with him. They had been excavating these ruins for weeks now, with Cruz's very own company that he was leading.

He had jumped at the chance to lead the US excavation team after he had left Astrid's side. Joey and Hannah had been very hesitant to return, but had done so primarily to offer their friend some support.

"Hey, Cruz... I thought this site wasn't opened to the public," Joey said.

"It's not," Cruz replied. He looked in the direction that Joey was facing.

There was a silhouette standing in the distance. He was wearing a black cloak and what looked like a plain white mask.

"Who the hell is that?" Cruz wondered.

"Mr Cruz?" a young dark-haired member of the excavation team, who went by the name of Demetri Matherson, addressed him. "You said you wanted me to inform you of anything odd about these ruins?"

"Yeah, Demetri, I did. What have you got for me?" Cruz asked turning to the young man. Joey left to give them some privacy.

"Well, some of the locals have been hearing word that there's some Greek mythology cultists around these parts... Apparently, they started up right after the pithos was opened."

Cruz glanced back into the tunnel where he had seen the silhouette standing earlier. He had now disappeared.

"Thank you, Demetri. Let me know if you hear anything further. Also, prepare the rest of the team. The president will be sending some of his men to check up on our progress tomorrow. We don't want them finding anything wrong and cutting our funding. Also, let me know when they arrive so I can meet with them."

"Yes, sir!" Demetri said.

Cruz smirked. "Demetri? Don't call me sir."

"Sorry, sir... I mean, Mr. Cruz..."

Cruz shook his head and headed back to the tent to join Joey, Hannah and Jessie.

#

Astrid stood in her room with Tash and Stacey, trying on maternity outfits that they had recently purchased. Over the past six months, the president, after having run extensive testing on

Astrid's immunity, accepted the group's proposal to work for him to find a cure for the Seven Deadly Sins curse.

He provided them with enough resources, accommodation and money to continue on with their work. As they fulfilled their research, they resided in Washington in close proximity to the president, promising to report any new findings to him directly.

While they had not yet turned up any new leads, after the president had ordered an entire clean out of the military divisions, Astrid had been sitting on a theory that Cruz had mentioned to her a long time ago, that maybe the military no longer held the artefact and had gotten sloppy, having it end up in the hands of someone else.

"Seriously, Tash. I look like I'm wearing a table cloth!" Astrid said, staring at herself in the mirror of her bedroom suite.

Tash smiled back. "And you look like you're hiding a very tiny ball under that tablecloth... I mean, you don't even look six months... more like three?"

"Don't be silly!" Stacey said, joining them. "Those dresses are the latest trend in maternity wear... Okay, maybe it does look a little bit like a table cloth... Not like it matters, though. Buzzkill thinks you look hot in anything... I bet he would rather see you in nothing at all, even with that tiny ball under that tablecloth."

Astrid and Tash stared at Stacey, making her smile cheekily. "I'm sorry... but while Tash is normally the one who says it like it is... I really couldn't help myself. It's just too damn obvious. He may as well just wear a sign over his head that says 'Astrid, I love you'!"

"Cruz and I broke up six months ago... I'm carrying his child and the world is still ending... I think the last thing that I should be thinking about is another relationship... especially if it's with Buzzkill!" Astrid snapped.

"...Stacey's right, though..." Tash said, "...and I'm not just saying that because she's my girlfriend... You are a strong, independent and beautiful woman! Don't miss out on great opportunities because some guy knocked you up and left! Besides, every time Buzzkill sees you, there's this super weird straight sexual tension, which his medications do not curb in the slightest. Don't tell me that you've never thought of him in that way... and don't use the 'it feels like I'm cheating on Cruz card' because he dumped you, remember?"

"He broke up with me to end the curse. It's not the same thing."

"Er... Astrid, we were all there..." Stacey added. "He broke up with you... he even told you to be with Buzzkill... and then he left without so much as a word... and it's not like he ended the curse, either... So, I'm pretty sure that means that you're a free woman..."

Astrid stared back into the mirror and changed the subject. "Buzzkill will be here shortly... He apparently needs to talk... and I'm going to ditch the tablecloth and wear the pants instead," she said picking them up.

"Just like with everything else..." Tash said smugly.

"Hey! Enough about..." Astrid began. She stopped midsentence as Samuel entered the room through the open door, addressing her directly.

"Sorry to intrude... but that dress looks..."

"...It looks like a tablecloth, yeah, we get it," Astrid grumbled.

"No, it actually looks really nice. But it won't offer much protection against the hot sun. Dr. Reynolds said that he wouldn't miss this trip for the world. It's really funny to think of that man anywhere but in his lab. Especially at a stinking hot excavation site."

"Is that the only reason you came in here? To tell me that?" Astrid asked him.

"Actually, no..." He looked around at Tash and Stacey who were staring at them with very humored expressions on their faces, then he looked back at Astrid. "What's going on in here?" he asked her, awkwardly.

"See? There's that tension again..." Tash said in her humored sing-song voice. She took Stacey by the hand and they both left Astrid and Samuel alone, closing the door behind them.

"What was that all about?" Samuel asked looking from the door to Astrid.

But she just shook her head and opened the door again with a smile. "Nothing, don't worry about it... So, you never told me where we're going exactly... Why's it going to be so hot?"

"That's actually why I came up here... We're going to Olympia. We have actually been given the go ahead to meet with the excavation team ourselves this time," he replied, leaning up against the door of the built-in wardrobe.

"We're going to Greece?" she asked him.

"Yeah, it's pretty exciting, don't you think?"

"What changed their mind? Why are they all of a sudden going with my theory?"

"You did! You changed their minds. They know better than to doubt a Sutherland."

"You talked to them, didn't you?"

"A little bit... I mean, they still value the opinion of a man before a woman, but we're a team, so I managed to convince them to succumb to your side... to succumb to the dark side!"

"A team?"

"Yes, we are. You, me, Reynolds, Tash, Stacey... and that little ass-kicker in there. Are you okay? We can always cancel the trip if you need to... Or just send those other guys instead."

Astrid had been brought back to her last conversation with Cruz when he had broken her heart. She had used that same word 'team' and he had given her the impression that it was not the case. She knew that she needed to move forward and end the curse with her own team.

"You miss him, don't you?" Samuel asked her, pulling her from her thoughts.

"Who?"

"You miss Cruz. You can tell me... I guess that it would be hard not to, considering you're carrying his baby."

"You know me too well," she said with a smile.

"I'm just glad that I know you at all. You should probably put on something that's a little more suitable to the European climate. We leave in an hour."

"You really want to go to an excavation site with a pregnant woman?"

"It's you... so yeah, of course I do. And we're only going to meet with the excavation team... It's not like we're going to be doing any digging.... I'll see you out there."

He placed his hand on her shoulder as he went to pass her, leaving it there for a moment longer than he probably should have. She looked up at him. There certainly was a lot of tension between them.

His lip quivered. She knew that he was wanting to kiss her. But before he could, Dr. Reynolds entered through the open door. Samuel removed his hand from her shoulder as fast as he could.

"Get ready, you two. We leave in an hour... Sutherland, are you really going to Greece in that? It looks like a tablecloth. Have either of you seen my... oh, here it is." He picked up the metal suitcase with his treatment supplies and left the room without even looking up at them.

"I should... probably go and take my medication and leave you to get ready," Samuel said, giving her a polite smile. He went to leave the room, hesitating.

Astrid hated when Tash was right. This was just another one of those times.

She considered what Tash had said earlier about not feeling guilty about Cruz. She hadn't seen him in six months, that same night that he had broken her heart. She had wanted to feel like a team when it came to him.

She had loved him, and was even willing to declare the news that she was pregnant, but there was something in that moment where she felt that he already knew, and yet, he still left just the same.

Astrid was not going to force Cruz to stay, as much as she had wanted him to. And as much as she wished that he would come back to her, she was giving up believing that it would ever occur.

Samuel would always be there for her and she knew that. There was also an aching inside of her that wanted him. She had felt it that moment when they had been on the road together, when he had attempted to kiss her. She could no longer let it eat away at her.

She decided to take control. So, before Samuel could leave the room, she called him back. "Hey, Buzzkill?"

He turned to her. "Yeah?"

The moment he turned around, Astrid ran to him, cupped his jaw in her hands and kissed him on the lips. Samuel was taken aback for a moment.

"Astrid, are you sure?" he asked, pulling away slightly.

She smiled at him. "Don't be a buzzkill," she joked.

He smiled back down at her and gave in to her kiss, holding her tightly in his arms, not preparing to let go for anything. She could feel his strength and a sense of belonging and protection that would always be there if she needed it.

She brought her arms around his waist as he leaned her against the wall. He closed the door, while not removing his lips from her own for a second. He was taking charge, which was entirely what she needed of him. He brought his other hand to her cheek, caressing it gently. She was completely lost in him.

In that moment she remembered his words from back at the truck, 'we could be good together', and she knew that they were true. They could be good together. In fact, they could be great together.

A loud knock at the door made them both jump to attention, and the door swung open instantly.

Astrid and Samuel tore themselves apart from each other. Their faces were red with embarrassment as Tash entered the room.

She clearly knew what had happened between them as she said, "So, this is what it's like to be the Buzzkill... Sorry, guys... We've gotta go over our last minute checks!" She smiled at Samuel as she spoke.

Samuel had the look of someone who had been caught stepping out of his house and onto a busy street completely naked. He smiled at the pair of them and left as fast as he could with his red-blushed face.

"Naww... You made Buzzkill's day, didn't you?" Tash asked, grinning at Astrid. "It's about damn time you two hooked up... but now you need to change out of that tablecloth, and let's go."

#

It wasn't long until the group had gone over all their last minute checks, including the pilot's mental stability, and were sitting in their own private jet.

As Astrid sat over with Tash and Stacey, who were insistent on talking to her stomach, Samuel sat over with Dr. Reynolds, exchanging flirtatious glances with her every so often.

Once again, Dr. Reynolds was doing his best to explain his updated medical treatment to battle the virus. It didn't matter how often he would synthesize a new treatment, the virus always seemed to evolve and become even stronger than before.

Samuel smiled back over at Astrid, who subtly excused herself from her friends and made her way to the aircraft's bathroom. Before she entered she motioned for Samuel to join her.

Just as he got to his feet, Dr. Reynolds addressed him. "Davids, would you be willing to trial out my new formula?"

"I'm sorry, new formula?" Samuel asked.

"The one that I have just spent a good ten minutes discussing with you... If all goes to plan, it should curb your virus enough for you to stand right next to her and keep your own composure. A distracted soldier is an unreliable soldier."

Samuel's eyes were still on Astrid. She was waiting for him. "Yeah... sure," he said to him. "Just let me know when you're ready," he said, barely listening. He hurried towards the bathroom with Astrid and closed the door behind them.

"Could you have made that all the more obvious?" she asked him.

"Sorry... it's just... it's not every day that... you know..." Before he could finish his sentence she was kissing him again. She leaned up against the sink and he continued to kiss her back, bringing his lips directly to her neck.

It took all the strength he could muster to stop himself from going any further. "Astrid... what is this? Is it just a fling, or something more?" he asked her, trying hard to keep his own composure.

"You're asking me now?" she asked him, puzzled.

"Sorry... again... but I'm fine either way. Really... Look, don't worry about answering, let's just get back to it..." He brought his lips back to hers and brought his hands to her waist.

Instead, she shook her head. "Why did you have to bring that up now, Buzzkill?"

He sighed. "I'm sorry... just forget about it... We'll talk about it later, okay?"

"No, maybe we should stop," Astrid said. "For now... whatever this is... we shouldn't rush things..."

"Okay... If that's what you want," he said, once again putting her needs above his own.

"God, Buzzkill! Why do you have to be so...?"

"Such a buzzkill?"

"That, too... but I was going to say... perfect."

"Sorry? What do you mean by perfect?"

"Never mind." She opened the door in an attempt to leave, but he closed it in front of her.

"No, what do you mean? How am I perfect? How do you find me perfect?"

"Look at you. You're good looking... You have muscles that are... well, perfect... And your history with women... that just explains itself... So anyone would think that you're a big narcissistic jerk... but you're not... you're anything but."

Samuel raised his eyebrows again. "You think I'm perfect? Hi, I'm Samuel Davids. I don't think we've ever met..." He put out his hand for her to shake it.

Astrid laughed at him. "Let's go back out there."

"Wait, you were being serious before? Okay, as long as you're sure..."

"I'm sure... I promise we'll talk about it later."

"I await that conversation..." he flirted. "So, who goes out first? Me or you?"

Astrid opened the door and peered outside. "I will," she said.

Before she could leave the bathroom, Samuel cupped her head in his hands and kissed her again. "Okay, now you can go," he said with a big grin.

She blushed at him and then left the bathroom again, making her way back to Tash and Stacey. Samuel followed not long afterwards to sit back with Dr. Reynolds.

#

When they had finally made their way to Greece, they were met with the country's ambassador and brought over to the excavation site. Tash, Dr. Reynolds and Stacey had gone off on their own, while Astrid and Samuel addressed one of the site's young supervisors.

"Have the men found anything in relation to the pithos," Astrid asked him. He was a young man by the name of Demetri Matherson.

"We haven't found any physical artifacts that could be related to Pandora's Box so far, but my boss asked that I let him know when you arrived. Do you mind if I go and get him now?"

"That would be great. We can just wait here until you return," Astrid replied.

Demetri nodded and left Samuel and Astrid alone in the tent.

"So this is where it all began!" Samuel said looking around at the books and equipment in the tent excitedly.

"I think the little ass-kicker is excited, too," Astrid exclaimed, getting his attention. "It's kicking."

"Oh? Can I feel?" he asked her.

"Mm hmm." She took his hand and placed it on her stomach.

"That's pretty cool," he said smiling down at her. He brought his face in closer, ready to kiss her again as she brought hers closer to his with a flirtatious smile.

"I came in here expecting to see a bunch of the president's men in suits, but you could imagine my surprise at finding all of you here, instead." Cruz's voice broke them up as he entered the tent.

As Astrid and Samuel turned to face him, entirely shocked that he was standing there, Cruz glanced down at Astrid's pregnant stomach.

"Huh!" he scoffed.

Chapter 21

Cruz continued to stare at Astrid and Samuel, waiting for either one of them to speak. The fact that his expedition had been entirely funded by his ex-girlfriend, and none of them clearly knew about it, was a shock.

But his eyes could not stop resting on her stomach. He knew that that was his kid in there. There was no doubt in his heart. He wasn't stupid.

Before he had gotten their attention, he had witnessed the moment that Buzzkill had placed his hand on her stomach and had gone to kiss her. That was why he had spoken out in the first place. It had been his attempt to stop them before they did.

Astrid had everything that Cruz wanted for her to have, with only one exception; he wanted her to have them with him.

Suddenly, Stacey voiced up as she entered the tent. "Hey, Astrid! You would never guess just who is..." She looked up at Cruz and stopped mid-sentence. "Oh!"

"Hi, Stacey," Cruz said. "Hi Tash!" Tash had just entered the tent after her.

"Wow!" Tash said awkwardly. "Hey, Stacey... I think that we should go..."

"No, you two can both stay," Cruz said in defeat as he looked back up at Astrid and Buzzkill. "You're the ones who invested in my expedition."

Astrid stepped forward and said, "We had no idea that this was your expedition. The president gave us the money and we saw that there was an anonymous man wanting to search for anything related to the pithos... We couldn't just say no."

"Would that have changed things?" he asked her. "If you had known that I was the person running the expedition?"

Astrid was speechless. She didn't know what to say. Yes, of course it would have changed things. He should have been with her, but he wasn't. However, she couldn't tell him that.

"I'm surprised that you don't even have an answer for that. You used to always have the last say!" he said sternly.

"Seriously? You left me! One minute things were fine and then the next..."

"...There it is... that final say," Cruz joked.

"Oh, shut up, Cruz!" she snapped at him.

"It's nice to know how quickly you moved on with Sergeant Buzzkill, huh?" he said angrily.

"Really, Cruz?" Samuel said to him.

"Whoa, whoa, whoa! Time out! Time out!" Tash intervened. "Now, we could all keep fighting, just remembering that Cruz was the one who dug his own grave here... Or we could do what we should be doing."

"Tash is right," Astrid said bitterly. "Let's not kill each other. We're here to talk business. Cruz, have your men found anything at all in relation to the pithos?"

Suddenly, Dr. Reynolds entered the tent. "Oh, hi Cruz... Did Sutherland tell you the news?"

Cruz shook his head in frustration. "I thought you weren't coming this time around... but I suppose that it all makes sense, considering that she is..."

"Wait... Reynolds, you knew that Cruz would be here and you never even told us?" Astrid snapped.

"Yes, frankly I did... I've been communicating with Cruz for the past six months, and personally, as a father myself, I believed that he should know that you were carrying his child. I pulled a few strings so you could come and see him yourself... and so he could see you..."

"I can't be in here in here dealing with all of this right now..." Astrid said, taking a few anxious breaths as she stormed out of the tent. Samuel followed after her.

"Samuel... please, I just need a moment to myself," she said frustrated.

"Okay, that's fine. Just let me know if you need anything." He left her in peace and went for a walk.

Astrid was then joined by Cruz. "Look, just save it! Alright, Cruz?" she snapped before he could get a word in.

"Astrid... I'm sorry. I'm sorry for leaving you when I did... I just... I need you to understand that I didn't do it to hurt you."

"Well, you did. I have been dealing with this for the past six months now! I waited for you to come back! Let's face it, deep down you knew that I was pregnant... and you still left! So, whatever it is that I have with Samuel... it's none of your business!"

"I'm sorry... but it is my business. That's my kid in there. I'm pretty sure that I should get a say in who should be..."

"Oh, no! Don't you dare say that! You can't tell me who can be around my baby. You left... You lost your right! And before you ask... this thing with Samuel and I... it's new... it's..."

"Cruz?" They were suddenly joined by Jessie Maxwell. "Joey, Hannah and I were knocking off for drinks later... were you coming?" she asked him. She stared at Astrid and then back at Cruz. "I don't think an excavation site is the place for a pregnant woman to be," she added in Astrid's direction.

Astrid glared back at the disrespectful woman with the temptation to knock her one, but resisted, instead.

"Jessie... I'll be there in a bit... Can you just... can you meet me there?" Cruz asked her, trying to get her to leave.

"Sure." She smiled at Cruz and did as he asked.

"Sorry about that... this girl... she..."

"No need to explain... So please, don't try. Let's just talk business and be done with... But don't worry, when this is done... you won't have to worry about seeing us again."

"What? Why?"

"Well, we won't be coming back! Me, Samuel, Tash, Stacey and the baby... we'll be out of your hair for good!"

"Why do you have to make everything so hard? Please... I just wanted to apologize..." Astrid shook her head and walked back into the tent with Cruz following in after her. The truth was, seeing him there hurt her more than words could express.

"Well, that was like ripping off a band-aid..." Tash said as they emerged. Astrid sat at the table beside Stacey.

"Tash is right... let's get to work!" Dr. Reynolds said. "Now, you mentioned earlier that you were onto some kind of cult?"

"Yeah... a cult of people who call themselves 'Zeus'. Earlier, I thought I saw..."

"Astrid!" Hannah interrupted as she entered the tent with Joey. "It's good to see you. It's been so long!"

Once again the intrusion frustrated Cruz. He was trying to explain the situation, but every time he did, they were interrupted. He leaned against the post and waited for an opportunity to continue speaking.

Hannah went to give Astrid a hug from where she was sitting and saw her belly. "Wow!" she gasped. She immediately looked over at Cruz and then back at Astrid's stomach.

"You're pregnant?" Joey gasped, too. "Is that Cruz's?"

"Yes, guys... it's mine!" Cruz snapped. "Now, before the two of you barged in here, I was telling them about the cultists."

"Sorry, man..." Joey said. He leaned over and hugged Astrid. "Congratulations... Don't mind him! If I had known..."

"Joey!" Cruz snapped again. Joey stopped speaking, and Cruz continued, addressing Dr, Reynolds as he spoke. "Well, these cultists have been sneaking into the tunnels. I think that they might have a hideout around these parts, so we're going to have to be careful. We have reason to believe that they may have somehow acquired the pithos. Do any of you remember when I mentioned that I was getting those dreams?"

Astrid nodded her head. She remembered all too well.

"Well, I feel that we're very close... and until just recently, I thought that the pithos was in the ruins again... but now, I'm not so sure. If these guys are anything like the crazy cultists we normally hear about on TV... it could be dangerous for Astrid."

"Dangerous how?" Samuel asked as he stepped into the tent and stood behind her with a flower in his hand. He handed it to Astrid, making her blush as she accepted it.

"Well..." Cruz said begrudgingly, "she's the descendant of Pandora. If they have the pithos, they could be looking for her next."

"Maybe we could use that to the best of our advantage," Astrid said, thoughtfully.

"What do you mean?" Stacey asked her.

"If they know who I am, they could come after me... I say we let them."

"What? No!" Cruz said, raising his voice.

"I see where you're going with this, Sutherland," Samuel said. "What's worse than bait that's secretly a lethal weapon in disguise?"

"When that weapon has soldiers for friends," she said with a smile meant only for Samuel.

"No! Astrid, these cultists could be dangerous. You're not risking yourself or our child for this thing!" Cruz snapped. He was letting his jealousy get the better of him.

"Well, do you have a better idea?" she asked him.

"Not really... but I'm sure that I'll come up with something," he replied in defeat.

"Sutherland," Dr. Reynolds began, "I'd hate to say it... but Cruz is right... you should be thinking about what's best for the baby."

"Seriously, Reynolds?" Astrid raised her voice at the doctor. "You're the one who tricked us into coming here in the first place. Look, we need to stop fighting. It's getting late and I'm dealing with some serious jetlag. Besides… Cruz, Hannah and Joey have drinks to get to with that woman outside... So maybe we should all just call it a night."

Samuel helped Astrid to her feet, and Tash and Stacey followed them out of the tent making their way over to their hotel, while Dr, Reynolds stayed back with Cruz, Hannah and Joey.

"Wow, man. She's pregnant!" Joey said. "Did you know?" Cruz stared at his friend, not wanting to answer. "You knew, didn't you!" Joey said angrily. "I get that you did all of this to try and save their lives... but as someone whose father was never around... I can't forgive that. I never thought that I would say this... but at least she has soldier boy by her side."

#

"Well, that was something," Tash said as the four of them made their way into Astrid's hotel room. Astrid and Samuel sat on the bed, while Tash and Stacey remained standing.

"How are you doing, Astrid?" Stacey asked her.

"I am actually fine... I mean, I never expected Cruz to grow so... angry over time."

"It's to be expected," Samuel said. "I don't mean to sound like I'm defending him or anything, but he left because he wanted to save the world and he wanted to save you the burden of having to give up your own life. He's just trying to build up a wall to protect himself."

"That was too deep... Way to kill the Cruz bashing session, Buzzkill. Remind us not to invite you to the next one!" Tash joked.

"Sorry, but it's true. Anyone with eyes can see that he regrets his actions. He still loves you, Astrid," Samuel said as he gazed up at her.

Astrid looked up at him and placed her hand over the top of his. Her tone softened as she spoke. "I get that, Samuel, I do. And while the intention was good... the consequences... well, he needs to live with them."

"Hey, Stacey... Maybe we should leave Buzzkill and Sutherland alone for now," Tash said, heading towards the door. She had been watching their body language and knew that giving them some privacy would be the best option.

"Definitely!" Stacey said with a smile that lit up her face. They left out the door and closed it behind them.

The moment that the door was closed, Astrid and Samuel both felt the nervous tension return again.

"Those two are very... strategic, aren't they?" Samuel asked.

"They are! I don't know how we've put up with them for so long... but at least it gives us some time to chat."

"Yeah... Do you mind if I go first?" he asked.

"Sure... I'm not sure where to begin, anyway."

"Thanks... I get that yesterday and today changed a lot between us... Especially after seeing Cruz... but it didn't change the way that I feel about you. Nothing will. I want you to know that I'm fine with whatever you pick... or... whomever you pick. I also get that you're having a kid, and... well, it doesn't change things for me. I'd love that little ass-kicker as if it were my own... even if we don't get together. But then, you could say 'let's just fool around' and I'd be okay with that, too. Because, ultimately, you need to put your baby first. So, whatever you want... whatever you need, I'm willing to give it to you. Even if its space."

Astrid gushed. "Damn you, Buzzkill. Stop being so perfect. Stop saying all those perfect things."

"I'm sorry. I'll stop," he said with a laugh.

"Okay... do you remember back when you and I were on the road together and you... well... you had been trying to savor your medications?"

"Please don't remind me... That was one of my biggest regrets!"

"No, don't... because it always had me thinking... what if we did give in? Of course, I never would have cheated on Cruz... but you managed to get under my skin. I really couldn't shake you."

"Really? I got under your skin? That was ages ago... Have I been under your skin since then?"

She blushed again and continued. "I'm just saying that I wouldn't mind exploring that... just seeing how good we could actually be together."

"Astrid? Do you know what you're saying? Because all I'm hearing is that you want me under your skin."

Astrid laughed. "Yeah... I guess that I am. So, what do you say?"

He leaned over and whispered, "Absolutely!" and then kissed her. Perfectly.

\#

Instead of going out for drinks with Joey, Hannah and Jessie that night, Cruz accompanied Dr. Reynolds to a bar instead.

"Today was probably the biggest disaster since I opened Pandora's Box," Cruz mumbled as he drank a mouthful of his bourbon.

"Yeah, it was. I'm just glad we finally managed to synthesize a treatment that is compatible with alcohol... It makes being a deadbeat dad all the more bearable."

"You're not a deadbeat dad... Did you happen to find out what happened to your family?"

"I did... which is why I know that you're doing the right thing."

"Why? What happened?"

"They got the treatments while I was being tortured... and my wife met someone new... A soldier no less. I still see my son and my daughter from time to time... but it's not the same."

"Ouch," Cruz said, sipping his drink again, "which is why you arranged for Astrid to come... Unfortunately, there won't be any rekindling of romances between us... Sergeant Buzzkill is destroying that chance."

"He shouldn't get all the blame... You played your part, too... which brings us to this pithos and those dreams of yours. What do you need to do after you find it?"

"Wait, you believe me about my dreams? I thought you were a skeptic."

"I was, until I found that I was working with the descendant of Pandora... But then, while I was working under the president... I was privy to a few extra pieces of information that astounded me."

"Yeah? Like what?"

"Well, for one thing... Astrid wasn't the only descendant of a Greek icon. So many Gods and heroes from way back went on to sow their wild oats. There are many people out there who descended from the beings that we once thought were nothing but legends..."

"Are we talking about Hercules and Percy Jackson?"

"Along those lines... but not in the same way that Hollywood has painted them. Those myths had to have come from somewhere. You would understand my amazement, to learn that I actually knew a few more descendants of Greek Mythology figures.

"What do you mean? Like who?"

"Samuel. His heritage comes from Jason. Do you remember the story about Jason and the Argonauts? Well, I looked into Samuel's family heritage... I couldn't believe it."

"Seriously? Well... doesn't that just suck! I mean, now he's all the more special! But you said there were others.... Anyone I know?"

"Actually, it would surprise you... Do you remember when I ran a blood test on you back at my old clinic?"

"Yeah? You said that there was nothing special."

"I lied, Cruz... I lied because I didn't understand it at the time... When I was tortured relentlessly, I found out the real reason that you were able to open the pithos... To anyone else it would have proven impossible... but not to a descendant of Zeus."

"I think you've had a little too much to drink, Reynolds."

"No... I've barely touched my glass."

"Yeah... but you're telling me that while Astrid and Jason are descendants of human heroes... that I'm some descendant of a Greek God... Do you get how crazy that sounds? For one thing, I'm not even the right nationality..."

"Think about the whispers, Cruz... Why was it you, of all people, that found and managed to open that pithos? It could have been anyone, but it was the descendant of the God who opened it. Not to mention, those Gods did procreate with humans on a regular basis..."

Cruz drank the last of his bourbon. This information was far too much for him to handle. It was absolute nonsense. He was feeling dizzy, like his whole world was spinning.

"Hey, I don't feel so well," Cruz said as he got to his feet. "I should go back to my hotel room."

Cruz's world continued to spin until he had collapsed onto the floor, unconscious.

"I'm sorry, Cruz... but a whole lot of Rohypnol will do that to you," Dr. Reynolds said as picked the man up onto his shoulder and led him out of the bar.

Dr. Reynolds led him back to the old ruins where he had arranged to meet with his fellow associates, followers of the cult known as 'Zeus'.

Dr. Reynolds applied his white mask and pulled up his cloak. He carried Cruz's unconscious body down the dimly candle-lit hallway, where he met with the rest of the cloaked figures in a large chamber in the heart of the ruins.

He dropped Cruz's body onto the floor and said, "It won't be long now, and we'll have the girl as well."

Chapter 22

The next day, bright and early, Astrid met with Joey in one of the tents. He was going over some of the books that Cruz had been reading over the day before, while Astrid was looking for Cruz to apologize.

"Joey, have you seen Cruz?" she asked.

"Not this morning... I've been looking for him, too. He never came out with us last night, and he never showed up to work this morning, either. Last I knew, he was going out with Dr. Reynolds... Maybe he's seen him?"

"I'll see if I can hunt him down. If I find Cruz, I'll let him know you're looking for him, too."

"Thanks, you, too," Joey replied, but as Astrid went to leave, he pulled her back. "Hey, Astrid?"

"Yeah?"

"Look... I might not agree with his actions... but he comes from a good place... If you need anything, Hannah and I will be there for you... and I know you can depend on..." Before Joey could finish his sentence, Samuel entered the tent.

"Hey, is everything okay?" Samuel asked.

Joey nodded and went back to reading the books, as Samuel wrapped his arm around Astrid's shoulders and followed her out of the tent.

"Everything's fine," she said. "Have you seen Cruz?"

"Not since yesterday. Why? Is something up?"

"I'm not sure... I just have a really bad feeling about something that I can't seem to shake," she replied.

"Do you need my help looking for him?"

Before she could answer, Dr. Reynolds' voice cut in. "Hey, Astrid... Can I have a word? It's about Cruz."

Astrid was still angry at Dr. Reynolds, but knew that it would be best to let it go.

"Fine, Reynolds... Have you seen him by any chance?" she asked.

"I have, actually. He had this theory about the pithos, which is why I needed to speak with you." He stared at Samuel and then added the word, "Alone," with emphasis.

"I'm okay, Samuel. Really," Astrid replied.

Samuel kissed her on the mouth, and she followed Dr. Reynolds over to the old ruins and past the boundary line.

"I take it that Cruz is in there?" she asked curiously, referring to the underground ruins.

"He sure is," Dr. Reynolds said as he led her deeper into the ruins. "He actually believes that he might have found the pithos and wanted to show it to you first."

"Why me?"

"Beat's me, it's Cruz... He probably just wanted to run a few theories past you before the rest of the group. You know him. We actually stayed up last night having a few drinks and we had a good heart to heart."

She was hesitant at first, but she knew that she had doubted Dr. Reynolds in the past. He had even saved her life when they had first met. Even Samuel and Cruz trusted him now.

She knew that he was a good man. Why should she doubt him?

They entered even deeper through the tunnel until they reached what looked like a large dimly lit crypt.

Astrid looked around at their surroundings as Dr. Reynolds ran the torch along the walls. "Wow, this place is... it's magnificent," she gasped.

"It's about to get a whole lot better," Dr. Reynolds said with a cheerful grin. He removed a brick from the wall slightly, which made the entire wall shift.

"A secret passageway?" she asked. "Let me guess, Cruz showed you that one! He would have just loved that!"

"Somewhat." Dr. Reynolds stepped through the open doorway and led her through.

Astrid continued to address Dr. Reynolds. She still felt bad for the way that she had treated him the day before.

"Look, I'm sorry for being mad at you yesterday," she said. "I get it! It wasn't fair for me to try and keep the baby from Cruz... okay, what's with all these candles? Please don't tell me that he has some romantic scheme planned... We're no longer together!"

But her question was answered as she saw Cruz chained to a post. He had been drugged and his head was currently lolling about.

"What the hell?" she gasped at the sight of him.

She and Dr. Reynolds were suddenly joined by the cultists who were dressed in black cloaks and wearing white masks.

They seemed to have appeared from out of nowhere. Astrid went to run, but as she turned around, someone injected a syringe into her back, and she fell to the floor unconscious.

#

"Hey, have any of you seen Sutherland?" Tash asked as she and Stacey entered the tent.

She was addressing Joey, Hannah and Samuel. There was another woman standing with them that Tash had never met before who was clearly a friend of Hannah's.

"She went looking for Cruz with Dr. Reynolds, earlier," Samuel said. "I'm surprised they're not back yet. They've been a while."

"Do you think that maybe we should go looking for them?" Hannah asked.

"Didn't you say that that woman was the mother of Cruz's baby?" Jessie asked. "Maybe they just needed a little time to talk things through. It would make sense... especially if there's a baby involved."

"I suppose so," Hannah replied, going over her books.

Samuel shook his head. "Something just isn't sitting right. There's something going on. Astrid had a bad feeling this morning, too."

"This morning?" Tash joked. "Was that when you were laying in each other's arms between the bedsheets or after?"

"Tash, not the time," Samuel replied.

"He's right," Stacey said. "I think we should go looking for them... Astrid wouldn't just leave without letting one of us know... Didn't Cruz say something about cultists yesterday? They could be in trouble."

"I'll get the first aid kit," Hannah said immediately.

"I'll get the torches..." Joey said. "Cruz was pretty keen on venturing into those ruins yesterday... Maybe Dr. Reynolds took her there to look for him."

"Hey, I'm sure they're fine!" Jessie said, sounding a little nervous. "I saw them yesterday outside the tent... before we went out for drinks... Those two seemed pretty... well... chummy! Maybe we don't want to know what they're doing."

"Excuse me?" Samuel snapped at her, on edge. "You don't even know her!"

"Jessie, I get that you're into Cruz," Hannah said, "but I really doubt that that's the case." She had just collected her first aid kit and went to leave the tent.

As she did, Jessie restrained her and pulled out a pistol. She held it against Hannah's temple. "Hannah, I'm sorry, but none of you will be leaving here today," she said.

As she said this, Samuel pulled out his own sidearm and aimed it at Jessie. "Let her go!" he demanded.

"What are you doing, Jessie?" Hannah pleaded.

"Mr. Prescott!" a voice said from outside of the tent.

"That's Demetri!" Joey exclaimed. "Don't hurt Hannah... let me get rid of him... please!"

Jessie said, "Fine!" and allowed for Joey to leave the tent.

"Please, Jessie... why are you doing this?" Hannah pleaded again. "Does it have to do with the pithos?"

"In part..." Jessie replied. She glanced over to the opening of the tent where Joey had re-entered.

He had the look of terror on his face and the group understood why, as they saw that both he and Demetri had both been taken hostage.

There were eight hostage takers all dressed in black cloaks and they were wearing white masks. They pointed their guns on Joey, Demetri and the rest of the group.

At that point, Jessie threw Hannah to the floor, where Stacey leapt to her aid. Jessie turned her gun onto Samuel.

"Now that we all have your attention..." she began, "none of you will be making it out of here alive. Hannah, you might need to check up on those epi-pens... they might not be very effective within the next half hour!"

"What do you mean?" she gasped.

But Jessie just ignored her and continued on. "Joey, Hannah... let me thank you for this opportunity to work with you... It got me that much closer to the descendant of Zeus... and my word...

that was exciting! None of you know what is to come next..."

"What's that supposed to mean?" Joey snapped. He stopped talking as he could feel the cold metal pressed up against his head.

Jessie went on to recite a verse from Hesiod. "But the rest countless plagues, wander amongst men; for earth is full of evils and the sea is full. Of themselves diseases come upon men continually by day and by night, bringing mischief to mortals silently; for wise Zeus took away speech from them. So is there no way to escape the will of Zeus... I believe that's how Samuel's little love letter went... It's actually pretty accurate, if you consider what's going to happen!"

"How do you know that?" Samuel asked, remembering the message that he had written for Astrid.

"Oh... Dr. Reynolds told me... You see... when Cruz opened the pithos he was only fulfilling his destiny... All of this... it's just the beginning. That pithos allowed for not only the Seven Deadly Sins to inhabit earth... but also for countless other creatures... Where Cruz and Astrid are now, you'll never find them... and if you do... it will be too late. You see, their child... that child is the key! The key to everything!"

Jessie stared back at Hannah. "I really think you should be careful about your medications in the future, Hannah.... and be careful who you trust."

Suddenly, Joey was overcome with anger and a strength that seemed a little strong for a regular person. He pushed his hostage taker away from him and began to punch into him in a frenzy. He was becoming chaotic.

Jessie shot a bullet just past Joey's head. It missed him and got one of her fellow cultists instead. Then she slipped away unnoticed.

Tash stood beside Samuel. "What do we do, sir?" she asked. Her fear was taking over her.

"Tash, do you have your gun ready? Because I think we're going to need it."

#

Deep in the candle-lit crypt, Astrid and Cruz had been chained from the roof by their hands. Their clothes had been removed and replaced for old brown rags. Cruz had been awake watching their environment, trying to determine the cultist's next course of action. He had heard more than he had wanted to hear while Astrid was still asleep.

"Astrid... you need to wake up." Cruz's pleading voice continued to whisper to her, encouraging her to wake from her deep sleep.

It seemed to be working. She stirred and then opened her eyes, immediately looking around at her surroundings.

"Cruz, what's going on? Why are we tied up? Where are we?" she asked. She remembered the cultists from before. Dr. Reynolds was among them.

The cultists were chanting in a different language. "What are they saying?"

"Don't worry about that. We need to get you and the baby out of here."

"We're getting you out, too."

"If it comes to it, I will risk my life for you both. You know that."

"Enough of the risking your life crap... okay?" She had gotten the attention of some of the cultists, but they carried on with what they were doing.

"Astrid, there are some things that you need to know," Cruz whispered. "I got the answers I sought. There was a reason I was able to open the pithos... and I managed to find out why my blood will help us end the curse."

"What do you mean?"

"You won't believe it... but it just so turns out that I'm a descendant of Zeus. It's funny, hey?" He was doing his best to be witty in the face of danger. A means to hide his inner fears. "It was our ancestors that created this whole thing... and that's why it was always you and me that were needed to end the curse... It's what brought us together in the first place! Our child is the answer!"

"You mean... I'm the metaphor for Pandora's Box? Our child is the world's only chance of hope... and you... you're the one that caused this whole mess to begin with?" she asked disbelievingly.

"It's rather poetic, don't you think? I get it now. It's meant to be love that ends the curse. It makes sense. Vengeance started it... and it was my love for you that created the key."

"While it is a little poetic... I don't think that this is the right time to start talking about our feelings for one another... We need to find a way out of here." Astrid rattled the chains that bound her. They would not come free. For the first time that she had been there, she noticed that someone had changed her clothes. "Oh my god! These creeps saw me naked," she exclaimed.

"Don't worry, they didn't do anything to you... But that's the least of our worries... especially after what they have planned."

"And what do they have planned?"

"Please... don't make me say it!"

"Cruz? What do they have planned?"

Cruz shook his head and stared at her sternly. "They want to remove our baby from your stomach."

"They what? But it won't survive! It's not old eno..!" She stopped mid-sentence as some of the cultists turned to look at her and she realized just how barbaric these people really were. She gasped. "No..."

She saw that they were standing around a table. On the table, the pithos stood open.

"Is that... Pandora's Box?" Astrid asked.

"Yeah... it doesn't look like much, but it packs one hell of a punch. Do you see that brown wool that it's sitting on?"

"Yeah? What about it?"

"That's the Golden Fleece... In fact, this whole crypt is filled with ancient artifacts from Greek mythology. If I wasn't bound up and about to be sacrificed, I would be in my glory right now! But it had me thinking... if Pandora's Box was able to do all that damage... then the other artifacts should hold powers, too."

Astrid stared at him. That childlike optimism in the face of danger had been one of the things that had made her fall in love with him in the first place. She shook her head. Her feelings for him needed to stop getting in the way of them needing to escape.

"Cruz... what are you suggesting?"

"Whatever happens, we will make it out of here. I promise that you and our baby will make it out of here alive."

"Why are you so optimistic? Look at us!"

"Astrid... I'm optimistic because I have you here by my side. Whatever is going on with Samuel, fate brought us together for a reason and we will get through it together. We're a team. You give me hope to believe in that."

She wanted to argue with him, to have the last say, but Dr. Reynolds approached them.

"Fate did bring you both together... Fate caused Cruz to find Pandora's Box in the first place. It wasn't just to end the curse, but to bring about a new world... with a new leader that would lead the old beasts and wipe out humanity from existence... and to bring forth the new Gods."

"What the hell are you rambling on about, Reynolds?!" Astrid snapped out.

"I'm not sure if either of you have noticed, but the wool that the pithos is sitting on... it's the Golden Fleece. Your child will be wrapped in it and protected. Your child will lead the new world. But you will both die... I can't let you foil our plans."

"You're crazy, Reynolds!"

"It's funny... that's what I thought before I met you... But I'm a scientist... I've done my research... You can imagine my disbelief when I saw just how true all of this really was. Sure, I was rescued by the U.S. government, but in my time working with them I met other like-minded individuals... and while I was able to keep you and the descendent of Jason under my watch... one of my colleagues accompanied Cruz and his friends back here in Olympia... keeping watch over him. It's funny... I always thought that the descendant of a God would have powers... but clearly not!"

"Jessie!" Cruz exclaimed angrily. "So what? You just wanted to get us here in one place? In Olympia? Why here? And why now?"

"We needed to ensure that the baby would pass the first trimester... not to mention we needed to make you trust us... which we've done, and now all of our plans are coming together."

"Ha! I hate to annoy you, but Samuel has always been such a buzzkill... he will stop this!" Astrid said cockily.

"You really think so? Something tells me that he is a little in over his head right now... We switched Hannah's treatments, not to mention my own... Your friends will be the most unreliable they have ever been... Unless they're put out of their own miseries first..."

"You have got to be kidding me!" Astrid snapped.

One of the cultists stepped forward with a tray that contained a syringe and handed it to Dr. Reynolds.

"Now, Astrid... it's time for you to take your medication... When we remove the baby from you... you won't feel a thing... Maybe you should just say your goodbyes now."

As he readied the syringe, tears began to emerge in Astrid's eyes. "Cruz... I..."

"No," Cruz stopped her. "Look at me... I'll think of something... Just look at me. I love you. We will get through this. I promise you, we will!"

Astrid shook her head as the doctor injected the serum into her arm. She tried to struggle free, but there was no use in trying.

"Leave me alone!" she screamed at the doctor.

"Astrid, please... mi amor! Look at me!" Cruz pleaded with her. "I love you. You won't die here. I won't let you die here!"

As the serum seeped into her bloodstream, she began to feel drowsy, her eyes growing heavy. The drug was potent and she could no longer stay awake.

Her body gave into sleep.

Chapter 23

Back at the excavation site, just as Dr. Reynolds had spoken, the group had begun to give in to their Seven Deadly Sins. Tash was huddled up behind the desk, afraid of the scene that was playing out before her.

Joey was in a fit of rage throwing objects across the tent. He was all the more angry at Samuel and Hannah who were currently enraptured in each other's arms, giving into their lust.

Stacey was sitting on the floor counting stones. Demetri had disappeared, as had Jessie and the rest of the cultists.

Tash continued to wipe the tears away from her eyes. How had this become the reality that she was living in? She remembered back to what had happened to her own family, the reason that she had joined up under General Sutherland in the first place.

Her brother had given in to pride. Her father had killed her brother out of jealousy. Her mother had killed her father and then herself in a fit of rage.

Tash had been hit by fear the moment she had come to visit her family on holiday. She had given into her fears and had taken to hiding away in a wardrobe.

She had not moved from her parent's closet for weeks. She had been starving and close to death when the military had gone through the house, looking for survivors and had witnessed the carnage that had become of her family.

Samuel had heard her whimper out in fear, and as she watched, he had approached her hiding place, wishing that she too had died when her family had.

But then, when Samuel opened the wardrobe door and knelt down in front of her, he had been the most stable and most calming person that she had met in a long time.

He had put down his gun and held out his hand to her. "Hey, it's okay," he had said. "We won't hurt you."

She had been too frightened to trust him at first. So he had requested that General Sutherland come and assess her. The General had injected her with the treatment, which stabilized her instantly.

They had then invited her to join them, to train with them for survival. She had no choice but to accept.

Samuel had always been like a brother to her. Just like the one that she had lost. But then she had met Cruz, Astrid and the rest of the group, and they too had become her family. They had accepted her as one of their own, which was something that she had not felt in such a long time.

Now, her new family was just as unstable as her old one had been.

Joey threw a book across the tent, just missing Tash's head. She tilted her head down, making herself even smaller than before.

As Joey stormed past Stacey, he kicked through some of her rocks which clearly meant a great deal to her. She stood up to him. "Joey! They were my rocks!" she yelled.

"None of that matters, Stacey! They're just rocks!" he yelled back at her.

Tash remembered something that Samuel had told her. Something about letting fears drive her to be brave.

Right now, the woman that she loved was being threatened. She needed to fight for her. She needed to help her. She had to stop being afraid, as hard as it was, and stand up for the one she loved.

Tash got to her feet. "Joey! Leave Stacey alone!" she said, shivering with fear.

Joey turned his anger onto Tash this time. "Excuse me? What's that, soldier girl? Do you want to fight me? Come on, take out your gun and shoot me! I dare you! You can't do it, can you! You're such a scaredy cat! Why don't I just put you out of your own damn misery!"

Somehow, Samuel could hear Joey threatening Tash in a fit of his own anger. He stopped and looked down at what he was doing.

He had been kissing Hannah. "What the hell?" he gasped. Somewhere, he remembered Astrid. She was in danger. He needed to fight this curse and rescue her.

He looked over at Tash. She was still frightened. Her hands were trembling as she held out her gun.

"Oh no, Tash!" Samuel muttered. His lust was slowly subsiding. "Hannah! Hannah! You need to get a grip... the medications! We need proper treatments!" he demanded of the doctor.

"What do you mean? What treatments?" she murmured to him as she ran her hands up his shirt and went to kiss him again.

Samuel pushed her away from him. "Hannah, please. Cruz and Astrid, they're in danger! Look at Tash... Look at Joey!" he told her.

"Joey? Joey!" she exclaimed as she realized just what was going on. She was battling with her own lust for the sexy soldier before her. She looked over at Joey, who was threatening Tash.

"Joey, no!" she gasped. She managed to pull herself away from Samuel and went straight for her metal briefcase. She checked over the epi-pens. They had been tampered with. "Oh my god!"

She ran over to the edge of the tent to look for her secret supply. She found her lockbox and opened it. There were enough in there for all five of them. She administered the dosages and watched as they all came to.

"Oh my god!" Tash said as she stared down at the gun in her hands. She had been ready to shoot Joey. She placed the gun onto the desk.

Joey stared down at her. "Tash... Stacey, I'm so sorry!" he apologized. They all looked over at Samuel and Hannah.

Samuel shook his head in remorse and then got into action. "No time for apologies, you guys... We need to save Astrid and Cruz, now!" He picked his gun back up and left the tent with the others close at hand.

"It's the cultists!" Joey exclaimed as he picked up the torches and followed Samuel out. "They'll be in the ruins!"

"I'll get the first aid kit!" Hannah said. "God, I hope they're okay!"

Stacey looked over at Tash. "You... you almost shot Joey. For me? You overcame your fear... for me?" she stammered, on realization.

"Yeah, Stacey... I guess I kind of did. I couldn't let anyone hurt you. I love you," Tash replied.

Stacey stared back at Tash. Instead of saying the words, she ran up and kissed Tash. "I love you, too... Now let's go save the others!" Tash picked her gun back up and left after her friends.

As Samuel kept his pistol at the ready, he stormed through the excavation site. The young man Demetri was heavily wounded on the floor. He had been shot in the stomach.

"Oh my god! Demetri!" Hannah cried. She knelt down beside him to stop the bleeding. "You guys go on ahead... Let me help Demetri and I'll join you all soon!"

Joey took the lead, showing Samuel the way to the ruins. They continued to travel deeper into the tunnel with only the torches to light the way.

They continued until they came to a dead end. A thick wall positioned right in front of them.

"It doesn't look like anyone's down here, Joe!" Samuel exclaimed. "We're wasting precious time!"

"It's an old crypt! Haven't you ever seen Indiana Jones? We saw one of those cultists in here yesterday... I can feel it! There's something about this place!" He shone his torch all around, and then onto the floor. "Look... Fresh footprints. They stop at this wall here," he said.

Samuel stared down at the footprints. "They're Astrid's. She has the smallest feet I know... and she was wearing boots this morning!" he said.

"You really pay close attention to her, don't you, Buzzkill?" Tash joked.

Samuel looked at her and then turned away. "It's my job, Tash."

Joey got back up to his feet and shun his torch around on the walls. He felt his hand around as he did so, until he felt a part of the concrete at the very top give in. He pushed it in, but nothing happened, so he pulled it out.

To their amazement the wall in front of them moved and slid open, leading them into the next chamber. The shock that beheld them forced them to immediately jump into action. In the distance, they could see Cruz hanging from chains on the roof. He was yelling and fighting with all his strength to break free.

Astrid had been strapped to a table with a group of cultists surrounding her. She wasn't making a noise.

Tash and Samuel both pulled out their weapons and started shooting as they led the rest of the group into the chamber.

The cultists dispersed from the table and began fighting against the group as if their lives depended on it.

Stacey ran towards Cruz to find a way to set him free. "Stacey! That lever over there!" Cruz exclaimed. "Quick, hurry! And don't look at Astrid!" he demanded.

Stacey listened to him and pulled the lever, but as she did so she couldn't help but witness the sight of her best friend. Her body lay lifeless, and the cultists had created a messy incision in her abdomen. They had removed the baby.

"Oh my god! Astrid!" Stacey cried as she ran over to her friend's body.

Cruz, who had managed to break free, joined Stacey at the table. With Astrid's ragged clothes, he attempted to compress her wound to stop the bleeding.

"Come on, querida! Wake up, mi amor! Please!" he cried.

"Cruz... where's the baby?" Stacey asked, with fear instilled within her.

"Dr. Reynolds! He took her! Get Hannah! Astrid isn't breathing!"

Stacey nodded her head in a state of shock and ran as fast as she could out of the chamber to find Hannah.

Samuel, who had managed to fight off and kill most of the cultists, ran over to the table that Cruz was sitting at.
"Oh my god, Astrid!" he said angrily. "What the hell! Cruz! I thought that you would never let this happen! Look at her! Look what those butchers did to her!"

"It's not my fault!" Cruz yelled back.

"Buzzkill, Cruz! Stop fighting! Where's the baby? Where's Reynolds?" Tash snapped at them.

"He went through that corridor!" Cruz exclaimed, not moving from his spot.

Samuel got to his feet and reloaded his gun. "He will not get away with this!" he snapped. Cruz continued to sit over Astrid's body in a state of shock, willing for her to come back to him.

Tash stood beside the table and took a hold of Astrid's wrist, checking her pulse.

"Cruz... she hasn't got a pulse," Tash said as the tears began to emerge.

"I know that, Tash!" Cruz snapped.

Joey, who had been watching all of this unfolding, looked around at the artifacts before them.

There had to be something that could help. He managed to find a staff which resembled two serpents intertwined.

It had once belonged to Hermes and was believed to have special healing powers. "Cruz, try this!" he said, handing over the staff.

"Why? What will it do?" Tash asked, barely able to make out her words loud enough for them to hear.

"It's supposed to have healing powers," Joey said.

Cruz took the staff and held it over Astrid, willing for it to work... to bring her back to life. But it wasn't working. He kept trying, when suddenly they were joined by Hannah and Stacey.

"Oh my god!" Hannah gasped as she saw the sight of Astrid. "Give me some space!" she demanded of the group. Cruz could barely get himself to move away from the table. He had broken his promise, and for that, he hated himself.

Joey supported him and tried to pull him away to give Hannah room to work. They all knew that Astrid was well and truly dead, yet Hannah continued to work. She managed to give her some medication to stop the bleeding and then bandaged her up tightly.

Knowing it was pointless, she attempted to preform CPR on their friend. To nobody's surprise, it wasn't working.

#

Meanwhile, Samuel had found Dr. Reynolds attempting to make his escape with the crying baby. The child had been wrapped up in an old woolen blanket.

"How fitting that you would find me with this possession," Dr. Reynolds said.

"It's a baby, not a possession! Now give me the child, Reynolds! I don't want to shoot you." Samuel said calmly.

"We wouldn't want that now, would we? You can kill me... but this child will only bring on the end of life as we know it. Astrid's blood already broke the curse, but the Seven Deadly Sins were only the beginning of what was yet to come."

"What's that supposed to mean?"

"Do you remember Hesiod's words? The Seven Deadly Sins curse was just the beginning. That pithos not only paved the way for humanity's own inner demons... but also so much more... New mischiefs will be set afoot. Spirits, demons, old and new Gods... This child is just the beginning. But we both know that you will keep her safe... That's why it's rather poetic that she's wrapped in the Golden Fleece, an artifact that relates itself to one of your ancestors..."

This was news to Samuel's ears. "How am I related to Jason?"

"Same way that Astrid is related to Pandora, and Cruz is a descendant of Zeus... It doesn't matter what you do with me here... Now, it's all out of my hands. So I will give you the child, and you can kill me, if you wish... But my bit has been done!"

Samuel looked down at the crying child. It was so small. But then, it was born at only six months. How was it still alive?

Samuel continued to hold up his weapon, just as Dr. Reynolds approached him with the baby. The doctor handed Samuel the small child, and it stopped crying instantly.

As Samuel was mesmerized by the baby, Dr. Reynolds attempted to slip away. But before he could, Samuel shot at him.

The bullet lodged into Dr. Reynold's upper leg. He would surely bleed out and die if he didn't seek medical attention.

Nonetheless, Samuel bypassed him with the child in his arms. It seemed fitting that a descendent of Jason would carry the Golden Fleece with such a precious child wrapped inside.

He walked back into the chamber and stared over at Astrid's body and the rest of the group. The spell had been broken, and at that point he knew that he truly loved her, and that it wasn't just the curse that made him feel the way that he did.

Cruz continued to weep over Astrid's body as Samuel approached him with the baby. But Cruz would not lift up his head from the woman that they both loved.

"I'm sorry... I couldn't save her," Hannah said softly.

"Dr. Reynolds isn't dead, but he's been shot. I won't take his life. We once trusted him," Samuel said.

"You should have killed him where he stood!" Cruz spoke through gritted teeth as he held Astrid's hand in his own.

"Trust me... I wanted to," Samuel said. "So... you have a daughter..."

Cruz raised his head, but his expression did not change. "How can I be a father when I had to watch the way that they killed her mother?"

"We will help you," Tash replied. "We're a family. We all are."

Samuel nodded in agreement.

Joey approached them, holding the pithos in his hands. "You guys, it's been closed!" he said in a mere whisper. Sure enough, the jar was tightly sealed shut.

"Yeah... and I have a bad feeling about what's to come next," Stacey said as Tash put her arm around her.

Cruz stood up beside Samuel, who handed him the child. "We will call her Hope," Cruz said. "It seems fitting."

"We should go," Samuel said. "And we should apprehend Dr. Reynolds."

"No! He killed Astrid! He will not get away with this!" Stacey snapped. She picked up Tash's gun and aimed it at the doctor who was slowly limping across the chamber to make his escape.

"Stacey... don't!" Tash pleaded. But, as there was a loud bang, they knew that Stacey had taken Dr. Reynold's life.

Stacey dropped the gun and collapsed to her feet, while Tash tried to comfort her.

Samuel began to make his way out of the chamber. Hannah, Joey, Tash and Stacey went to join him. But Cruz would not leave. "No! I'm not leaving her here!" he exclaimed.

"Cruz, we need to go... We will come back and collect her after," Hannah said.

"No!" Cruz demanded.

Samuel and Joey approached him. Samuel took the child and Joey went to lead his friend out of the chamber.

"Get off me, man! I'm not leaving her!" Cruz demanded of his friends.

As Joey released him, Cruz collapsed back over Astrid's body. "Come on, mi amor! Let's go... Come on! Vámonos! I'm not leaving unless you come back to me! Please!"

His tears continued to fall down his face. He kissed her on the head and then on the mouth. "I won't leave you." he whispered.

Samuel felt uncomfortable by the display, but knew that the man was grieving in his own unstable way.

Suddenly, there was a moment, an aura about them. Something had shifted in the air.

"Do you hear that?" Cruz asked.

"Hear what?" Joey asked him.

"The whispers!"

"What whispers?" Samuel asked.

But Cruz was in his own mind. He was certainly hearing something.

Tash felt the urge to say something about the man's instability but chose to bite her tongue instead.

"Hannah, can you check Astrid again?" Cruz
asked pleadingly.

"I don't know what that will accomplish,
Cruz!" Hannah said doubtfully.

"Please! I'm begging you."

Hannah shrugged and checked Astrid's pulse
again. Her eyebrows instantly raised in surprise. "I
don't understand... Her pulse... it's faint... but it's...
it's there!"

End

CPSIA information can be obtained
at www.ICGtesting.com
Printed in the USA
LVHW051730180719
624531LV00005B/819